Small, Dark, and Handsome by Kevin D. Patterson

Published by Dark Peak Publishing
Copyright ©2014 by Kevin D. Patterson

Small, Dark, and Handsome
by Kevin D. Patterson

Dark Peak Publishing
PO Box 560396
The Colony, TX 75056
www.kevindpatterson.com

Cover design by Julius Dawson

Acknowledgments

Everything that I've ever accomplished, or will accomplish, including the completion of this novel, is due to my faith in God.

————

After talking for years about my passion for writing and my desire to write at least one novel, I met a woman who dared me to live my dream. That woman is now my wife and I can't thank her enough for everything she's done for me, including all the love and support she has given me in every step of this project. I also want to thank my sister, who has been a positive influence on me throughout my life and has provided me with a constant source of inspiration. Of course, I have to thank my mother for the many sacrifices that she made so that I could have all of the opportunites that she never did. If I were to properly thank her for everything that she has done for me, this acknowledgment section would be longer than the novel itself, so I won't even try.

I'd like to thank members of my initial focus group for giving me their candid comments on my early attempt at a book. I'd also like to thank my editor, Jeff Hill, for helping me to focus on the reader, and for teaching me the importance of "showing" and not just "telling" the story.

Special thanks goes out to Julius Dawson, my book cover designer, who patiently dealt with me and my often conflicting direction, even though I brought him into the project far too early in the process.

And don't worry, whoever you are, you are not in this book. I purposefully did not model any of the characters after anyone I've ever known, in order to minimize lawsuits and maintain friendships.

Finally, I'd like to thank you for taking the time to check out this novel. I hope you enjoy reading it as much as I enjoyed writing it. Assuming that you do, you would then become part of my marketing team, and as a member, your only assignment would be to tell as many people as you can about how much you liked the book you just read. :-)

Small, Dark, and Handsome
by Kevin D. Patterson

Stiletto Stilts

Thou shalt not hit on a taller woman. It wasn't anywhere in the Bible, but it was a dating commandment that I was learning to live by. This meant no initiating conversations with them, no flirting with them, and above all, no dating them. Based on my thirty-seven years' worth of experience, I was convinced that most women wanted nothing to do with men that didn't measure up to them in their highest heels. At 5'6", that usually didn't leave me with many women to choose from, but I'd have to work with the cards I had been dealt in order to one day find my queen.

Based on what I had seen, I doubted that I'd be able to discover my soulmate in the Saturday night crowd at the Urbia Lounge, Oakland, California's newest meat market. The place was packed with a host of WNBA-looking women who, judging by the uninviting scowls on some of their faces, seemed like they'd much rather dunk on me than dance with me.

I was supposed to meet up with my best friend, Fritz, over an hour ago, but he had clearly stood me up, and I would have left earlier if it weren't for the DJ who had been holding my ears hostage with an assortment of old school hip hop classics. After I reached the bottom of my second overpriced cocktail, I took a seat at a table near the small dance floor and watched some of the happy-go-lucky Millennials who seemed to be having the time of their lives. As the music transitioned into some obscenity-laced songs that were much more popular with the youngsters and much more of a mystery to me, I started to feel like a fish out of water until I felt a gentle tap on my shoulder. I spun around and was shocked to see a breathtaking 5'10" woman with the friendliest smile I had seen all night. Although it was tempting, I didn't allow

6

myself to get too excited because she probably thought she knew me, and the first words out of her mouth were bound to be an apology.

"Hi!" she said.

I stood up and then recognized the hint of surprise in her eyes. She clearly expected it to take me a bit more time to reach my full elevation, and was probably caught off guard when it didn't.

"Uh... hello."

"Hi! What's your name?"

"My name is Ethan."

"It's nice to meet you, Ethan." She extended her hand and said, "My name is Lisa."

"Hi, Lisa. It's very nice to meet you and I've gotta say, that dress looks fantastic on you!"

Hearing the words that had just slipped out of my mouth, confirmed that I had somehow shifted into partial flirt mode, and before I knew it, I found myself straining to see through Lisa's short black, see-through dress without being caught.

"Thanks, Ethan, and I hate to bother you, but I was wondering if you could do me a favor?"

"Sure!"

By that point, I was completely mesmerized by her smile, and was far too deep under her spell to put up any resistance. So, with the exception of robbing a bank, I was ready to help her do anything she asked.

"Could you take a picture of me and my girlfriends?" she pleaded as she pulled her phone out of her purse.

"No problem," I said while mentally kicking myself for flirting with a woman beyond my reach, and thereby breaking my commandment.

It took Lisa and her two friends a total of three minutes to "prep" for a pic that took me three seconds to take, and after I returned the camera, I half-heartedly asked her if it came out okay. I got my answer when I saw all three of their smiles fade at the same time, while they stared silently at the mess I had apparently just made.

When Lisa finally looked at me and said, "It's all good," I translated her response to mean, "It's not good at all," as I watched the three of them scamper away from me. My guess was that same picture would have been "just perfect" if I was 6'3", like the guy Lisa was now giving her camera to in the opposite corner of the lounge.

I decided to take one last lap around the place before calling it a night, but as soon as I placed my empty drink on a nearby table, a woman caught my eye. She was sitting at a small table near the edge of the dance floor, and I studied her intensely for a few minutes as she rocked back and forth to the beats that were pumping through the oversized speakers. She was alone, so if I was going to make a move, at least for the moment, I didn't need to worry about finding an unknown wingman and begging him to run interference on a potentially unfriendly girlfriend. She also didn't have a drink in her hand, which meant that she couldn't rely on the classic "I need to finish my drink" excuse. Best of all, she looked to be about 5'5" from my vantage point, which was right in my sweet spot.

After procrastinating for as long as I could, I finally decided to approach her, but instead of going with a bland "would you like to dance" line, I planned to throw in a "with me" at the end while motioning to my heart, implying that she'd surely break it if she turned me down. I tried to look casual as I nonchalantly made my way toward her, but I could sense that my window of opportunity was closing fast, as other male patrons were starting to take notice of the woman who had already been locked on my radar screen for the past five minutes. Adding to my anxiety was something inside, telling me that I was going to find a way to screw it up, as usual, but I was determined not to end the night on a sour note.

Just before I reached her table, she stood up and immediately my heart sank. While she was seated, I hadn't noticed her four-inch stiletto stilts, which gave her a height advantage on me that was at least three inches. The size of the challenge now standing in front of me dampened my mood faster than a busted condom. After the camera phone disaster just moments ago with Lisa, my first impulse was to race right by her and just pretend that I was in a hurry to catch up with an old buddy who looked a heck of a lot like the brick wall a few feet behind her. But, my only two friends in the place (Gin and Tonic) wouldn't allow me to turn back, and they quickly drowned out every negative thought that threatened to keep me from completing my mission.

"Would you like to dance with me?" I asked as I motioned to my heart.

She took one look at me (good sign), thought about it for the longest three seconds of my life (bad sign), looked around in both directions (worse sign), and then said, "No, I… uh… don't like the music in here." (Check please.)

Not waiting until she stood up was a rookie move that I was far too old to make, and before things could get any worse, I bolted toward the exit without saying another word. If nothing else, my encounters tonight with Ms. Quick Pic and Ms. Music Hater had validated the importance of always obeying my eleventh commandment in order to avoid these types of depressing and embarrassing episodes. I needed to just stick to my own kind: vertically disabled. They had to be 5'5" or shorter in heels, which meant that my son would be short, his son would be even shorter, and my great grandson wouldn't be tall enough to even ride a roller coaster.

Height Thing

I lived in a two-story townhouse in Hayward, California, which was about thirty-five minutes southeast of San Francisco without traffic... and in the Bay Area, there was always traffic. My little housing community was about five years old and had attracted a good mix of age groups and ethnicities, but as a single guy with no kids, I had always felt more at home in the larger nearby cities like Oakland and San Francisco, that had constant energy and a vibe that was nowhere to be found in my minivan-friendly 'hood. Through a recent conversation with a nosy elderly lady who deemed herself to be the leader (and the sole member) of our unofficial neighborhood watch program, I learned that most of my neighbors considered me to be a loner. This wasn't too surprising, since my cousin Mia had started calling my place the Bat Cave years ago, because, as she said, everyone figured it existed, but no one knew where it was, and no one had ever met anyone who had been there. On one hand, it made me seem fairly mysterious, which I liked. On the other hand, it implied that women didn't go near my place, which, although true, I didn't like at all.

This morning, however, I was expecting a visitor, and at 9:45 A.M., a series of loud bangs on my door announced Fritz's arrival. Why he never used the doorbell that was right in front of his face, I had no idea. I opened the door and there he stood without an ounce of guilt in his shameless expression.

"Nice of you to show up!" I said with as much attitude as I could muster. "Fritz, I waited over an hour for you last night! No text, no call, no nothing!"

His real name was Frederick Fitzgerald, but, as a kid, he insisted on being called Fritz, and I suspected it was to keep everyone from calling him "Double F," the nickname that aligned much better with his grammar school report cards. By high school, Fritz was actually one of the top students in our class, but he was also the undisputed class clown. Most of the time, he didn't have an off button, and if you sat too close to him, the guy could make you laugh out loud during a funeral.

"Hey, I'm sorry, but I got a better offer at the last minute, if ya know what I mean," he said with a stupid grin. "Besides, I know you had your hands full with all those dimes up in that spot. I would've just slowed you down." Fritz paused a moment for some form of confirmation from me, until he realized it wasn't coming. "Dammit Knox, don't tell me you left that place empty-handed!"

When we were kids, Fritz found out that my dad was originally from Knoxville, Tennessee, and he had called me Knox ever since. I guessed he didn't want to be the only Black kid in the neighborhood with a jacked up nickname.

"I asked a 5'9" woman to dance," I said.

"You did what?"

"Actually, she was about 5'5", but with her four-inch heels, she could have busted my windpipe with either breast. Too bad I didn't see the heels before I stepped to her."

"How did you know that she was 5'5" and how did you know that her heels made her 5 9"? Did you just whip out a measuring tape and ask her to stand still for a sec?"

"Just trust me, Fritz. If there's one thing I know, it's height."

"Okay, fine. So, what did she say?"

"She said she didn't like the music, but whatever. I didn't sweat her about it. I figured that she was just as embarrassed as I was, and didn't want to be seen talking to someone beneath her."

11

"Dammit, Knox, you can't possibly believe that you're beneath her or any other woman for that matter!"

"I was last night."

"Knox, I'm serious, and how many times do I have to tell you? You're not beneath anyone! You're not a shrimp, you're not a little guy, and you're not small! But when it comes to this height thing, you're small-minded as hell. And I know how you think, Knox."

"Do you?"

"Yeah—I do. You think that if you were just a few inches taller, everything would be perfect and you'd be bonin' babes left and right."

"Bonin' babes left and right isn't my definition of 'perfect,' but, yes, I've always thought that my social life could benefit from a few more inches. There's nothing I can do about that, of course, but I don't have a 'height thing.' I just know my strengths, and attracting women who want taller guys isn't one of them. It never was, and it never will be. Am I happy about it? No. But, I've come to accept it. So, why can't you?"

"Well, I don't know the clinical term for what you've got, but you definitely have 'something,' and there's only one sure-fire cure that I know of—we gotta get you laid."

Throughout our friendship, 'getting me laid' seemed to be Dr. Fritz's sole recommendation for a stomach ache, a sprained ankle, the hiccups, or any other ailment that I had ever mentioned.

"I'm trying my best, Fritz, but I can't find anyone you haven't slept with already. Speaking of which, have you hit the 925 area code yet? If not, promise me that you'll hold off and give me a head start, at least until the weekend."

"Very funny, but you know I'm right."

"Whatever."

Fritz looked like he had run out of patience. He pulled out his phone and pressed a button before sticking it in my face so that I could see my own reflection on his screen.

"Knox, you might not believe in this guy, but I do! Take a good look at him. He's got everything that these women say that they want. A six-figure income? Check! A nice crib in a nice neighborhood? Check! A late-model, European luxury ride? Check! An MBA from fuckin' Stanford? Check! No kids? Check! And if another woman tells me how cute or handsome he is, I'm just gonna vomit all over her!"

"What's your point?" I asked.

"My point is that none of this stuff will ever do you a bit of good if no one, besides us, knows about it. Does a tree in the forest make a sound when it falls?"

"Your analogy sucks, and you messed it up anyway. The correct question is, 'If a tree falls in a forest and no one is around to hear it, does it make a sound?'"

"Well, how about this one? Does your mattress squeak if no woman is around to hear it?"

"That analogy is even worse, but I guess you're suggesting that I need to change things up and start flossin' a little. Correct?"

"It's not just that. Knox, you need to be more proactive and start putting yourself out there. And you also need some more exposure. Have you ever thought about online dating?"

Since he had never mentioned online dating before, Fritz had caught me completely off guard with his suggestion, and he could probably tell by the stunned look on my face. "Are you talking about a real, legitimate dating site, or are you talking about a virtual brothel? And don't even pretend to be offended, because you know it's a valid question if you're suggesting it."

Fritz smiled before he said, "Offense taken, but I know that you're not ready for any of the advanced, big-boy sites yet."

Before I could defend myself, Fritz cut me off.

"Look, Knox, I know that socially, you're pretty damn conservative, but I almost cry when I think of all the talent that you're always leaving on the table. Trust me— they're out there, just waiting for a guy like you to scoop them up. You just need to forget about height or any of your other lame excuses and start using what you've got to get what you want."

Although I appreciated the fact that Fritz was trying to help in his own weird way, it sounded like the kind of advice a pimp would give to one of his girls before he pushed her out on to 'the track.'

Thirty-Seven-Year-Old Baby

Since my San Francisco 49ers had a bye and weren't playing, after Fritz left, I used the rest of the morning and part of the afternoon to take care of few errands. As soon as I got back home, the phone started ringing. When I saw Mom's name and number on the caller ID, I picked up the receiver.

"Hi, Mom!"

"How's my baby doing?" she asked.

"Your thirty-seven-year-old 'baby' is doing fine, Mom."

"And you'll still be my baby when you're sixty-seven, even if I'm no longer around."

"No longer around? Mom, I hope that's not a hint about why you called. Should I be sitting down or something?"

"Calm down, Ethan. There's nothing wrong with me. Of course, you would know that if you checked on me once in a while."

When I was a kid, I thought I had mastered the art of guilting my parents into doing things for me or giving me things I wanted, but somewhere down the line, the tables had turned, and when they did, I realized that I had always been an amateur compared to my mom, the real pro.

"I just called you yesterday!" I said.

"Yes, but you were returning my call from a few days earlier. You weren't calling just to chat or find out how I was doing."

When my father passed away two years ago, my mother was devastated, and since that time, I had made a conscious effort to see and speak to her on a regular basis. Despite the fact that she only lived fifteen minutes away from me, my brother and I didn't want her living alone, and we tried our best to convince her that she would be much better off living with his family in their suburban mini-mansion. I was worried about how she would cope without my father after forty-one years of marriage, and although she would never admit it, her pain was becoming more evident each month. By the slightly combative tone in her voice this morning, I realized that I was fighting a losing battle, so I decided to do what I did best: give in.

"I'm sorry, Mom. You know that you're everything to me, and regardless of what I think, if you feel that I'm not calling enough, then I'm not calling enough. I'm not planning to set a daily reminder on my calendar or anything like that, but I promise that I will call more often."

I could feel her smiling through the phone. "Okay, Ethan. That's all I wanted to hear. So what's going on with you these days? How's the job?"

"The job is fine, and before you ask, no, I'm not dating anyone special."

"Didn't you tell me yesterday that you were planning to go to a party or something like that last night?"

"It was a lounge."

"And did you go?"

"Yep."

"Ethan, your father and I didn't break our necks to send you to private schools that taught you to say 'yep' instead of 'yes.'"

"Sorry, Mom. Yes, I went to the lounge."

Ever since I moved out of her house almost twenty years ago, most of our calls had followed a predictably painful pattern, beginning with Mom peppering me with a few general questions, before going in for the kill and grilling me with questions about my glacial love life. Since my older brother, Malcolm, who was my only sibling, had literally cut his cord after having two sons, I represented her final hope for additional grandchildren, and I guess this line of questioning was her way of keeping hope alive.

"Well, didn't you meet anyone there?"

"Not anyone who would be worth bringing home to you one day, but I'll keep looking."

"Well, where else are you looking? Did you try online dating yet? You know they have a lot of different dating sites these days and on most of them, you can even see a woman's height before you decide to contact her."

"I've heard," I said as I wondered if my mom and Fritz had conspired to double-team me.

"What about speed dating, Ethan? Have you looked into that?"

"I tried it, but they said I was too slow."

"Ethan, can you be serious for a second? I'm trying to help!"

As my mother continued to rattle off suggestions for dating vehicles, something told me that she knew a lot more about online and offline dating than I ever did, which, given the fact that she was almost seventy years old and only recently widowed, kind of creeped me out.

After a few more minutes of sharing her free dating advice, Mom realized that she needed to get off the phone because her favorite TV game show was coming on in a few minutes. I considered reminding her about the DVR I had bought her last Christmas, and how I had showed her how to record all the game shows she could ever want, but I was ready to get off the phone as well. After we hung up, I thought for a moment about what she had said. Although her approach was slightly different, her message was basically the same as the one Fritz had shared earlier: if I was going to find the woman for me, I had to really start searching.

Online Lovin'

Although I hated to admit it, the quickest and easiest way for me to start my quest would be to follow Fritz's and my mom's advice by signing up with an online dating site like Match.com. In the past, I never had the time, energy, or patience to deal with online dating, but I did get a strange sense of comfort seeing first-hand all the profiles of other people who were also looking for love. Nothing screams "you are not alone" like a database of over 20 million available singles.

I wolfed down a steak salad for dinner, and after pulling up the Match.com website and opening up an account, I was ready to embark on my first online lovin' adventure. I signed up with a fake name and a generic user ID (justsomeguy291). Then I completed the "about me" section of my profile, but I didn't spend much time on it because I was anxious to dive head first into the pool of eligible women who would fit my yet-to-be-determined criteria.

When I clicked on the "Customized Search" link, I was confronted by an overwhelming list of criteria categories, but I stopped when I saw the first category under the "Appearance" section: Height. Though she innocently tried to slip it in, my mother's comment earlier about height got me thinking about my eleventh commandment. There was no doubt in my mind that my size had limited my available pool of dating prospects, but were most women really against dating shorter guys? More importantly, were the women I wanted really against dating shorter guys? It was something I always felt and assumed based on my personal experiences, but I never had any hard core, objective proof. So, in order to set the record straight once and for all, I decided it was time to conduct an experiment that would confirm what I already knew in my heart to be true.

At a high level, my project seemed to be pretty simple. First, I would need to generate a listing of female profiles that had my ideal criteria for a mate, and then I would compare the difference between their average heights and the average height of their ideal matches. In particular, I selected women who were single or divorced, between the ages of thirty and forty, lived in California, and had listed their ethnicity as Black/African descent. I was tempted to open up my criteria to women of all races and was fairly confident that my results would be race neutral, but I decided to just keep a narrow focus for this experiment.

When I hit the search button, the results generated over two thousand profiles, which was way too many. By the time I made it through all of them, I'd already be receiving reminders to renew my AARP membership. In order to speed things up, I decided to limit my search geography to women who lived within fifty miles of my place, and I also decided to just include data from every fourth profile in my analysis. The perfectionist in me wanted to make sure the process would include a statistically significant number of profiles, but the experiment felt less scientific by the minute, and by the time I was done, I would have a tough time getting my project admitted into a second grade science fair.

Two hours later, I had a spreadsheet filled with data on 186 profiles. I had only captured screen names, heights, and preferred heights for a mate, but that was all the ammo I needed. I spent another thirty minutes slicing and dicing the data like a Benihana chef, creating graphs and tables with details that only someone in a straitjacket could truly appreciate. It was time to present my findings, or at least find someone who would listen and pretend to care, and the first person I thought of was my cousin, Mia.

When she answered the phone, I gave her a warm, friendly greeting. "M-I-A, whatcha say!"

"Is this my freakin' cousin who knows good and damn well that I've gotta wake up in a few hours for an early morning flight across the country?" I had been so consumed by my project that I had completely forgotten about her trip, and suddenly my research didn't seem that important. "Your aunt felt compelled to call and wake up her loving daughter thirty minutes ago, and after I finally convinced her that she hadn't picked up a damn virus on her computer, here you come."

"I thought I was the only employee working her 24/7 free tech support line. And wasn't she worried about a virus last week?"

"Yes, and the week before that, and the week before that. But I'm guessing that you didn't call this late to talk about my mom's virus phobia."

"No, but I did want to talk to you about something computer-related," I said.

"Sorry, you've reached 'us' after business hours. Please call back tomorrow."

"Okay, I'll catch up with you another time," I said reluctantly.

"Wait! What the hell are you calling me this late about computer stuff for, Ethan? You're way more technical than I'll ever be."

"Well, it's actually about a website—Match.com."

"Oh my God! You went out with someone you met on Match?"

"No."

"Someone contacted you through Match?"

"No."

"Someone winked at you?"

"No."

"Someone viewed your profile?"

If I didn't feel like a loser already, the fact that Mia got excited about the possibility of someone merely viewing my profile made me want to crawl into a deep dark hole.

"Look Mia, I just signed up for the first time, so I don't have anything juicy to report yet, but, I did use it to do some research."

"Did you say 'research?' Don't tell me that you're one of those weirdoes who only logs on to use women as unsuspecting lab rats."

"I didn't *use* anyone. I just took a look at some information that they willingly listed on their profiles."

"Information? What kind of information? I bet it has something to do with height."

"As a matter of fact, it does." I heard a faint "Oh, Lord" muttered under Mia's breath, but I carried on. "Now, haven't you heard me say that most women I'm interested in prefer taller guys?"

"Repeatedly."

"Well, thanks to Match, I can prove it."

I could picture Mia's eyes rolling upward right before she said, "Okay, let's hear your proof."

Before she could change her mind, I quickly emailed her all of the data that I had compiled for my experiment, and after she confirmed that she had pulled it up on her laptop, which seemed to be on and near her at all times, I proudly started to explain my approach and the steps that I used to set up my project. I then took her through the data at a high level, and finished my late night presentation off with a big conclusion, which I had summarized on the final slide. "So, as you can see, over seventy-two percent of the women in my study indicated that their ideal height for their mate is at least three inches greater than their own height."

"So?" Mia said.

"So, combined with my personal observations of thirty-seven years, this is yet another data point to prove what I've been telling you for years about women and this height thing."

"First of all, let's be clear—you're the one who has a 'thing' about height, and you always have. Secondly, you have absolutely no data to prove that these women wouldn't go out with a guy who is shorter than their stated ideal height, especially if he seems to have a lot of other attractive qualities. And third, I doubt that the criteria that you used allowed you to generate a representative sample of the type of women you would date in real life. For example, it doesn't look like you included any height limitations, but I seriously doubt you'd go out with the woman in row seventeen who's 6'4", now would you? And you wouldn't go out with the woman in row thirty-two who's 6'2", would you? Hell, would you even go out with the woman in row fifty-seven who's 5'11"?" I didn't answer, but Mia took care of that. "No, you wouldn't! And that means your data is flawed and that your study can't tell you jack shit… And don't forget, twenty-eight percent of the women in your screwed-up experiment didn't have the height preference that you mentioned, and that's still a large number…" I couldn't even respond. "Ethan, you're a great guy and I know that you've had a tough time finding the right woman, but instead of looking for reasons why it may not be happening as quickly as you'd like, why don't you focus more energy on just finding her?"

I had to hand it to Mia. She knew how to take the wind out of my sails, but I knew she'd never leave me drifting aimlessly.

"And where should I be looking?" I said. Given the recent advice from Fritz and Mom, I expected her to tell me that looking online at a site like Match was a good start, but that I just needed to quit experimenting and start searching.

"Well, I'm glad you asked! It just so happens that my girlfriends and I are throwing a party and we all have to bring a single guy who we're not dating. So, if you're not busy next Saturday night, I'd love for you to come with me."

Assuming I heard her correctly, my cousin had just invited me to a "Feed your Friends" party, and I wasn't quite sure how I should feel about it. While I was kind of flattered that Mia thought I might be good enough for one of her girlfriends, I could picture myself among a group of other misfits being paraded around her fellow "judges" all night like show horses, with little to no insight into their scoring system and final assessments. Not knowing what the night might have in store for me, I at least wanted to confirm that I'd have a decent amount of eye candy to snack on if all else failed.

"Well, what do your friends look like? Do you have any pictures?"

"Pictures? What is with you guys and pictures? Why do you always need to see pictures before you make any decisions?" Mia's strong reaction took me by surprise, but since she had already sacrificed enough sleep time dealing with me, I decided to let it slide for now.

After I agreed to go blindly into whatever Mia and her friends were cooking up, we decided to touch base soon to discuss party logistics before we said our good-byes. As I began to collect the pages of worthless data that I had printed out for my research project, I couldn't help but smile at how Mia turned my almost three hours' worth of work into a meaningless mess in less than thirty seconds. I walked over to the trash bin, but before throwing everything out, I glanced at the spreadsheet one last time and noticed that the 5'11" woman in row fifty-seven had listed a range between 5'5" and 6'5" as her preference for an ideal mate. During the experiment, I had pulled up all the profiles of the women who were part of the random sample, but I had only focused on data, not faces. I did a quick visual scan of the spreadsheet and realized that she was the only woman who had indicated a willingness to connect with someone much shorter than she was, so, I plugged her username to pull up her profile again, this time with the intention of taking a closer look.

I expected to see an eyeball in the middle of her forehead, but was stunned to see a headshot of a very attractive woman with a warm and inviting smile. I clicked on the three other photos in her profile and was equally impressed with each one, although the action shot of her spiking a volleyball while wearing shorts that showed off her long, athletic legs was also a little intimidating. After reading her intro and the rest of her profile, I could see that we had some common interests and might possibly get along well, but as I reminded myself, I had an eleventh commandment that had to be followed. So, once again, I picked up the printed pages from my experiment, but this time, I fed them into the shredder until the evidence of my failure was gone.

Primetime

The house party was scheduled to take place at the apartment of Mia's friend, Paula, and in the days leading up to it, I spent several lunches, coffee breaks, and phone calls trying to convince Mia that we didn't need to show up at the listed start time on the invite.

"Come on, Mia! You know it'll just be you, me, and Paula there if we show up at eight o'clock. Nobody shows up on time to a party, and if we did, I bet you Paula would put us right to work! I'm sure it'll take you at least an hour to do all of your woman stuff in order to get ready, and you can't tell me that after all that prep, you'd be willing to help Paula mop her floors and scrub her toilets."

I was trying to paint Mia an ugly picture of what an early arrival might mean for her, but I was more concerned with the possibility of Paula introducing me to her vacuum cleaner.

"Ethan, Paula's my girl, and if she needs help, I want to be there for her. She'd do the same for me."

"Wouldn't you rather show up at Primetime?" I asked.

"And exactly what time is that?"

"That's when all of the food is ready and the party is in full swing."

The definition that I gave her was partially correct. I learned long ago that the best time for me to show up at any party, event, or function was the half-way point between the time that the majority of the food was ready, and the time that the majority of the women (who drink) were as tipsy (and receptive to my weak rap) as they were going to get. That was what I called Primetime, but I knew that if I gave Mia the full definition, she would, no doubt, give me an earful.

"Ethan, *I* invited *you*, so I'll be the one to determine when we get there. Not you. Besides, we both know that your social life has turned into more of a solo life these past few months, so I thought you'd be eager to get the first crack at each woman that shows up."

"Look who's talking! I haven't even heard you mention a guy since your high school crush on what's-his-butt."

"His name was Craig, and just because I don't always choose to share details about my personal life with you, doesn't mean there's nothing worth sharing."

"Okay, then. Let's make this party a bit more interesting for both of us. Let's make a bet!"

"A bet? Ethan, given your victim mentality these days, it's a pretty safe *bet* that you walk away empty-handed."

"And I bet you do, too. So, whoever goes out on at least one date with someone they meet for the first time at the party, gets a free lunch at a restaurant of their choice." It sounded like a good way to motivate us, but given Mia's champagne tastes, I literally had a lot on the line.

"Okay, you're on, Ethan. But I'm still planning to have us there at eight."

"Why don't we just take two cars so that we can both show up when we're ready?" I asked.

"No! I told you the rules of the party. My girlfriends expect me to show up with a respectable young man, and even if I have to drag your triflin' ass out of your house, into my car, and into the party, you're coming with me like you promised!"

I wasn't sure how I could be triflin' and respectable at the same time, but regardless, I still didn't want to show up too early. Thankfully, Mia called me the night of the party and said that she was running twenty minutes late, which turned out to be forty-five minutes. We were further delayed by an accident on the freeway, and by the time we made it to the party, it was almost half past nine. Based on the scents of all the tasty hot dishes coming from the kitchen, the number of empty and half-empty glasses scattered around the apartment, and the sight of various women giggling and wobbling around like toddlers taking their first steps, I felt like there should have been a giant "Mission Accomplished" banner behind me as I proudly entered the apartment.

"Mia! There you are. I've been looking all over for you! Where've you been?" said a 5'8" woman with a short afro.

Before she could answer, Mia heard her name coming from another direction.

"Hey, Mia—I was getting worried! What took you so long?" said a 5'4" woman wearing tall brown boots that almost went up under her jean skirt.

Under the brim of her tilted black hat, I could see Mia shooting a sharp glare in my direction, which made it clear that she was not a happy camper. But, she knew that she couldn't blame me as she responded to those and a few more "what took you so long" questions from various girlfriends within the first few minutes of our arrival.

As I watched these exchanges, it soon dawned on me that Mia wasn't introducing me to anyone, which led me to believe that she had taken our little bet a bit more seriously than I had hoped. After a while, "Bootsy," as I had nicknamed the woman in the high boots, noticed as well.

"Hey, Mia, aren't you going to start introducing your friend, or are you just gonna keep him leashed up to that lamp he's been guarding since you two arrived?"

I don't think they knew that I could hear them, but it didn't matter. My wallflower act obviously wasn't scoring me any cool points, so, with or without a tour guide, I decided it was time to start my own expedition. Before I could get going, a 5'5" woman stumbled over to Mia and whispered something in her ear.

Begrudgingly, Mia said, "Kendra, this is my cousin, Ethan. Ethan, this is my friend Kendra."

Kendra eagerly reached for my hand, but just based on her exterior, I could tell right away that she wasn't my type. She had a full figure, which, in most cases, was fine with me, but thanks to her questionable fashion choices, every inch of it was fully on display, which was not fine at all. She also had a terrible weave that had more visible tracks than New York's Grand Central station, and highlighted a head full of recycled hair that surely looked much better on its original Indian owner.

"Hi, Kendra. It's nice to meet you," I said.

"You, too, Ethan." She turned to Mia and said, "I didn't know that you had any male relatives in the area."

Something about the way she said "male relatives" made it sound like a dish specifically created for her consumption. Before Mia could answer, Kendra turned her attention back to me.

"Are you just visiting, or do you live here in the Bay Area?" she asked.

Mia cut me off and said, "Ethan usually stays hidden in his Bat Cave. No one really knows where it is, but he keeps showing up, so it must be around here somewhere."

I gave her a touché-type nod as I wondered how quickly we could move away from this conversation, and more importantly, away from this woman.

I got the feeling that Mia wasn't feeling Kendra's vibe tonight either, because it wasn't long before we broke away and she introduced me to another one of her friends. "Hey, Paula, I forgot to introduce you to my cousin, Ethan. Ethan, this is Paula, and since this is her place, I guess she's technically the hostess."

"It's nice to meet you, Ethan, but just so ya know, I am nobody's hostess tonight! So, if you need one, y'all betta host yourselves."

Even though she was about 5'9" in her sizable heels, there was something about Paula that I kind of liked. With her short stylish haircut, big deep dimples, and comforting smile, she easily stood out from the crowd. But I had a commandment to keep, which meant that she was off limits.

"Mia never mentioned a cousin. Are you from around here?"

"I am, but I've apparently been stashed away in my cousin's witness protection program for quite a while." I shot a quick glance at Mia who shot me one back, and then I turned back to Paula. "I grew up in Fremont."

"So did I! Where did you go to high school?"

If there's one game I couldn't stand, it was the one I called "Education Disconnection." It always started with the "where did you go to school" question, and usually ended in an awkward moment of frustration after it became clear that one person didn't know any of the people the other person thought they should know and/or vice versa. So, to avoid getting caught up in it, I often threw out some off-the-wall answer to my fellow contestant, which tended to end the game pretty quickly.

"I didn't finish high school, but I got my GED last year," I said with a straight face. I was almost certain that Mia was going to blow my cover and tell Paula that I was messing with her, but since she didn't interrupt, I guess she was interested in Paula's reaction as well.

"Oh... uh... that's cool. Well, the drinks are in the kitchen and there are a couple of people coming around with some trays of some fancy-schmancy appetizers. If you guys need anything else, just let me know. I'm going to welcome some more of our guests. Ciao!" I had to laugh at how quickly my GED line had turned Paula into a hostess after all, as I watched her depart, presumably in search of some better-educated guests.

As I continued to feast on hot Buffalo wings and check out a few of the buzzed female guests who seemed to be struggling with gravity, I was confident that it was still Primetime. But, other than an extra 800 or so calories from my wings, and an embarrassing wet spot from a cocktail that a slightly drunk woman spilled near the crotch of my pants, I had absolutely nothing to show for it.

Bad Boy

We had been at the party for over an hour, and while I had met quite a few women on my own, I wasn't feeling any of them. Even worse was the fact that I had almost forgotten about Mia. She wasn't at the party to just babysit and make introductions for me. She was hoping to make her own love connection, and from the looks of things, she wasn't having much luck either. Like me, she had her own history of dating challenges to deal with. In particular, Mia had spent a lot of time trying to convince me how much the deck was stacked against Black women in the game of love. Yet, she remained an eternal optimist, despite enduring several relationships with men who turned out to be in several other relationships at the same time, and even though it might cost me a steak and lobster lunch, I truly wanted her to find a great (or at least a decent) guy who deserved all the wonderful things she had to offer.

I decided it was time to check in with her, but first I wanted to make a pit stop in the kitchen to reload my empty right hand with another beverage. After finding a beer in the cooler, I reached down to grab it while I looked out into the living room in hopes of spotting my cousin. All of a sudden, something in the cooler grabbed onto my thumb, causing me to jump back and knock several ice cubes out on to the floor.

"Oh shit! I'm *so* sorry," said the woman who had grabbed me instead of a beer. If I hadn't known better, I could've sworn that she gave me a quick head to toe scan before she stretched out her hand and said, "By the way, I'm Claudia."

She was about 5'3" with sparkling eyes, a milk chocolate complexion, and a short, curly hairstyle that was well suited for her cute rounded face. To say that she was

31

easy on the eyes would have been a gross understatement, and as I touched her for the second time, I had a sense that the real party was about to get started.

"Hi, I'm Ethan. Sorry for the cold wet hands."

"No problem. I've seen where they've been," she said with a sweet smile. "And, I'm sorry for scaring you."

My chest was still heaving when my ego forced me to respond. "I wasn't scared, just a little startled."

She chuckled and said, "Well, Ethan, I'll try my best not to 'startle' the crap out of you again."

I laughed and said, "I'd appreciate that."

I noticed Claudia sort of looking around before she said, "So, Ethan, who brought you to the party?"

"My cousin, Mia, invited me. Do you know her?"

"Oh, yeah, I know Mia! I met her a few years ago. We only run into each other once in a while, but she seems real cool."

"Yeah, she's cool, but she's been a terrible hostess. She should have introduced me to you immediately." After only a couple of words, I felt like I was already coming on way too strong, and although I couldn't see them, my fangs were undoubtedly visible and glistening. Fortunately, Claudia didn't look scared at all, and judging by her body language, she seemed willing to at least hear me out. "So, you know that Mia brought me here, but who did you bring?" I asked. Based on the rules of the party, she wasn't supposed to be dating whomever she brought, so I shouldn't have been concerned, but I was still a bit curious.

"Honestly, I just couldn't think of anyone, so I just came by myself." If she were a contestant on my game show, I would have congratulated her on giving me the answer that I was looking for.

"Well, I hope you weren't just going to grab a beer and go drink it in some lonely corner by yourself?"

She smiled and said, "No, I was talking to some girlfriends who are waiting for me over there." She pointed

32

to three women in the far corner who were doing a very bad job of pretending they weren't spying on us.

I gave her a grin that was undoubtedly more scary than sexy and said, "Well, I hope you don't mind making them wait a little longer."

Claudia flashed another smile, and even though she gave no indication that she was going anywhere, I suddenly felt like I'd been given just two minutes to impress the hell out of the late night crowd at the Improv.

To my surprise, she was in a talkative mood and before I knew it, I had stretched my two-minute audition into a thirty-minute routine. By the time we both cracked open our next beer, I was actually starting to feel good about the impression I was making on her.

"I don't know, Ethan. You kinda come off as a square and geeky guy, but I can tell that you've got something to hide. I just can't figure out what it is yet."

"Square and geeky wasn't the look I was going for. Can you give me a quick bad boy makeover?" According to my dream script, Claudia was supposed to seductively whisper something erotic to me like, "Not now, but maybe later," as she lightly brushed the bottom of my earlobe with her juicy bottom lip, but even though she looked like she had a sexy comeback line for me, it quickly became apparent that she had the wrong script when she started laughing loudly in my face.

"Ethan, I hope I'm not offending you, but I just don't think you have an ounce of bad boy in you, which is okay."

"Well, do you ever hang out with boys who aren't initially that bad, but show some potential and eventually prove to be worse than you could ever imagine?" I joked.

The music was thumping loudly, forcing everyone's conversation to be even louder, including ours. Unfortunately for me, someone chose the wrong moment to kick a cord that temporarily paused the beats right when Claudia was in the middle of shouting her response.

"And what do you mean by 'hang out?' Do you mean, like, go on a date with you or something?"

As the phrase "go on a date with you" echoed loudly throughout the party, everyone seemed to stop what they were doing and turn in our direction, while I just stood there helplessly praying that Scotty would quickly beam me back up to the Enterprise. Fortunately, the music kicked back on a few seconds later, much to the disappointment of our fellow party people who slowly turned away from our cliffhanger and reluctantly went back to their conversations.

I was still a bit shaken from the momentary interruption when I heard Claudia's voice again. "Ethan, I hope you don't take this the wrong way, but I'm a grown woman, and I don't 'hang out' anymore except with my girlfriends. So, are you or are you not asking me out on a date?"

Now I knew what women meant when they complained about men taking all the romance out of a situation. Still, I always had a thing for assertive women, and Claudia's willingness to call me out somehow made her even more attractive.

"Yes, Claudia. I, Ethan Anderson, being of a semi-sound mind and body, do hereby ask you to join me, for an evening on a date yet to be determined."

She didn't answer right away, and instead, she gave me a weird, uncomfortable stare. Judging from the look in her eyes, it appeared that she was having an internal debate, and while there could have been a million reasons why she might be hesitant, I found myself slightly standing on my tiptoes to make me appear to be a half inch taller, just in case.

"Okay, Ethan, I'll give you my number."

She sounded almost defeated, but I felt victorious as I slowly came down off my ballerina pose. I whipped out my phone and was ready to categorize her contact info as a "favorite." After I entered her number and called her back to ensure that she had mine. I looked around to see if I could get a visual high-five from Mia or anyone else who had witnessed my moment of triumph. Unfortunately, Claudia was the only one paying attention to me, and since I had no confidence in my ability to avoid saying something stupid that might make her regret or even change her mind about what she had just committed to, I realized that I needed to break away.

Someone above must've heard my prayer because the next thing I knew, Mia walked right up to us and said, "I guess I can cross this intro off my list!"

I gave Mia a cheesy grin to let her know that I was well on my way to winning our bet, but I'm not sure she picked up on it.

"Hey, girl!" Claudia said with a smile as she gave Mia a light hug. "How's it going?"

"Pretty good, but not as good as you! You look great!" Mia's enthusiasm made it sound like she was referring to her friend's recent and substantial weight loss, and my smile quickly faded as I suddenly pictured a chubby Claudia pushing our chubby little son in his XL stroller. "When did you cut your hair?" Mia asked as she admired her friend's 'do.

I glanced at Claudia and I let out a silent sigh of relief after I realized that our kids wouldn't be short and fat... just short.

It must've looked like I was watching a tennis match as I politely turned back and forth from Claudia to Mia while they played several sets of girlfriend catch-up as if I wasn't even there. Eventually, Claudia excused herself to get back to her girlfriends, and once I noticed that there weren't any guys in the direction she was headed, I silently gave her my blessing and promised to call her the next day. She then gave me a tight, full-body hug, which I hoped we would reenact sometime in the near future.

When I turned around, Mia was staring at me with her arms crossed, expecting me to give her the full details on what went down between me and Claudia. But, nature had been calling for a while, and could no longer be ignored. So, Mia would have to wait a few minutes for her update.

"Hey, Paula, where's your bathroom?" I screamed across the room.

Paula came closer and told me in a more appropriate volume that it was "down the hall to the right." By the time I had locked the door and lifted the toilet seat, I was doing a wild and frantic pee dance that Michael Jackson couldn't have duplicated in his prime. While I was redistributing my beer, I looked over to my right and saw that there was another door to the bathroom that I hadn't noticed before. Fortunately, it was already locked, which meant that I didn't have to worry about any unwanted surprises from that direction. I washed my hands and was about to go catch up with Mia when I heard some voices coming from the second door. It sounded like two women, which piqued my interest, and when I recognized Claudia's voice, I quickly found myself down on my knees trying to listen in through the crack under the door.

After suffering through five minutes of basic girlfriend chitchat, I was bored to death and was hoping that I'd find Claudia to be much more entertaining on our date. I was about to put an end to my brief career in espionage when they started talking about a subject that I actually cared about: me.

"Dang, Claudia! I still can't believe it! I mean, I thought you were just gonna chill tonight."

"I was."

"Well, what happened? Audrey said she saw you all huddled up in a corner with some dude!"

"Girl, trust me, I was just as surprised as she was. After all that damn drama that Tony just put me through, I wasn't tryin' to talk to any guys tonight and I almost stayed at home. I really just came to catch up with you and the rest of my girls, but when I saw this cutie heading over to the cooler, I didn't see any harm in just checking him out for a second."

"Now, Claudia, I know you didn't just go up and start talking to him! I can't imagine you doing anything that bold. Did he come up to you?"

"No, he wasn't even looking my way, and I didn't know what to do. So, I just kinda… I don't know… 'accidentally' grabbed at him while he was reaching for a beer."

"Grabbed at him?"

I couldn't tell for certain, but it seemed like Claudia was reenacting our intro scene for her friend who, by this time, was laughing hard, and even I had to smile at the way Claudia had convinced me that her smooth move was purely accidental.

"So, what's the scoop? Tell me all about him."

"Well, his name is Ethan, he's super cute, he's from the Bay Area, and he lives in Hayward. I don't know much more about him yet, but he seems really sweet and he's got a pretty good sense of humor."

"How tall is he?"

"Well, I think he's only 5'5" or 5'6", and as you know, I normally prefer them a little taller…"

The light knock on the door that I had apparently been ignoring for a while was now a loud series of bangs. But it didn't matter because I had heard enough and I was ready to leave. Claudia was only five freakin' three at best, and less than an hour after she had given me her number, she said that I wasn't tall enough for her. It didn't make any sense to me, but if she preferred guys who could rest their balls on her forehead, I wasn't going to waste my time with her. I erased her contact info from my phone and hoped that it would be just as easy to erase her completely from my mind.

When I came out, I was greeted by four pissed-off faces, but their desire to get into the bathroom had possibly been tempered by the thought of whatever I had been doing in there for the past ten minutes. I mumbled an apology to the first person in line and quickly walked away.

I was pissed off and ready to leave, but I wasn't ready to talk about what I had overheard, and I didn't want to ruin Mia's night just because mine had been. When I scanned the room, I saw my cousin near the bottom of a staircase.

"Hey, Mia!"

"Hey, Ethan, what's up? How are things going with Claudia? It looks like you two hit it off!"

"Yeah, we exchanged numbers and we'll see what happens."

"That's great," she said before pausing a moment and saying, "but, why am I happier about it than you seem to be?"

"I'm actually not feeling too good, and I think I'm going to just jump in a cab and head home."

"Don't be ridiculous, I'll drive you," she said, "let me just say some quick goodbyes."

"Mia, don't even think about it. There's no way I'm letting you leave this party because of me. Trust me, I'll be fine."

"Ethan!"

"Mia, please don't worry about me!"

She looked at me for a moment with her hands on her hips, as if she were trying to determine why I was being so stubborn.

"Okay, Ethan. I can see that I'm not going to talk you out of it, but promise me that you'll text me tonight to let me know that you made it home safely, and that you'll call me tomorrow when you're feeling better."

I smiled and gave Mia a big hug and said, "I promise."

As I let Mia go, I looked up at the guy who had been standing next to her. After he gave me a friendly head nod, I made eye contact with Mia and tried to non-verbally ask her if I had interrupted anything. When she shook her head, it was clear to me that tonight we probably were both losers, and unfortunately, there would be nothing memorable about this house party for either one of us.

My Little Big Brother

By the time I got home, I was still fuming and way too wound up to go to sleep. I needed to talk to someone, but since it was past midnight on Sunday morning, my options were limited. Normally, I did my venting with Mia, but more than likely, she was still at the party and I wasn't ready to speak with her anyway. I considered calling Fritz, but at this hour, unless he heard a female voice moaning in the background, he wouldn't be interested in anything I had to say. My third option was my brother, Malcolm, who was two years older and two inches shorter than I was. He was the proudest 5'4" man I had ever known, and if anyone could help me understand women and this height thing, it was my little big brother.

Although Malcolm was a family man with a wife and two young sons, he was a night owl and usually stayed up watching TV and surfing the web most evenings. I never missed a chance to tease him about his late-night habits, and I had recently sent him a virtual postcard I found online of a little girl praying with her eyes closed. The caption on the card read, "Dear God, please send some clothes to those poor ladies on my daddy's computer." In response, Malcolm sent me a picture of his fully naked middle finger a few days later.

I didn't want to risk waking Malcolm's wife, Anita, and my two young nephews, so, knowing he'd be online, I sent him an email and asked him to call me back right away. I knew that my cryptic message might alarm him, but I didn't want to risk getting a call in the middle of the night, which was always a possibility with Malcolm. Two minutes later, my cell phone rang.

"What's up? Is Mom okay?"

"I don't know. Why don't you call her sometime to find out?"

"Ethan, don't tell me she's got you helping on her latest guilt trip campaign?"

"You'll be happy to know that she pulls the same thing on me, but I didn't call about Mom. I just got back from a party."

"A party? Let me guess—you met a woman and you need some advice."

I didn't know if I was more annoyed at Claudia for what she had said about my height, or at Malcolm for correctly guessing why I called. "While you're at it, can you give me the Super Lotto numbers for Saturday? I promise to buy the hostages some nice stuff with part of the money I win." I occasionally referred to my nephews as 'the hostages' to remind my brother that I hadn't seen them in a while and that it was about time for him to prove that they were still alive and well.

"When your frugal-ass starts talking about spending money on your nephews, I know you've been drinking."

"I know your family-man ass hasn't been to a party since New Edition was on top of the charts, but trust me, they still serve alcohol at them," I said.

"And I see that your perpetually single-ass is still having problems with women."

All this ass-talk was getting us nowhere, and though I was starting to second guess my decision to get my brother's advice, I still wanted him to know what set me off. "Oh, this one acted fine in front of my face, but as soon as my back was turned, she showed her true colors."

"Go on," Malcolm said.

I spent the next few minutes giving Malcolm a blow-by-blow account of my exchange with Claudia, including what I overheard on my knees in the bathroom.

"So, that's the story," I said.

"Okay, here's what I'd do. I'd call her as if I never heard anything in the bathroom."

"Didn't you hear what I said? I specifically heard her say that she prefers taller guys!"

"So? Anita would prefer that I didn't snore myself to sleep every night and I'd prefer that she didn't wear her Halloween-looking, avocado dip mask to bed all the time. Anita would prefer that I didn't watch so much football and I'd prefer that she'd stop watching those damn house-hunting shows 24/7 and start appreciating the big dream home that she already has. Anita would prefer that I lost ten pounds and I'd prefer that she lost fifteen pounds. Anita would—"

"Malcolm, I get your point."

"So, are you gonna call her?" he asked.

I honestly didn't know and said, "I'll think about it."

"Good. And for the record, I never said one word about Anita's weight."

Restraining Order

When I woke up eight hours later, my thoughts were on Claudia, just as they had been when I finally hung up with Malcolm. I had memorized her number shortly after she gave it to me, and although I had re-entered it into my cell phone, I had no idea if or when I'd ever use it. I decided to mull it over some more at the gym, while burning off some of the beer and fattening appetizers that I had consumed at the party.

I packed my gym bag, grabbed a banana from my desolate fruit bowl, and began to devour it as I scrolled through my personal email box on my cell. As usual, it was stuffed with miscellaneous sales promotions, requests to complete surveys, invitations to free seminars, and far too many e-newsletters, all of which went directly into my trash bin. One email that did catch my eye was from Match.com, which indicated that someone had sent me a message. Given the fact that I hadn't posted a picture on my meager profile, I was immediately suspicious. I clicked on the email and was stunned to see the same profile picture of the 5'11" woman from row fifty-seven that I had briefly checked out a few days ago. She had probably received a note alerting her that I had recently reviewed her profile. I clicked on her message:

Hi! Thanks for checking out my profile. I checked out yours as well and noticed that we have some things in common. I think it would be fun to connect sometime, so if you're interested, let me know.

Regards,

Anna

Although I was intrigued, knowing that she decided to reach out to me despite my sparse profile had me pretty skeptical. Having never met a Black woman named "Anna" had me even more suspicious, even though I had never met another Black man named "Ethan." Of course, my overly optimistic ego didn't want it to be a scam, but as tempted as I was to send her a brief reply, I had to remind myself that she was 5'11", and I wasn't. I had learned my lesson about breaking my commandment, and there was no doubt that I would be better off with a 5'3" Claudia who would prefer a taller man, than a 5'11" woman who, more than likely, wanted much more than I had to offer.

Historically, I tried not to work much on the weekends, but I spent most of the afternoon developing an important slide deck that I was scheduled to present two days later. As the product marketing manager for a small software company, I was often called upon to give key presentations and demos to help our salespeople close big-money deals. While they were all experts on the golf course, most of our sales reps couldn't even spell PowerPoint at gunpoint, which gave me some comfort in terms of job security, but also intensified the importance of every client-facing move I made.

I had cleared my calendar at work the next day so that I'd have ample time to put the finishing touches on my presentation before sharing it internally. When I woke up, I got dressed, and headed straight to Starbucks to pick up a copy of the paper and get some caffeine into my system before heading into the office. As I got closer to the store front displaying the familiar Starbucks logo, I could see the long line inside through the glass windows. Fortunately, I had left much earlier than usual and had plenty of time to spare, so I went inside and waited patiently in line as it stubbornly inched along. The newspapers were kept on a rack near the register and I was almost there when I heard a familiar voice.

"Sorry, Ethan, but we're out of the Journal already," said Stan, the fourteen-year-old-looking "barista."

"Stan, you've gotta be kidding! I've never seen you guys run out and I almost never come in this early!"

"I don't know what to tell you, but maybe you can piece one together from the copies that people have left behind?" The thought of embarking on a treasure hunt in order to piece together the *Wall Street Journal* from the various newspapers scattered randomly throughout the crowded café didn't thrill me. So instead, I headed across the street to pick up a fresh copy at the corner store.

The tiny bells tied to the inside of the door announced my arrival, and after stepping into the store, I went directly over to the newspaper section where I spotted a short stack of *Wall Street Journals*. I took a quick glance at the headline before I picked one up and headed toward the register. Ahead of me was a tall brunette woman wearing a business suit and heels that made her at least six feet tall. She had placed a few feminine products on the counter and was now pointing to a pack of cigarettes in the case behind the register. She didn't notice me at all, and out of curiosity, I got a little closer to see how it might feel to accompany a taller woman in public.

I allowed my mind to drift and for a moment, we were a couple. The way she towered over me was a little intimidating and somewhat uncomfortable. As I inched even closer, instead of feeling like her man, I felt like a little kid again, waiting for Mom to pay for her items, and hoping that she didn't notice the pack of Starburst that I quietly placed in her basket.

"What the hell are you doing?" the brunette lady said as she stepped back and pulled her purse close to her body.

Her voice snapped me out of my daydream, and made me realize that I was close enough to justify a restraining order.

"I... I'm sorry. I'm really sorry," I said.

Apparently, she didn't want to hear it because she grabbed her purchases and stormed out of the store. The cashier, who witnessed the whole thing, tried his best to suppress his laughter, but finally gave in after I paid for my paper and started to head toward the exit. Assuming the store's security camera worked, I had no doubt that he'd be laughing again, real soon.

Behind the Podium

I finished up the first draft of my presentation around half past three, and then I emailed copies to my boss, Charles Egan, and Alex Higgins, our rainmaker sales rep who had brought HealthPath, the prospect we were meeting with tomorrow, to the table. An hour later, Charles swung by my cube.

"Hey, Ethan! How's it going?"

His overly friendly tone immediately put me on high alert.

"Not bad. I take it you saw my presentation?"

"I did. In fact, I just finished reviewing it with Alex, and we both think it's pretty much good to go. I gave you a couple of minor edits to consider and the revised version should already be in your inbox."

"Okay, I'll take a look at it."

"Good. Now, Ethan, I don't have to remind you that HealthPath could be our big chance to break into a new market with huge potential, and the guys upstairs with the corner offices and big paychecks are really counting on us to bring this one home."

I had met a few of our overpaid execs during my interview process a few years ago, but I doubted that any of them would even be able to pick me out of a prison line up as being one of their current employees. This meant that Charles, our VP of Marketing, would ultimately be held accountable for the success of my presentation, and from what I could tell, the thought scared him to death. For his sake, I tried to sound confident when I said, "Don't worry, Charles. I got this."

When I got home that evening, I spent an hour making some final touch-ups to the HealthPath presentation. Charles' suggested edits added absolutely no value to anything beyond his own ego, and for the most

47

part, I ignored them. But, before shutting off my computer, I checked my work emails and noticed several "good luck" and "go get 'em" messages from Alex. I considered him to be one of my few close friends at work, and he heavily relied on what he called my "marketing magic" to continually help close deals to fund his golf membership, his Maui timeshare, and his child support payments. I wanted to believe that he didn't share these obligations with me in order of priority, but it was hard to imagine how he could keep his natural, year-round tan glued to his face if he was making frequent visits to Vancouver in order to see his estranged kids.

I woke up the next morning feeling energized and confident. My presentation was scheduled to start at eleven o'clock, but shortly after I connected my laptop to the projector in our main conference room, someone from HealthPath called to say that their team would be about twenty minutes late, giving me some more time to relax and Charles some more time to worry. As I flipped through the slides that were now displayed on the projector screen, I noticed the giant patches of sweat that had seeped through Charles' shirt, and then glanced at Alex who was in the corner. As usual, Alex was working his cell, trying to bait another hook while waiting for his big fish to arrive.

A few minutes later, the team from HealthPath was escorted into the conference room. Justin Rivers, the company's founder and CEO, introduced himself first and I tried my best to focus on him, even though my eyes tried desperately to wander over to the cute 5'3" woman with long braids who was part of his crew. Her name was Melody Bishop and although she was officially Justin's Chief of Staff, she was, as Justin soon explained, the "real CEO of the company." Next to Melody stood someone whose name I couldn't retain as it rapidly traveled in one ear and right out the other, and for a brief moment, I was solely focused on Melody who, for the next forty-five minutes, would be solely focused on me.

Before we could get going, Justin had to step away to make some urgent calls. Melody took the opportunity to initiate a business card exchange, but unfortunately, I had run out after handing out all my remaining cards the week before at a conference.

"Thanks, Melody. I'd love to give you something in return, but I just ran out… of them." I could feel a few eyebrows rise with the 'something in return' part of that sentence, which confirmed my poor choice of words and didn't bode well for my suddenly wavering confidence.

"No problem, Ethan. And please call me Mel."

I took note that Melody had given me, and only me, permission to use her nickname, despite the fact that Charles and Alex were sandwiching me as she spoke. Historically, I had never even considered mixing business with pleasure, but up until now, that rule had been easy to follow. Before my mind could wander too much further, the sound of Justin re-entering the room and closing the door brought me back down to earth and signaled that we were finally ready to begin our game of three on three. Alex kicked things off with a brief, innocuous intro, and then turned the floor over to me.

During my preparation for the meeting, I had decided that I wanted to minimize my use of PowerPoint slides, and incorporate some brief video success stories, illustrating how our software solution was able to help a few of our customers solve some of the major issues that HealthPath currently faced. About half-way through my presentation, I thought things were going smoothly when Justin spoke up.

"Ethan, I'm going to be honest with you. Nine times out of ten, when it comes to big software and IT decisions, I usually go with a combination of what my team here tells me, and what my gut tells me. Right now, my gut isn't telling me anything other than the fact that I should have had a bigger breakfast. So, in the time remaining, I want you to convince me that this is the right solution for us."

Without directly looking at him, I could tell that Charles' face was now red as his tie, and that Alex's had turned blue, which told me that he was holding his breath. I glanced at Melody who gave me a quick, reassuring head nod, and with that, I calmly walked over to the white board.

"Justin, if it's okay with you and your team, I'll take a moment to sketch out your current inventory system with your help, and then point out specific areas in which I think our solution can help to make a substantial and measurable difference in your business."

"Okay, Ethan, let's see what you've got," he responded.

I diagrammed their high level inventory management system as best I could, and fine-tuned some of the areas with input from the HealthPath team. After completing my illustration, I said, "So, are we all in agreement that this represents an overview of your current system?"

The three HealthPath teammates looked at each other before Melody said, "Yes, Ethan, that's a good representation."

"Great!" I circled four areas on the diagram and said, "Now let me explain how these points represent areas of opportunity where our solution can help you to reduce overall costs by moving items through your system faster and improving the overall quality of your tracking process."

By the time I made it to the Q&A section thirty-five minutes later, I could tell that our visitors were impressed. In addition to Justin's challenge, they had posed some tough questions throughout the presentation, but I had anticipated most of them, and was well prepared with my responses. One thing I wasn't prepared for was seeing Melody occasionally sucking on the tip of her pen. I doubted that she realized what she was doing or what she was doing to me, but I needed to remain behind the podium for a while or else it would soon be rather obvious… to everyone.

"Thanks, Ethan! That was exactly what I wanted. I think we can work something out, but before we go any further, let's take a break and regroup in five minutes."

Charles said, "Sounds good to me!" which turned out to be the extent of his contribution to the meeting.

One by one, everyone stood up and slowly headed toward the door. I had planned to stay where I was until the room was empty, but then I looked up and saw Melody slowly approaching me.

"Hey, Ethan! I just wanted to tell you what a great job you did. I was glad that you didn't get fazed by Justin's gut challenge. He pulls that line during almost every vendor presentation, and most people end up folding like a bad poker player."

"Like a bad poker player? I never heard that one, but I kinda like it. I expected you to say 'like a cheap suit.'"

Melody gave me a rather seductive smile and said, "I like to do the unexpected," and as I watched her strut toward the door, I knew that I would need to remain standing behind the podium for the full five minutes.

After everyone finally returned to the room, we spent another twenty minutes discussing the steps and timelines needed to move toward a deal, and by the end of the meeting, it was looking like my boss would keep his job, Alex would keep his time share, and I would keep thinking about Melody sucking on her pen.

Pray for Me!

After work, Alex insisted that I come out to celebrate his impending HealthPath deal with him and some of our local and outside sales reps who were in town for a quarterly sales meeting. I wasn't really in the mood for a wild weeknight, but after Alex shot down every weak excuse I could come up with, I finally agreed. Given the success of my presentation, I figured that I actually did have a good reason to celebrate, and with Alex's commission on the impending $1.2 million deal that I just helped to tee up for him, I was pretty sure that I wouldn't be pulling out my wallet for a while in his presence.

On the surface, Alex and I had little in common beyond the logo on our business cards. He was a thirty-year-old kid from Canada, with two ex-wives and three estranged children, and I was a thirty-seven-year-old guy from Northern California who had never been married and had never touched a diaper in his entire life. Despite our different backgrounds, Alex and I actually got along well outside the office, and if it weren't for his well-known addiction to strip clubs, we would have hung out more often.

"So, where to first?" asked Alex.

I looked around at the four sales guys that Alex had invited to see if any of them were going to respond to his question. We all knew that we were eventually going to end up at Sliders, Alex's favorite strip club, so part of me wanted to just go straight there and get it over with so I could get home at a decent hour. The one time I had allowed Alex to drag me into one, I wasn't too impressed, but given their undying popularity with men throughout the years, I wondered if they had some kind of weird intrinsic value for single guys like me, perhaps acting as a therapeutic bridge to fill in the gaps in between our relationships with women whose G-strings weren't as visible where they worked.

Brandon Lee, the northeast sales rep, finally spoke up. "I already made a six-thirty reservation for us at that new steakhouse on Second Street. It's kinda pricey, but when I heard that the A-Team was treating, I just picked the most expensive place I could find."

After a few laughs and high fives, Alex, who never cared for his A-Team nickname, said, "Fine, but try to take it easy on the wine tab this time! Don't forget that I've got three kids to feed."

"And at least eight strippers!" I shouted.

One of the things that I liked best about the crew Alex had assembled was that, with the exception of Earl Thomas, our southeast sales guy, they were all short. None of them were over 5'7", but if they had any issues about what little height they had, you'd never know it, and most of them acted like they could pull any woman, anywhere, at any time. While I could do without their cockiness, I admired their confidence and hoped that some of it might rub off on me.

After devouring our entrees at the restaurant and draining five bottles of wine, we were finally ready for dessert. I wanted the key lime pie, Brandon and Chris wanted the woman in the booth across from us, Earl wanted the hostess, Vinnie wanted whoever would take him, and Alex just wanted to get to Sliders as soon as possible. While we waited for the waitress to take our dessert orders, I felt my phone vibrate and when I pulled it out of my pocket, I saw a text from Mia: *How are things going with Claudia?* She was still waiting on the update that I had promised to give her, but after looking around at my collection of drunken co-workers, I had a strong suspicion that any promises ever made to anyone were in jeopardy tonight. I quickly typed a response: *Sorry—Out with the sales team. Pray for me!*

In spite of our best efforts to empty the restaurant's wine cellar, Alex kept his word and took care of the entire bill. He even promised to pay for our lap dances, which left no doubt as to where we were headed next, but despite his good intentions, we all knew that once Alex got a pair of D-cups wrapped around his head, it would literally be hard for our ATM buddy to hear our requests for withdrawals from his wallet.

By the time we finally piled out of the restaurant, it was almost nine o'clock, and though none of us seemed sober enough to even recognize our own car keys, I could sense that several of our party people were plotting an escape. Chris' phone had been buzzing all night, and I assumed it was his pregnant wife wondering if he had lost his damn mind being out on a weekday and leaving her to deal with their three kids by herself. After reading his latest text, Chris took a few steps toward Alex, but decided not to say anything when he saw the "don't even think about bailing now" look in Alex's eyes.

Though it wasn't a pretty sight, we were able to stumble six blocks from the restaurant to our inevitable destination. When the bear-sized greeter at the entrance to Sliders saw Alex and his merry band of fresh meat, his eyes lit up. After some quick and meaningless introductions, the greeter whispered something to Alex about his "usual booth " before we were swiftly escorted to a VIP section, which gave us a great view of all the action, and gave "the action" a great view of all of us. Since it was a Tuesday night and still fairly early, I assumed that the place would be kind of dead, but one look around reminded me to never underestimate the demand for naked women anywhere, at any time, on any night.

The comfort level that I had felt with the guys throughout the night had vanished as soon as I stepped into the club, and I tried my best not to make direct eye contact with any of the dancers who were already buzzing around us like we had pools of golden honey in our laps.

Of course, all of them knew Alex by name, and for a moment, most of them were snuggled around him and undoubtedly telling him whatever he wanted to hear. With their five-inch heels, they were all at least four inches taller than Alex, and as I watched my 5'3" friend being gently stroked and cuddled by three of Sliders' finest, I was reminded of how strip clubs served as a great equalizer to the vertically challenged. Outside these walls, most of the women in here wouldn't even notice us, but inside these walls, they were sticking to us like salesmen at a used car lot. Outside, we couldn't touch them. Inside, they'd let us stuff dollar bills in places on their body that would embarrass a gynecologist.

I had turned my phone to vibrate at the beginning of the night, and it started buzzing just after a young "staffer" known as Cinnamon Bunz decided to jump into my lap. She made some lame joke when she felt the buzz of my phone beneath her, but to my surprise, she didn't move an inch. As I reached into my pants to pull it out, she playfully jerked her shoulders and nearly knocked me out with her left boob. I looked at the screen and saw that Mom had sent me a text, which read: *Hey—Can you talk?* By now, Cinnamon was begging for attention and had practically stabbed my right eye with her left nipple. To get some breathing room and regain my blurred vision, I gave her a twenty and begged her to give Alex a lap dance on the next song. I wasn't sure what my mother wanted to talk about, but I knew I'd have trouble finding out with 2 Live Crew's "Me So Horny" blasting away in the background. I decided to just send her a reply, which read: *Out with the guys. Is it urgent?* She replied back a minute later with: *No, but I hope you find me a daughter-in-law tonight, wherever you are.* ☺

Right after I put my phone away, two dancers decided it would be a good time to share my lap. Alex had most likely sent them over after stuffing them with enough financial incentives. Like most of the strippers at Sliders, they were wearing the standard uniform consisting of an overflowing bikini and high heels that made them at least 5'9". Without even introducing themselves, they gyrated on me for almost two songs, but were unsuccessful in their attempts to accomplish what Melody was able to do in her business suit with just a simple pen.

By the time Alex finally reached his ATM withdrawal limit, it was almost midnight, and as the gang rapidly dwindled down, I sort of felt sad for him as he sat alone in the corner, sipping on what appeared to be an empty bottle.

"Hey Alex—"

He cut me off and said, "Let me guess—you had a great time but you gotta go."

"Actually, I was heading out, but I wanted to see if you were ready to share a cab. What do you say?"

"I'll leave on one condition."

"What's that?" I asked.

"You pay for the cab."

"No problem."

"And for my last two beers."

"Deal."

"And the money I still owe Ginger for the last four dances she gave me."

"Now hold on!"

"I'm just fuckin' with ya, Ethan. But seriously, you gotta admit that this is the life. Great food, good friends, lots of booze, and all the naked women you could ever want!"

I forced a smile in Alex's direction and then flagged down the cocktail waitress to settle his tab. By the time we stepped outside, there was a row of cabs all lined up and down the street, which was yet another reminder of the seemingly endless number of industries that were consistently able to cash in on horny and possibly lonely men. While I admittedly fell into both of those categories all too often, the club had left a bad taste in my mouth.

Unlike Alex, this definitely wasn't "the life" for me, and there was nothing therapeutic about Slicers at all. I couldn't deny that most of the women were gorgeous and built like the brick houses that once inspired a group called the Commodores to pen a song, but in the end, they were just actresses playing their part in a play that didn't have a good role for me, and I knew I'd be much better off stuffing dollar bills down my own butt crack than down any of theirs.

2:17 A.M.

With Alex passed out on the other side of the taxi, I started thinking about Melody and how much I'd enjoy a dance from her. Throughout the night, I had done a decent job of keeping her out of my mind so that I could try to enjoy my evening out with the sales guys without any distractions. But, after Alex rolled out of the cab in front of his luxury apartment building, the strippers were a distant memory and she was a present problem that would remain top of mind until I figured out what, if anything, to do. Even though she had given me her business card at the beginning of the meeting, it wasn't like there was an imprint of her lipstick on it. It was simply part of a standard business ritual, which also required her to give cards to Alex and Charles. Still, she made a point of giving me sole permission to call her Mel, and assuming that she only carried one phone, I did have her cell number. In addition, as the main presenter during our meeting, I figured that I had a legitimate reason to send her a follow-up thank you note.

When I finally got home, it was almost two in the morning, but before pulling out my laptop and doing something I'd regret, I took a moment to think it through. I still hadn't decided what to do about Claudia and I had no proof that this Anna woman was even a real person. And even if she was, given our height disparity, I seriously doubted that she would give me a real chance, despite what Mia had said about my experiment, and despite what Anna had said in her email. So, my dance card was clean at the moment and technically, there wasn't any reason why I should feel guilty about sending Melody a simple email. Besides, she had already told me in a somewhat flirtatious manner that she likes to "do the unexpected," which, I reasoned, may have been a green light for me to do something slightly unexpected myself.

After changing my mind far too many times, I decided to just pull out my laptop and draft a quick message to Melody before I could talk myself out of it again.

Hi Melody—

It was nice meeting you and your team. I've attached a copy of my presentation for your review in case you have any questions or need to share the information we covered with anyone else in your organization.

I'm sure that Alex will follow-up soon with a draft of the contract, but if you have any questions or need anything in the meantime, please don't hesitate to call.

Best Regards,

Ethan

I ended the message with my contact info, but I really wanted to end it by telling her that she was welcome to suck on my pen any time. After re-reading the email several times, I determined that it was appropriate enough and decided that I would send it out in the morning. I wasn't sure if this "business" email would give her any indication that I was also interested in possibly exploring a non-business relationship, but, for the moment, I wasn't going to worry about it.

As fate would have it, I was very worried about it only a few seconds later. Apparently, my motor skills and few remaining brain cells hadn't fully recovered from the night's earlier festivities with the sales team, and instead of clicking on the "draft" button, I hit "send." A properly-worded email sent the morning after a meeting might subtly say, "I'm still thinking about you," but that same email sent at 2:17 A.M. screams, "I'm still thinking about you while I'm making love to the one I love the most." One is kind of cute and the other is downright scary.

I immediately started to panic, and even though I had never done it before, I considered trying to recall the message. But, given the fact that I couldn't even hit the "draft" button properly, I figured that it wasn't a good time to experiment with an unfamiliar email feature. With my luck, I might've sent it out to our entire company. So, instead, I decided to just put it out of my mind temporarily, and a few minutes later, my eyes were closed and Melody was finally giving me a much-needed lap dance.

A Center for the Lakers

The theme from *Mission Impossible* woke me up at seven in the morning. After several years of receiving countless last-minute work requests that were better suited for someone with a PhD in Miracle Work, I thought it was an appropriate ring tone for my cell. Since I was too dazed to even look at the caller ID, I greeted the caller with a menacing grunt, which made it clear that I wasn't looking forward to a conversation.

"You sound like you've had about an hour of sleep. What time did you get in?" Mia's voice reminded me that I still hadn't spoken to her since the party on Saturday.

"Who says I ever made it home?" I responded.

"Your scratchy voice says you just woke up and need some more sleep. I can call back if you want, but don't you need to get up soon and head into the office?"

As I listened to Mia, I began to slowly piece together the details of last night in my mind, starting with the fun I had with the sales team at the restaurant and ending with my keyboard nightmare. My slight headache wasn't bad, given the amount of wine we went through, but Mia's loud voice wasn't helping.

"Besides, Ethan, you promised that you'd call me the morning after the party to tell me about what happened with Claudia, and I'm still waiting for the damn text you promised to send after you got home safely."

"Uh… yeah. Sorry about that."

Mia said, "If you need it, I'll give you ten minutes to crawl out of your coffin and sober yourself up, but you owe me a call before you head to the office!"

"Okay, okay. I'll call you back in a couple of minutes."

After gulping down quite a few glasses of water, I picked up my cell and was about to call Mia back, but first,

I took a quick look at my work emails to see if Melody had responded to my message. She hadn't, but then I remembered that I had literally sent it only a few hours ago, and it was highly unlikely that she had even seen it yet. I did see a few work emails, which required my immediate attention, and after sending out some very short replies, I pulled up my phone contacts and pressed Mia's name.

"It's about time! What took you so long?"

"Sorry, cuz. I told you I was out with the sales guys last night, so you shouldn't be surprised that I'm a wreck right now."

"Don't blame them. You've always been a wreck."

"I'm sorry, Miss, I think I dialed the wrong number. I was trying to reach my loving and supportive cousin who wanted me to fill her in on what happened at a recent party. I'm sorry for disturbing you so early in the morning, and it won't ever happen again. Bye."

"Nice try, Ethan."

I spent the next few minutes providing Mia with all the details about what happened with Claudia, including the comments she made about my height.

"Is that it? Damn, Ethan, I was really worried about you! After you left, I heard someone say that you had been in the bathroom a long time and had possibly puked your guts out. Hell, I almost left the party to check on you after you didn't return my call or my text that night."

"Oh, I got sick all right. I got sick of hearing Claudia talk about how she prefers taller guys, right after she gave me her number! I mean, who does that?"

"Ethan, how many times am I gonna have to listen to you get all bent out of shape about women and your height issues? You got your little feelings hurt and then ran home to pout? Is that it?" She sounded a lot like Malcolm, and although she didn't emphasize the word "little," we both knew that she didn't have to use it.

"How badly could she have hurt my feelings? I'd just met her!"

"Come on, Ethan. You're like a woman when you see someone you like. It doesn't take you long to picture where you'll get married, the house you'll buy together, and what your kids will look like."

"Do you want me to go through life as a pessimist?" I asked.

"But that's what makes you so frustrating! When it comes to relationships, sometimes you go from being an optimist to a pessimist in five seconds flat. One moment I bet you were ready to run off with Claudia forever, and the next, you're ready to toss her back in the ocean, without even knowing what she said."

"What are you talking about? I told you exactly what she said!"

"Yes, but 'a little taller' doesn't mean she wants a center for the Lakers, and she said 'normally prefer' which sounds to me like she was prepared to make an exception in your case. And speaking of exceptions, don't you 'normally prefer' women with bras that have cup sizes a little further down the alphabet than hers?"

I wasn't ready to admit it, but Mia had made some good points that I'd have to chew on for a while.

"Well, it's a moot point anyway because I already met someone else," I said.

"Don't tell me you hooked up with one of those strippers last night? Good luck getting her through your mother's front door!"

"Who said anything about strippers?"

"Ethan, I'm not stupid. You said you were out with the sales guys, and even though I don't know how the evening started, I'd bet my next commission check that I know where it ended."

I tried my best to sound dead serious when I said, "Her real name is Chandelieria, but her professional name is Cinnamon Bunz."

Mia let out a light chuckle, and before we ended our call, we promised to reconnect in a few days. I didn't tell her about Melody or Anna, primarily because there wasn't anything to tell, and even if there was, after Mia's tongue-lashing about Claudia, I wanted to make sure I had something more concrete and positive to share the next time I mentioned a new woman in her presence.

Enlighten Me

When I got home from work the next day, despite my ambivalent feelings toward Claudia, I decided that it was finally time to fulfill my overdue promise to call her. I pulled up her name, which had been re-entered into my contacts, and hit the "call" button. It went straight to voicemail, which meant that I had to come up with an appropriate message.

"Hi, Claudia. This is Ethan. I'm calling you as promised…" I stopped mid-sentence to re-record the message. I didn't want to start off sounding like I deserved a cookie for calling her back, especially since I was calling her several days later than I had originally promised. "Hi, Claudia. This is Ethan, the guy you met at the party on Saturday…" I stopped again. As good as she looked, every guy at the party might've approached her at some point, so that message wouldn't work either. "Hi, Claudia. This is Ethan, the closet bad boy you met at the beer cooler on Saturday night. Sorry I missed you, but feel free to call me back when you get a sec. I'm guessing that my number showed up on your caller ID, but just in case, it's 415-555-1013." Now that I had left a message, my job was done and the ball was in her court.

After taking care of Claudia, I checked my work emails, as I did most evenings, in anticipation of some last-minute "fires" breaking out that my boss would inevitably expect me to help put out with my tiny squirt gun. I saw a message from one of our sales reps who wanted me to "look over" a presentation in the morning, which usually meant rewrite, proofread, and revise, but at least he gave me a heads-up. I much preferred his approach over a message I received from a frantic rep earlier that day who expected me to drop everything immediately and magically build a quota-saving presentation from scratch at the last minute.

In my haste to go through my inbox, I almost overlooked a message from Melody. I could tell from the subject line that it was a reply to my ill-timed email, and I felt a burst of excitement swelling up inside of me as I left-clicked my mouse and opened the message.

Hey Ethan—

Thanks for the follow-up note. We all enjoyed your presentation and I think it helped to seal the deal with our CEO. Alex should have the revised contract within a few days, and we look forward to working closely with your team in the near future.

Thanks again!

Melody

I re-read the note three more times, but couldn't find one word that I could cling to as a sign that she wanted to explore anything beyond our contract. Unlike most men I knew, I was never comfortable dating more than one woman at a time. So, part of me was relieved that Melody seemed to be all business, because it meant that I could now focus on Claudia, which was probably what I should have been doing all along. Watching guys like Fritz juggle multiple hearts seemed physically, emotionally, and financially draining. I always considered myself to be a simple guy who wanted a simple relationship with a simply wonderful woman. My approach might be slower, but I felt it would pay off in the long run, and I wasn't about to suddenly change up now.

I decided that the rest of my work emails could wait until the morning and then I took a quick peek at my personal email box. Hidden in between a Viagra trial email and a virus that was apparently being sent to a friend's entire address book was an email from Match indicating that I had another message, and without hesitation, I clicked on the link.

Hi again. I don't know if you saw my first message, but just in case, I wanted to reach out one more time. I hope you'll respond, but if not, good luck with your search.

Anna

Anna's follow-up message caught me off guard. Based on the impressive pics that she had posted on her profile, I assumed that she'd have her hands full trying to filter through and respond to all of the messages that presumably filled her inbox each day. The fact that she had reached out to the faceless profile of a guy who was almost six inches shorter didn't make much sense, and the fact that she had reached out twice made no sense whatsoever. I remained skeptical as I clicked on my profile in an attempt to figure out what she might have seen in me that 99.9% of the other women on Match seemed to have overlooked.

Overall, the profile was as bare-bones as I remembered. I hadn't really opened up about myself at all, and in the hobbies section I had listed:

1. Ironing wrinkle-free clothes

2. Watching recordings of weather forecasts

3. Telling bad jokes

I suppose that my stated affinity for steak burritos and the San Francisco 49ers may have matched up well with her love of Mexican food and football. We also both indicated that we were Christians, but beyond those few tidbits, I couldn't see much else that we had in common. Yet, I couldn't deny that she had made a real effort to connect with me, and despite my suspicions, I couldn't see any harm in sending a polite reply.

Hi Anna—

Sorry for the delayed response, but I really do appreciate you reaching out to me. I'm not too experienced with online dating, and I'm definitely not used to women initiating contact with me. So, forgive me if I seem a little shy and guarded initially.

I must admit that I was very impressed with your profile and blown away by your killer smile, but I can't quite figure out what in my profile motivated you to contact me… twice. Without having hardly any information about me and not having any pictures, you took quite a chance. Don't get me wrong, I'm very glad that you did, but I just can't figure out why. When you get a sec, feel free to enlighten me.

Regards,

Ethan

I guess I could've saved both of us some time by just coming out and asking her if this was some sort of money scam, but I didn't want to risk offending her too much in case she turned out to be legit. But, the fact that my thoughts went right to Claudia after I closed my laptop was a clear indication that my expectations for this Anna situation were pretty low, and even if she did turn out to be a real person in search of a real relationship, my renewed commitment to my eleventh commandment would prevent me from pursuing her any further. Still, at a minimum, I thought that an online pen-pal type of relationship with Anna would be a good way for me to gain some valuable experience with this online dating thing, and I hoped it would prepare me for something better down the line.

Cutz R Us

Claudia and I played phone tag throughout the day on Friday, but that was probably a blessing in disguise. By the time we finally connected, I hoped that it would be easier to focus on what she was saying to me instead of what she had said about me at the party.

On Saturday morning, after eating some breakfast and skimming the paper, I was ready to head out to Cutz, a local salon, for my 11:30 A.M. haircut. I actually called the place Cutz R Us because of all the kids and toys that seemed to dominate the shop floor, especially on the weekends. Normally they didn't take appointments at Cutz on Saturdays, which was their busiest day, but I was one of the few people who was willing to take a chance on my barber, Chuck, when he first started six years ago, and as a result, he told me that he'd be willing to hold up his Thanksgiving day meal in order to give me a haircut if I needed one. I'm sure that my sizable tips also helped to make his schedule a little more flexible for me than for most of his other clients.

Chuck had a chair in the back corner of the shop, and like most of his male customers, I always enjoyed my long, slow walk down the hall and around the corner to his area. It was a great opportunity to see a wide array of women getting their 'dos done. While it was well known that women loved to sport a "fresh from the salon" look, for my money, the look from within the salon wasn't bad either. As I opened the door to Cutz, a woman strutted by me on her way out as if she were modeling designer clothes down a walkway in a Milan fashion show. When I stepped inside, my nostrils were immediately overwhelmed by the scent of the various oils and sheens that were a standard part of a Black beautician's arsenal. Most of the salon chairs were filled with customers who were either reading magazines or were pecking away on cell phones as the stylists worked their magic.

When I finally made it to Chuck's corner, I was right on time for my appointment, and right on time to see someone else jump into his chair. I gave Chuck a puzzled look, but before I could say anything, he tried his best to diffuse the situation.

"Hey, Ethan—my man! Good to see you! I'm... uh... running a little behind today, but after I finish doing these twists for Dwayne, you're up next. He's trying out twists for the first time."

Based on my experience, waiting for anything beyond a traditional shave or haircut had the potential to suck up much more time than I wanted to spend in the salon, and there was nothing traditional about a twist hairstyle. Personally, it wasn't my thing, and I wasn't sure if it was going to work for Dwayne either. Each of the lengthy twists on his head looked as if they had organically sprouted up out of his scalp over time, and when viewed in unison, made him look like he had just been electrocuted. But, I'm sure it didn't matter. With his long, gangly legs, I sized Dwayne up to be well over six feet, which meant that his social life probably wouldn't even skip a beat if he decided to sport a neon wig for a while.

Like most barbershops in the area, Cutz had a few Black-oriented magazines scattered on a corner table, including a popular Black women's magazine with a headline that read "Against All Odds: The Challenge of Finding the Right Man at the Right Time." Based solely on the title, it sounded like something that Mia would write and it piqued my curiosity enough to pick up the magazine and flip to the article. Similar to my experiment on Match, it started out by using statistics to paint a dire picture about the chances of finding "The Right Man," which it seemed to define as a man who was single, straight, educated, employed, and didn't live at home or have a prison record. According to this definition, I should have been the right man for someone, but I certainly didn't feel like one. As a single, straight, educated, and employed homeowner who had only seen the inside of a police station or prison on TV, women often referred to me as "the exception," and from experience, I knew that exceptions to popular theories were often discounted or ignored.

I stopped reading, and as I thought more about the magazine's definition, I wondered what height a man had to be in order to meet the minimum criteria for the "Mr. Right" category. Although my flawed research project didn't really prove anything, I still felt there was an unwritten vertical threshold for some women, and while it might vary from one person to the next, I felt that only a bedridden woman would ever consider me to be tall, dark, and handsome.

The Firing Range

After my haircut, I went straight home and called Claudia. The phone rang several times, and as I tried to figure out what I was going to say in yet another voicemail message, my thoughts were interrupted by the sound of a real live voice.

"Hello?"

"Hi... Claudia. This is Ethan."

"Hey, Ethan. How are you doing?" I detected a surprising amount of concern in her tone, which threw me off for a second.

"I'm good."

"It's great to finally hear your voice again! After all the voicemails we've exchanged, I didn't think we'd ever reconnect."

"I know, but I'm glad we both hung in there."

"Me too. You know, Ethan, I looked for you again after we talked at the party, but when I caught up with Mia again, she said that you left early because you weren't feeling too well."

"Yeah. I'm actually allergic to beer. I can have a few, but by the sixth or seventh can, my stomach gets a little queasy." Claudia's brief pause reminded me that she wasn't used to my sarcasm yet, so I jumped right in before she got too carried away with the visual. "I'm just kidding. But I was upset... I mean... I had an upset stomach, and I did end up leaving early."

"That's a relief. I thought you had changed your mind about going out and were trying to avoid me."

"No, I wasn't avoiding you," I said, a little too defensively.

"Well... you haven't changed your mind about going out, have you?" she asked.

"Of course not!"

"Great! When do you want to get together?"

"It depends," I said.

"Depends? Depends on what?"

"Depends on when we can get reservations at Manger."

"Manger! Wow! Ethan, I don't know if you're trying to impress me, but if so, you're off to a great start."

"They say you never get a second chance," I teased.

"Well if you make a habit of taking me to places like Manger, you might get plenty of chances."

I supposed that Claudia was just trying to be flirtatious, but if we were contestants on the old $100,000 Pyramid game show, my response to that statement would have been: "Things a Gold Digger would say."

"It might be easier to get reservations on a weekday," I suggested.

"I could do a weekday, but Mondays are bad because I have classes after work."

"Classes? That sounds like fun. What kind of classes are you taking? No, wait. Let me guess. Yoga?"

"No."

"Cooking?"

"No."

"Spanish?"

"Well, okay, it's not exactly a formal class. On Mondays, I go out with a few girlfriends to the… uh… firing range."

My skin thankfully kept my jaw from hitting the ground. "Did you say 'the firing range?'"

She responded with a rather timid, "Yes, that's what I said."

"Really? Well, what do you do there? Some type of volunteer work, like setting up the targets, sweeping up the shell casings, or helping to reload guns? Or is that where you train and prep for your first dates?" Even though I was having a lot of fun at her expense, I had always been deathly afraid of guns, and the thought of going on a date with Claudia and her concealed loaded weapon was becoming less appealing by the minute.

"It's actually where I train and prep for final dates."

Part of me knew she was joking, but the rest of me didn't want to find out. I couldn't picture it when we first met, but now I could easily envision Claudia driving a massive pickup truck with a gun rack and one of those bumper stickers that read: *Is there life after death? Touch my truck and find out.*

Claudia must've sensed something was wrong when she said, "You know I'm just joking, right?"

"How do I know? I don't have a shred of evidence to prove that any of your ex-boyfriends are still walking this Earth, and if they're not, I just hope you took them out quickly and didn't make them suffer."

"Ha ha. Now, can we get back to Manger and the reservations? I've heard that it may take us a while to get reservations, so we should look into that first."

"Good idea. I'll check it out and get back to you."

"That sounds good, but if it turns out that the wait is too long, I'm fine with going somewhere else," she said.

We talked for a few more minutes about the party and I teased her about her "hand in the cooler" move without revealing that I knew it was intentional. She teased me about running away before the dance floor got going and warned me that there would be nowhere to hide next time. By the end of our conversation, it was clear that Claudia was genuinely looking forward to our date and her eagerness had helped to change my initial indifference about her, and my concerns about her gun "hobby," into mild optimism.

See You There

A few weeks ago, Malcolm had told me that one of his ex-college roommates was a chef at Manger, one of the hottest restaurants in the Bay Area. Seemingly overnight, the place had developed a cult-like following as a result of its expansive menu and innovative dishes, combined with its spectacular view of the Golden Gate Bridge. It was located at Fisherman's Wharf in San Francisco and was a short, but usually freezing cold, walk away from Twist, the biggest and most diverse dance club in the city. Based on the way Claudia's body was bouncing to beats that were playing the night I met her, I felt it was a pretty safe choice to offer to her as a second stop for our night out on the town.

Malcolm had said that his friend would have no problem hooking me up with reservations at Manger, as long as I reached out at least twenty-four hours in advance, and I had kept this piece of info from Claudia in hopes of making me seem much cooler and well-connected than I really was.

The next day, I decided to test out my new contact. As advertised, I had no problem getting us a reservation, although Anton, the chef, implied that I should "take good care of my waiter," undoubtedly in anticipation of a nice kick-back coming his way. I had intentionally chosen Tuesday evening to give us a chance to have a follow-up date on the weekend in case things went well. If we were longtime friends or had been dating for a while, I might have simply sent Claudia a text with the date and time of our reservation, but not knowing if she was the texting type, I decided that I would give her a quick call within the next day or two. In the meantime, it dawned on me that Mia and Claudia had spoken again after I left the party, and given my cousin's natural nosy nature and tendency to pry, there was a good chance she had some valuable insights about their conversation that needed to be shared.

When I called Mia later that evening, she answered the phone on the first ring.

"Hey, Ethan."

"Hey, Mia. You got a sec?"

"Sure! What's up?"

"Guess who I spoke to yesterday?"

"My mom?"

"No."

"Your mom?"

"It wasn't a relative," I said.

"Hmmm? Let me guess—you called Claudia!"

"Yep. Are you surprised?" I asked.

"Kinda. When we talked about her a few days ago, it sounded like you had already written her off, and I didn't think that any logic from me was gonna make it through that thick skull of yours."

I chuckled and said, "Well, you did get me to reconsider, and Malcolm also thought I should call her. But, honestly, I wasn't convinced I was doing the right thing until I spoke to her. I may be wrong, but she sounded like she really wanted to go out with me."

"Of course she wants to go out with you! Why do you think she gave you her number in the first place?"

"I know that I say and do a lot of regrettable things when I have enough alcohol in my system. Over the years, I bet I've asked for and taken numbers from women who would have made our Great Aunt Karen cringe."

Mia sounded puzzled when she asked, "Wasn't she blind?"

"My point exactly."

Mia said, "Claudia didn't seem too hammered to me."

"Well, she said that she caught up with you again. Did she say anything about me?"

"So that's what this call is about! You just want to find out if we talked about you!"

"And?"

"Well, she didn't say much other than that you guys talked about going out soon... but I did."

"Really?"

"Of course! If I'm going to sell products every day that I don't really care about, to people I don't really care about, then I wouldn't pass up an opportunity to sell someone I care about to someone I like."

I wanted to reach through the phone and give Mia a big hug for that one, but I was more focused on hearing the pitch that she used in order to "sell me" to Claudia. "Thanks, cuz. So, what did you say?"

"I just told her how happy I was about you two connecting and that I could see you guys really having a great time together. I tried not to overdo it, but I wanted to make sure that she was looking forward to seeing you."

I had a feeling that there was a little more to her pitch than that, but regardless, I had to admit that my cousin had come through for me again. "Well, we're going to dinner on Tuesday, and if things work out and we end up going out again on the weekend, I'll send you a commission check for successfully closing another deal."

"Something tells me I'll need every penny of it to pay off the bet that you're about to win."

"You might also look into a second mortgage," I joked.

"I'll consider myself warned. Now have you decided what you're going to do on your first night out with Claudia?"

"We're going to start with a simple dinner at a restaurant."

"Which one?" she asked.

"Manger. Have you heard of it?"

"Who hasn't? And are you going to pick her up or meet her at the restaurant?"

"Wait a minute. Is this my cousin or did I somehow get connected to Claudia's father? I thought I knew, but now, I'm not so sure."

"Ethan, just answer my question."

"Well... I hadn't even thought about it, but I guess I'll do the gentleman thing and offer to pick her up."

"Wrong answer!"

"Are you telling me that I shouldn't be a gentleman?"

"Ethan, even though Claudia knows me, she doesn't really know anything about you. So, she might not come right out and say it, but I doubt that she'd be comfortable with you picking her up at her place, or even knowing where her place is until you guys get to know each other a little better."

"I thought I was the only one who was allowed to have a secret Bat Cave."

"Ethan, can you be serious for a moment?"

"Sorry."

"Now, assuming things work out and she decides to eventually let you pick her up, she might still be concerned about feeling pressured to invite you inside, especially if she's still undecided about your potential together. So, what I'm saying is, whatever you do, just don't rush her."

"Are we talking about me and Claudia or you and someone else? Because it sounds like you're speaking from personal experience with some other dude."

"Maybe I am, Ethan, but just make it easy on her and offer to meet her wherever you're going, at least on your first date."

"Okay."

Mia's advice got me thinking about Fritz's Dominos rule. After narrowly surviving a supposed drive-by shooting on a date last year, Fritz came up with a rule, which is based on Dominos' deliveries. Before he commits to picking anyone up who lives in a sketchy or unfamiliar neighborhood, he'll simply call Dominos and begin the process of ordering a pizza using his date's address, and if Dominos won't go there, he won't go there—end of story. I couldn't picture Claudia living in a neighborhood that was too dicey for Dominos, but if I could be both safe and a gentleman at the same time by not offering to pick her up, so be it.

After hanging up with my cousin, I felt much better about my impending evening with Claudia, so I picked up my phone and gave her a call. Although things for our date were now coming together, I had been second-guessing my plan for dancing after dining at Manger. Tuesday was a perfect night for our dinner, but it was generally a slower night at Twist, and I could picture us bored to death all night in a club that was basically empty. So, when my call went to voicemail, I only left a message about our 7:30 P.M. dinner reservation and asked her to let me know if it would work with her schedule. I figured that if things went well, we could include a trip to Twist as part of our plans for the weekend.

An hour later, Claudia sent me a text, which said: *We're on for Manger. See you there!*

It was only a seven-word message, but it told me a lot about her. It told me that she was open to text messaging, and more importantly, it settled our first-date logistics. Since she had simply volunteered to meet me at the restaurant, I didn't have to worry about how we would meet up, and could, instead, focus on making sure we had a great time when we did.

My Own Mess

Thinking about my date the following day made Monday tougher than usual to endure, but Claudia and I exchanged a few check-in messages that helped to get me through it, and got me even more excited about our seeing her again.

Tuesday night, I pulled into the parking lot at Manger about fifteen minutes early for our date. I considered going in and getting a quick drink to help me loosen up before she arrived, but she had already seen me with a slight buzz at the party, and I didn't want her jumping to any false conclusions about my drinking habits. By the time I entered the restaurant, it was twenty minutes after seven. I took a quick peek around, but didn't see Claudia. Before I could check with the hostess to see if she had arrived early, I heard a car pull up to the valet in the front of the restaurant and saw Claudia tossing her keys to the parking attendant. She was wearing heels, but they weren't massive, which put us at approximately the same height and helped to put my mind at ease. She walked inside and took a quick look around before our eyes met.

"Hi, Ethan," she said as she greeted me with a nice warm hug. "I hope you haven't been waiting too long for me."

"I actually just got here a few minutes ago, so your timing is perfect."

I wasn't certain if Claudia wanted to jump right into dinner or run to the ladies' room to freshen up first. I figured that I'd leave it up to her and said, "Did you want me to check and see if our table is ready?"

"Sure!" she said as she took a quick scan of the place.

I walked up to the hostess stand and was told that they were running behind, and that our table wouldn't be ready for another twenty minutes. The hostess suggested waiting in the bar area and promised that she would come get us when our table was ready.

"Looks like we've got a twenty-minute wait. Do you want to hang out in the bar area until our table is ready?"

"That sounds good. It's been a long day and I think a drink will help me unwind. I need to run to the ladies' room first, but I'll meet you in the bar."

"Okay, I'll see if I can find us some seats," I said.

The restaurant's happy hour officially ended at seven o'clock, but it was clear that the happy hour crowd hadn't found their way home yet, and, judging from all the laughter and shouting, was still a little too "happy" for my tastes. All of the bar stools and tables were full, but I swiftly moved over to a long table in the corner of the bar when I noticed that the person seated at the end was signing the bill. After a few final jokes and swigs, everyone at the table got up at once and I quickly pounced on two seats while the other vultures, who had been circling the area, swooped down on the rest of them.

When Claudia returned, she was pleased to see that I had an empty seat and a drink menu waiting for her. She thanked me verbally, and then thanked me visually when she took off her coat, revealing an outfit that raised quite a few eyebrows, including my own. She was wearing a light blue ruffled mini dress that complemented her shapely build. At the party, she had a casual tom-boy look, which I liked, but tonight, she had a drop-dead diva look, which I absolutely loved.

"In case it's not clear by all the men who are looking this way, you look absolutely stunning," I said.

"Thanks! To be honest, I wasn't too sure about this dress. What do you think?" she asked with a grin.

"Let me put it this way… the moment you took off your coat, I forgot the name of the cocktail I had just picked out, the name of the appetizer I had planned to order, and the names of my two nephews."

"Thanks," she said with a shy smile. She started blushing the same way that she had the night we met, and I figured we were off to a good start.

"Now, why was it such a tough day at the office?" I asked.

"My boss is going on maternity leave soon and she's driving me and everyone else crazy with her last-minute requests and emergency planning. I'm second in command, but I feel like a kid listening to a parent who's leaving me at home alone with my siblings for the first time."

I thought back to my harrowing experiences babysitting my nephews when they were younger and figured that her boss would soon have her hands full. "Well, she'll be knee deep in wet diapers before you know it, and I doubt you'll have to worry about her much longer."

She chuckled and said, "That wasn't the most appetizing thing you could have said before dinner, but I'd still toast to it if we had something a little stronger than these waters."

"Okay. Do you know what you want?"

Claudia started flipping through the menu and said, "Gimme a sec."

We were facing each other and seated at the end of the long table filled with other couples and several small groups of people. The seats were squashed together so tightly, I felt like I was riding coach on a commuter plane, and I was worried that our "neighbors" would be part of our conversation, whether they wanted to or not. Of course, that worked both ways, so I was very relieved when the couple next to us got up and headed for the restaurant after they were told that their table was ready. Unfortunately, given the number of people standing up, I knew that the seats wouldn't be open for long.

As I took another look at the drink menu, out of the corner of my eye, I noticed a woman had taken the empty seat next to Claudia. Another woman, who was apparently with her, climbed into the empty seat next to me. Before I could look up, I froze when I heard Claudia exchange greetings with someone who had a very familiar voice. When I finally took my face out of the drink menu, I noticed that my ex-girlfriend, Stephanie, was sitting right next to Claudia, and both of them seemed to be staring at me. Up until this point in my life, I had successfully avoided these types of uncomfortable sitcom scenes, primarily because I didn't have many ex-girlfriends and I didn't go on many dates. Yet here I was, staring face to face with a woman who had devastated me by walking out of my life over eight months ago, and was poised to do more damage tonight.

For what seemed like an eternity, I sat in silence as I tried to figure out how to handle the situation. The fact that Stephanie didn't say anything directly to me might have been a sign that she wasn't going to bust my groove with Claudia, but there was something different about her face that made me uneasy. She had definitely put on some pounds, which was surprising. The Stephanie I had dated was blessed with curves so perfect they'd make a racetrack jealous, and within five minutes of meeting her for the first time, Fritz was calling her "Stiffen Me" behind her back. I could still feel her staring at me as my eyes went from her face down to the slight bulge under her blouse. When it finally hit me, I looked up at Stephanie and realized that she had been giving me a "Yes, you idiot, I'm pregnant" look for a while. Before I could pull out my mental calendar, the sound of Claudia's voice reminded me that I was still on a date.

"I think I'll start with a Cosmo. How 'bout you, Ethan?"

I wanted to order a paternity test, but settled on a light beer. Although Stephanie and I had been as sexually active as we could be when we were dating, we were careful to always use condoms, and while I knew that didn't guarantee anything, I felt the odds were in my favor. She also didn't look like she was ready to burst anytime soon, which meant there was a good chance that she wasn't anywhere near my body when her child was conceived. Still, I wanted to know for sure.

I turned my attention back to Claudia and purposefully kept the conversation as light as possible. I figured that Stephanie was straining to hear every word, and I certainly wanted to keep her in the dark about what was going on between me and the person sitting beside her, just as I was in the dark about the person growing inside of her. Stephanie's friend must've realized that something was up, because she got conveniently caught up in a lengthy text exchange, keeping her out of harm's way. By the time our cocktail waitress came back to check on our table, I started to perspire noticeably. Even if they weren't quite ready to seat us, I wanted to get the hell away from Stephanie. I still wanted to follow-up with her about the baby, but not here and not now. I had already gone eight months without knowing a thing, and I could certainly make it another day or two.

When I thought she wasn't looking, I stole a quick glance at Stephanie's wedding finger. It was bare, which confirmed that I was in the running for her baby daddy sweepstakes. Though Claudia made an honest effort to break the ice, there was minimal conversation at our table while I impatiently waited for our check.

"So, Ethan, Mia tells me that you're in high-tech marketing."

"Yeah."

"Well… do you like it?"

"Yeah, it's fun."

"What do you like about it? What makes it fun?"

"The fun people."

I almost leaped out of my chair when I saw the waitress arrive with our bill, and before she could escape, I handed my credit card to her. If I could, I would have volunteered to run the card for her myself, but thankfully, the credit card processing machine was right around the corner. When she returned, I quickly scribbled my name on the bill and stuffed a tip into the portfolio without even looking at the total. In my mind, it was time to go as soon as Stephanie showed up, but now that we had finished and paid for our drinks, we could make a graceful, yet swift exit.

Just when we were about to leave, I heard something hit the table. When I turned around, I saw the liquid that had flowed in my direction from the drink Stephanie had somehow knocked over. Fortunately, she had already downed most of her cocktail, but I instinctively grabbed some napkins that were on the table and started blotting what was left of her drink.

As I frantically tried to help, I took a peek at Stephanie who looked me dead in the eye and said, "Thanks, but you didn't do it, and I don't need your help. I can take care of my own mess."

Claudia gave me a confused look and I purposefully gave her one back, even though Stephanie had just clarified things for me. I almost said, "Okay, good luck with that," to Stephanie, but even as coded language, it would have sounded too insensitive. Instead, I grabbed Claudia's jacket and practically pushed her toward the hostess stand.

By the time we sat down at our dinner table, my heart was still racing and Claudia could tell that something was wrong.

"Are you okay? You seem a little uptight."

"I had some drama today myself, but I'm fine," I said.

"Really? You seemed okay to me until that pregnant woman showed up. Do you know her?" I had just dodged a major bullet with Stephanie, and five minutes later, another one had been fired at me from a woman who hangs out at shooting ranges.

"Yes, I know her."

"Who is she?"

"Her name is Stephanie and we used to date a while ago. I thought it would be awkward to introduce you and she didn't seem like she wanted to be introduced."

Almost without a pause, Claudia teed up her next question. "When did you stop dating?"

It was obvious that she had an idea of how far along Stephanie was and if the math worked out (or didn't work out), my answer would likely trigger an uncomfortable series of questions. "We stopped dating about eight months ago."

I could've kicked myself for saying "about." That mistake probably added a two-month margin of error, and in Claudia's mind, had increased the probability that Stephanie's kid would look at lot like the man she was currently interrogating.

"Has she been dating anyone else?"

"Claudia, I have no idea."

"Well, do you think the baby could be yours?"

"Look, Claudia, this is honestly the first time that I have seen or heard from her since we stopped dating, and as you may have figured out by now, when she said that I didn't do it, she wasn't talking about the drink that she conveniently knocked over."

Claudia paused for a second and sat with her arms folded across her chest. "I guess you're pretty relieved," she said.

It was a seemingly innocent question, but I knew it was a trap. If I said yes, I'd come across as another baby-dodging Black man who was just lucky enough not to get caught up in a situation in which he would have to "man up" and take responsibility for his actions. If I said no, I'd come across as either a liar or as someone who didn't care enough to be relieved. I decided that I might as well be honest and then just hope for the best.

"More than anything, I'm actually concerned for Stephanie. I didn't see a ring on her finger, which means that it probably wasn't a planned pregnancy, and unfortunately, women often end up shouldering most of the load in those situations."

For a moment, I thought my answer had helped to ease Claudia's concern and would allow us to transition to another topic. In fact, any other topic would have been better than the one that we were stuck on. Much to my dismay, Claudia continued to clench on to it with a pit-bull–type grip.

"Ethan, I'm curious. What would you have done if she told you the baby was yours?"

By now, I had lost my appetite and simply wanted to go home. Although I was very attracted to Claudia and wouldn't mind meeting up with her again, we were obviously starting out on the wrong foot, and there was a good chance that one of us would soon say something we'd both regret if we continued much further down this strange path we were on.

"Claudia, I don't like answering hypothetical questions because they often place you in extremely difficult situations and require you to make painful choices that in reality, you don't need to make, and also because my answer may not match my actual actions. I could tell you what I honestly think I'd do, but unless I was actually in that situation, neither one of us knows for sure what I would do. And that holds true for not just your question, but any question that involves a hypothetical situation."

That was all I had to give. If we were in a courtroom, I would've told the judge that the defense rests its case. Now it was up to Claudia, a jury of one, to decide our fate and where we would go from here.

"Well, I appreciate your honesty, but I'm not looking to get caught up in any drama, and it already seems like you have a little too much going on for me. I'm sorry, Ethan. We can still have dinner if you'd like."

Her arms were still folded and I could see a look of disappointment written all over her face. I glanced over Claudia's shoulder and noticed a mannequin wearing women's clothing in the window of a retail shop across the street. As I gazed at it, I realized that I would be more comfortable having dinner with that mannequin propped up in the seat across from me, than sitting through dinner with a woman who had so quickly written me off.

"Don't worry about it. You can leave and I'll explain things to our waiter when he returns."

I got up and helped Claudia slip on her coat. Instead of a hug, she gave me a handshake and said, "Take care."

That comfortable feeling that I had when I saw that her heels made us the same height completely disappeared once it was clear that we couldn't see eye to eye about anything related to Stephanie. As I watched her walk toward the front door, I felt like I had just failed an interview for a job that I didn't know much about, with a person I would never see or hear from again.

Check Her Out

I was more productive the next day at work than I had ever been as an employee at any company. I edited the technical portion of a sales training manual, finalized a customer success story for my marketing team, and made my way through my entire work email box, all in an attempt to keep my mind off the previous night's disaster at Manger. Somewhere around half past seven, I looked up and realized that most of my coworkers had stopped working for the day and had gone home to live their lives outside the office, something that I couldn't avoid any longer. As I slowly packed up my things, Alex stepped into my cube.

"Hey, Ethan! What are you still doing here? Got a hot date with the janitor? I think she's still doing the bathrooms, but you'd better pop some breath freshener, because she should be stopping by to empty your garbage can soon."

"I haven't been having much luck with dating lately, so I guess it couldn't hurt to check her out. Does she like short guys?"

"I don't think your work schedules are compatible, but forget about her. I know a place where short guys like us get all the attention we need."

"Getting me laid" seemed to be Fritz's answer to all of my problems, and Alex apparently had his own. "Is a trip to Sliders your answer to everything?"

"Come on, Ethan! You can't possibly tell me that you didn't enjoy yourself the last time we were there!"

"I didn't enjoy myself the last time I was there. But, it wasn't your fault. I'm just not into strip clubs."

"Well, were you into that Melody babe?"

"Melody? You mean Melody Bishop from HealthPath?"

"The one and only!"

"Why? Did she say something about me?" The mere mention of Melody's name had me on the edge of my seat, as if my doctor was about to give me some potentially life-altering news.

"Sorry, Ethan, but I heard through the grapevine that she only dates big pro athletes—big, like basketball players."

And just like that, the unexpected spark I had just felt was extinguished and gone for good.

"Then why did you even bring her damn name up?"

"Dude, calm down. I thought she was fine myself, but I wanted to know what you thought of her."

"She's top notch, no doubt, but since I'm not her type, she's not mine either."

"That's bullshit."

"What makes you say that?"

"Is Beyoncé your type?"

"What does she have to do with Melody?"

"Just answer the question. Is Beyoncé your type, yes or no?"

"What do you think?"

"I'm asking you."

"Of course!"

"And do you really think that you're Beyoncé's type?"

I conceded Alex's valid point with a smile and said, "Don't you have some deals to close or some strippers to feed?"

"As a matter of fact, I do. I'll see you around, Ethan."

Alex didn't tell me anything more about his next move, and I really didn't need to know. The fresh memories of my nightmare with Claudia, twenty-four hours prior, made me overreact when I got a whiff of

Melody's name, but it was time to put them both behind me and start moving forward.

Before packing up my things, I decided to check my personal emails to see if Anna, or whatever her real name was, had responded to my last message. When I saw that I had a new message from her, I opened the link:

Hi Ethan—

I want to start by thanking you for giving me your name. It sounds like that was a big step for you, which I can understand. I've heard there are women who reach out to men on dating sites, and after stringing them along for a while, start asking for all sorts of favors, gifts, and money. I'd tell you that you don't have to worry about that with me, but I know that can only be proven over time.

As to why I contacted you, I guess it's because I saw something in your profile that I found sort of unique and refreshing. Even though you didn't post any pictures and didn't reveal much of yourself, I still loved your off-beat sense of humor, and I liked the fact that you didn't seem too pressed about what other people thought about it. You were just... real. So, when I noticed that you had recently checked out my profile, I decided to take a chance and reach out to you.

I don't know if that answers all of your questions, but if not, please let me know. I hope to hear from you soon.

Anna Collins (1-510-555-0190)

I could tell already that Anna was a very bright woman. Without offending or patronizing me, she addressed my concerns head on about this possibly being a scam, and even provided me her full name and number, which she knew I could use to fully check her out online. And I did, as soon as I got home.

I started off by putting her number into a reverse directory lookup which confirmed that it was an Oakland, California AT&T cell number, the same city listed on her Match profile. So, if it was a scam, at least it was a local operation, which, if needed, might be traceable. Then I went to LinkedIn, and after doing some digging, I found out that she was the Director of Finance at a major pharmaceutical company headquartered in Los Angeles. She had worked out of the company's San Francisco office for eight years and had steadily risen up the company ladder. She did her undergraduate studies at the University of Texas in Austin, Texas, and had gone to the University of California at Berkeley for graduate school where she received an MBA. Unlike her Match.com profile pictures, she wore a business suit in the picture posted on her LinkedIn profile, and had tried, unsuccessfully, to tone down her 100-watt smile.

I couldn't find her on Facebook, but I did find various links to conference presentations she had delivered and published blog posts that she had written. From what I pieced together, I could tell that she was also very experienced with data analysis, so she might've gotten a good laugh out of my sandbox-type research project, which, ironically, first brought her to my attention. Overall, I had to admit that I was extremely impressed with what I was able to find online, and the more I read, the more I realized that Anna Collins was indeed looking like a real person.

Collateral Damage

I wasn't aware of the amount of time I had spent playing digital detective, and when I finally shut down my laptop, it was almost half past ten. I opened my fridge in search of something that could pass as dinner, but with the exception of a condiment sandwich, there were no viable options. I contemplated the thought of yet another night of fast food fine dining, and then decided that I was much better off going to bed on an empty stomach. While I made my way upstairs to the bedroom, I heard my phone ring, and as soon as I saw Mia's name on the caller ID, I answered.

"Hey, Mia! You got me just in time. I was about to shut my ringer off and call it a night."

"What about my mom's 24/7 tech support calls?"

"I reroute them to your line after hours." I listened for some laughter, but didn't hear a thing. "Seriously, Mia, what's up?"

"I just called to hear about what happened on your date with Claudia, and also to find out when and where the big winner wants to have his victory lunch."

"Actually, I don't feel like a winner at all."

"Really? Why's that?"

"Because Claudia and I just had our first and last date," I said.

"What happened?"

I proceeded to give her a verbal replay of the evening, and to her credit, Mia listened to the whole story without interrupting me, questioning me, or second-guessing any of my actions.

"So, Doc, that's my story. Now what's the prognosis?" I asked.

Mia gave a long pause before she began. "Well, it sounds like you have some real bad luck, and it also

94

sounds like Claudia isn't ready to start dating again. I heard that she had a bad break-up with some guy named Tony a while ago, but it might have just ended recently. I think she was caught in the middle of some baby momma drama with him, and that's probably why she freaked out at the mere thought of jumping into a similar situation with you and Stephanie."

"It sounds like this Tony guy really messed with her head. Did you ever meet him?"

"Yeah, I met him last year when they first started dating."

"I'm just curious—how tall is he?"

"Oh, I'd say he's about two inches shorter than you."

It felt like every vein in my body popped out at the same time. "You're kidding!"

"Calm down! I'm just playing with you. He's about 6'1," and I know what you're thinking, but I wouldn't jump to any conclusions based on his height. I honestly think that Claudia really likes you, and when she's finally able to put her last relationship behind her and move on, I think you should consider giving her another chance."

I knew Mia meant well, but if she thought that I was just going to sit and wait for Claudia or "The Sniper," as I was now calling her, to come back around just so that she could use me for target practice and eventually shoot me down again, she had another thing coming.

As we chatted a few more minutes about our mothers and their latest attempts to drive us crazy, I tried to decide whether or not to tell Mia about Anna. I wasn't sure if she had actually tried online dating herself or what she thought of the whole concept, but the way my life was going, she probably would have been happy for me if I met someone special in jail. I finally decided to hold off, at least until I had my first live conversation with Anna.

Shortly after we hung up, it hit me that our call had totally focused on Claudia and my soap opera. Not once did Mia share anything about how her social life was going. I hated to admit it, but my friendship with my favorite cousin was steadily turning into a one-way relationship that only benefited one person: me. I tended to avoid those types of relationships with other people at all costs, and I wasn't going to make Mia suffer through one with me another minute. I called her back and she picked up on the first ring.

"What's up?" she asked.

"I forgot to ask how your world is turning these days."

"What do you mean?"

"I mean, lately, most of our calls have turned into love therapy sessions with me on the couch and you holding the clipboard while asking questions and taking notes. It's time for you to finally lie down for a while."

She hesitated for a moment and then said, "Ethan, do you really want to know what's going on in my love life?" She was either relieved that I finally had the decency to ask, didn't believe that I really wanted to know, or both, but either way, I wasn't hanging up until she told me.

"Yes, of course. I know that I can come off a little self-absorbed sometimes."

"Sometimes?"

"You're not going to make this easy, are you?"

"We'll see. Continue please."

"I forgot what I was saying," I said.

"You were admitting how self-absorbed you are."

"Yes. Thanks for the reminder. As I was saying— I know that I can come off a little self-absorbed, but I do care about you, and I want you to find a guy who deserves you and makes you happy."

"Do you really think I'd be good in a relationship?" she asked.

It was kind of strange for me to hear Mia sound so insecure and vulnerable. "Why do you think I always come to you for relationship advice?" I responded.

"Because I'm a woman, and the only woman you feel comfortable enough with to ask the kind of questions you ask me." Mia could, at times, be extremely blunt, but she was usually dead on—and this was one of those times.

"Yes, you being a woman helps, but you've given me some great advice throughout the years and thanks to you, I've been able to avoid a lot of bad situations. It's about time that I return the favor."

I wasn't too sure that Mia would open up to me about anything, but I had, at least, laid the offer out there.

"Do you remember when we talked about your research project on Match a little while ago?"

"Yes," I said, remembering how strongly she reacted to my experiment.

"I've been dating online for the past few years, and besides Match, I'm on two other dating sites. I decided a while ago that with my crazy travel schedule, and the fact that I absolutely hate getting all dressed up and wasting my time at sleazy bars and clubs, I'd rather take my chances looking for love online in the warmth and comfort of my PJs. So, now I hope you understand why I was so upset when you told me about your little project that you conducted on innocent people who are actually trying their best to find someone. There are plenty of women on those sites, like me, who don't get a lot of attention, and if we do, it's a big deal for us. So, imagine how excited I was to see that I was checked out by a guy whose profile looked somewhat decent, and how disappointed I felt when I learned an hour later that the guy was my cousin who was just using me as another lab rat for his sick experiment."

I had felt pretty low before, but I don't ever remember feeling worse. One of the most important people in my life had been caught up in the collateral damage resulting from my attempt to prove a theory. I hated saying sorry because it never seemed to express what I felt.

"I screwed up," I said. "I didn't realize how badly at the time, but I really screwed up. It may take weeks, days, and months to make it up to you, but I will, no matter how long it takes."

Mia laughed and said, "Don't be so dramatic! Yeah, I was disappointed, but it didn't take me that long to get over it once you told me what you were doing. But, I hope you now understand that there must be some other women out there who saw that you checked them out, and may still be hoping that you'll contact them. Heck, I wouldn't be surprised if some of them already tried to contact you! Have you checked your Match messages lately?"

"I'll let you know if I get any messages worth mentioning, but before I let you go, help me understand something. You said that you don't get a lot of attention."

"I don't."

"But, I've never seen you take a bad picture. So, how in the world is your mailbox not stuffed everyday with new guys trying to get at you?"

"Who said I had any pictures posted? Maybe I'm only interested in guys who are more attracted by my personality and other things they can only discover by taking the time to actually read my profile and have a live conversation with me."

"Fair enough." Now I understood why Mia barked at me when I asked to see pictures of her female friends before I committed to attend her party, and while I seriously doubted that she could attract the type of guy she wanted without posting at least one picture on her profile, I couldn't fault her for trying.

"But forget about me, Ethan. I'm not finished with you yet."

"What now?"

"Since I gave you a chance to try and prove your little theory on Match, now it's time to check out my theory. I told you that your experiment sparked some hope and interest for some women, but let's see if I'm right."

"Okay, Mia. I'm game. But for the record, are you a 'mad scientist' or just a scientist?"

"Ethan, you don't want to make me mad, so just shut up and log into your Match account."

"Aye, aye, captain!"

Mia gave me a few seconds to log in before she started barking out commands. "Okay, tell me how many times your profile has been checked out since the day you ran your experiment."

"Let's see... fifty-two," I responded.

"Okay, now how many winks have you received?"

"Twelve."

"And have you received any direct messages?"

I hesitated a moment before I responded. "One."

"Really? Wait! I thought you said that you haven't received any messages worth mentioning yet?"

"I haven't. So far, we've just exchanged a couple of emails, but if anything meaningful happens, I'll let you know."

I pictured a suspicious look on Mia's face and hoped that she wouldn't try to dig any deeper.

"Okay, fine. But, make sure you compare the usernames of all the women who checked out your profile, winked at you, sent you a message, or expressed any interest, against the usernames of the women who were in your experiment. I'm guessing that most of them were part of it, which would prove *my* theory that your experiment was much more impactful than you thought."

By the time we got off the phone this time, it was almost midnight, which was way past my normal weekday bedtime. But, I was curious about Mia's theory, so I pulled the spreadsheet from my experiment out of the trash bin on my hard drive, and opened up the file. Based on their usernames, it only took me a few minutes to confirm that ninety-two percent of the women who had recently checked out my profile, and all of the women who had winked at me, had unknowingly participated in the experiment of a wannabe scientist. Mia was right. Some of the women had expressed their interest and were probably hoping that I would contact them. I tried to rationalize my actions with the notion that most guys check out tons of online profiles without ever contacting anyone, but Mia didn't think that I was like "most guys" and for better or worse, held me to a higher standard. I doubted that Mia felt that I should follow-up with all the women who winked at me, but I was going to follow through with my plan to call Anna who, by sending three separate emails, had clearly expressed a sincere level of interest that I could no longer deny.

Individual Contributor

When I woke up, I put together my daily "to-do" list, and right near the top was to call Anna after work. Shortly after joining my company, I attended a leadership seminar, and during a session on effective communications, I was taught the importance of having a clearly defined end-goal prior to participating in an important call or face-to-face meeting. My only goal going into my call with Anna was to complete the call. I didn't know what I wanted to say, or wanted to hear. I just wanted to break the ice and go from there.

The anticipation of my upcoming call couldn't make up for my lack of sleep, and by the time I got to the office, I was already struggling. Somehow, I was able to make it through the day without crashing at the wrong moment, although I certainly tried my best during our CEO's boring afternoon presentation at an all-hands meeting. Fortunately, a coworker who was sitting next to me gave me a timely nudge when he saw that I was drifting off and about to fall head first into the crotch of our VP of HR.

After sending off a final email, I was all set to head home and call Anna for the first time. However, before heading out, I decided to send her a quick heads-up note so that I wouldn't totally catch her off guard.

Hi Anna—

Thanks for your message. I'll try to reach you this evening around 7:30pm, but if that time doesn't work for you, feel free to suggest a better one. (I'm wide open from 7:30pm on).

Regards,

Ethan

I wasn't sure how she'd react to a last-minute email about a potential call, but I figured I'd find out soon enough. The clock on my laptop read 5:52 P.M. when I closed the lid and slid it into my backpack. I took my cell phone out of the cradle on my desk, but before I could stuff it into my pants pocket, I noticed that I had a voicemail from Mom. It wasn't like her to call me at work, so I immediately hit "play" to find out what was going on.

"Hi, Ethan. I'm sorry for calling you during work hours, but I really need you to stop by the house on your way home from work. My internet went down and you know that I can't survive without my computer! Please call me back to let me know when you'll be here."

I had timed my departure to allow me enough time to make it home, and still have fifteen minutes or so to figure out a good way to start off my conversation with Anna. Stopping by Mom's place would completely kill those plans. After addressing her computer issues, I'd be forced to stay for a fattening meal and listen to agonizing details about relatives I either didn't remember or didn't want to remember. Sending Anna another message to reschedule the time I had just proposed for our call would make me seem flaky and unorganized. So, it wasn't really an option, and I half-way considered calling my mother back to ask her what she wanted more: an internet connection or a daughter-in-law.

I was actually a little overdue for a visit with Mom, but I reasoned that she would forgive me as long as I got her back online before she started experiencing any website withdrawals. If I had time, I might have been able to help her over the phone, but I didn't. Fortunately, I wasn't the only one in the family who could help, and on my way back home, I called for backup.

"Hey, Mal. I need you to do me a favor."

"A favor? What, no hello? No romance? No foreplay? You just get right to it don't you? Now I see why you're still single."

"Mal, I'm serious. I need you to help Mom get her internet connection back up and running."

"Why can't you do it?"

"Normally I would, but I'm tied up with something."

"Tied up? Ethan, in case you forgot, as the CIO of a university, I manage a staff of eight people, including three fresh-out-of-college kids all day at work, and when I come home, I've gotta deal with two more kids who know they can't be fired, along with a wife who greets me with a lengthy new 'honey do' list every damn day. So, forgive me if I can't picture a single, individual contributor with no direct reports and no kids, like yourself, ever being more 'tied up' than me."

"You're right. Forget I asked and just put Anita on the phone. I've been meaning to tell her how much better her husband thinks their marriage would be if she could only lose fifteen pounds."

"You wouldn't!"

"No, I wouldn't. But seriously, Mal, can't you do me this one favor?"

I heard him grumbling to himself before he responded.

"All right, all right! But if I can't help your mother out over the phone, you're gonna have to call her or go over there yourself when you get 'untied,' and I don't care how late it is. Do you hear me?"

"Fine. Just give her a call as soon as we hang up and text me with an update when you're done."

First Impressions

Traffic was worse than usual on the drive home, and when I finally pulled into my parking garage, it was almost half past seven. As I got out of my car and headed up my stairs, I thought about some of my initial calls with women in the past. Most of them reminded me of the first round of a boxing match in which both contestants conservatively felt each other out, and looked for weaknesses and vulnerabilities that could be exploited later if needed. Looking back, that approach often resulted in some poor first impressions on both sides, and I was certainly looking to reverse that trend with Anna.

After dumping my backpack on the couch, I picked up my cell phone. Anna hadn't responded to my message yet, but that didn't stop me from touching the number that had already been entered into my "favorites." After two rings, she picked up.

"Hello?"

As pleasant as it was, Anna's live voice caught me by surprise. Most people let calls from unfamiliar numbers roll into voicemail, and I expected to hear a recording.

"Uh... hi, Anna? This is Ethan. You reached out to me through Match."

"Oh! Hi, Ethan! It's nice to finally speak with you live! How are you doing?"

"I'm fine. Is this a good time to talk?" I asked.

"Ummm... actually, I need to run to the babysitter in a few minutes. I just saw your email message a few minutes ago about the time, but I didn't have a chance to reply. Can I call you back around eight-thirty?"

I could feel my heart drop as soon as she said "babysitter." According to her profile, she didn't have kids, which now made me question everything else in her profile. I wasn't opposed at all to dating women with children, but I had never done it and, judging by my initial reaction, wasn't necessarily looking to start with Anna.

"Sure—eight-thirty sounds fine, and you can call me on this same number," I said.

Anna sounded genuinely excited when she said, "Great! Thanks again for calling and I'll talk to you soon."

I now had an hour to figure out what to say, but I was starting to doubt if I could even make it past her child. I pulled out a pad and jotted down a few potential topics. At the top was "Your kid," followed by "Babysitter," "Anna's Match profile," and "Lies." Although I certainly wasn't planning to bring it up, I also listed "five-inch height difference" at the bottom and unconsciously highlighted it in yellow. The list looked like a recipe for a disastrous call, which I was dreading more and more by the minute.

By the time eight-thirty rolled around, I had toyed with the idea of turning my ringer off. I couldn't see a future with a woman who seemingly had no problem lying on her profile about something so important, and I thought it would be best to nip the situation in the bud right then. My cell phone rang at 8:33 P.M. and my caller ID flashed Anna's name and number. All of a sudden, I flashed back to Mia lecturing me about my quick leaps from optimism to pessimism. Earlier in the day, I couldn't wait for my call with Anna, and now that it was time, I was about to let it roll into voicemail oblivion.

I forced myself to pick up the phone and said, "Hi… Anna?"

"Hi, Ethan! Sorry again for the interruption earlier, but I'm all yours now."

"No problem. Is your child asleep?"

Although I wanted to learn about her child and find out why she chose not to mention that she was a parent on her profile, I certainly hadn't planned to start out with a pedophilesque question about what her kid was doing at that very moment.

"Oh, she's not my child! She's my niece."

A huge sense of relief quickly came over me as I happily pushed my call topic list to the side.

"And yes, she's supposed to be asleep, but I'm sure she'll do her best to stay awake and fight off the sandman for as long as she can. What about you, Ethan? Do you have any nieces or nephews?"

"Yes," I said proudly. "My older brother, Malcolm, has two boys, ages seven and nine, but their mother doesn't let me babysit too often because we have too much fun together, and they usually end up babysitting me."

She laughed and said, "So, are you telling me that you're just a big kid?"

"Didn't you see that warning on my Match profile? It was one of the first things I mentioned!"

She chuckled at my weak joke, which I took to be a good sign.

"So, Anna, at the risk of sounding like a cheesy speed dater, why don't you tell me a little bit about yourself?"

"Is Velveeta sponsoring you or something?"

"Wow! That cheesy, huh? Okay, delete that one from your memory and let me try again. So, Anna, I noticed on your Match profile that you live in Oakland, but are you originally from the Bay Area?"

"I am. I know you rarely come across people like me these days in the Bay Area, but I was actually born and raised in the Richmond district of San Francisco. My parents divorced when I was only four, and my mom raised me and my younger sister on her own in a rickety old house that she still calls 'home.' What about you, Ethan? Where did you grow up?"

One of the things I liked about Anna right off the bat was the fact that she didn't ramble on about anything for long stretches, something I was guilty of on occasion. I didn't know if it was a conscious effort, but she made sure that the conversations were well balanced, giving each party equal opportunity to participate, listen, and learn.

"I'm from here too—Fremont, to be precise. I've spent most of my life in the Bay Area, but I went to the University of Michigan in Ann Arbor for my undergrad."

"So you're a Wolverine?"

"Only when our teams are winning," I said.

"And when they're not?"

"I suddenly realize that I'm not really into college sports."

Anna chuckled and said, "Sounds like someone's afraid to have his heart broken."

"Oh, I've had my heart broken before, but I plan to take much better care of it going forward."

The weird pause in our conversation indicated that my last comment had caught us both off guard, landing us in a ditch that we needed to get out of, quickly.

"So, Anna, where did you do your undergrad?"

I remembered from her LinkedIn profile that she had gone to the University of Texas at Austin for undergrad, but I didn't know that she had been such a jock and participated in a wide range of sports, including the track team, the softball team, and the volleyball team. I wanted to ask her if she ever thought about playing basketball given her height, but I didn't want to risk offending her with a "big girl" stereotype.

As we continued our light-hearted exchange of questions and answers, I started picturing us walking together. Anna was wearing flat shoes, and I was grinning from ear to ear as we walked down the street with our arms locked together. Anna's voice snapped me out of my daydream.

"Ethan, I have a confession to make."

"Okay... what is it?"

"I've never actually reached out to anyone on Match before contacting you, and I was a little worried about coming across as a bit too desperate."

107

"Anna, as long as you're paying Match's monthly fees, you have a right to be as desperate as you want to be, especially since you chose to reach out to *me*. And I'll be honest—I actually thought your first message was a little too good to be true. I'm not that experienced with this online stuff and I just assumed that most women don't make the first move, especially someone like you who's got so much to offer and who's also very attractive." I purposefully mentioned her attractiveness second, hoping it would earn me some kudos for not sounding like a typical guy.

"Well, I normally don't make any moves at all, but since that hasn't gotten me very far, I decided to take a chance," she explained.

Next to assertive women, nothing turned me on like women who were risk-takers, and while contacting me may have been the only risk that Anna had taken in years, based on the way things were going, I suspected that it might pay off big time for both of us.

As our conversation continued to flow smoothly from one interesting topic to the next, I decided that I wanted to skip right to the next step and meet up with her face-to-face. I wasn't sure where and I wasn't sure when. All I knew was that I wanted to have us both committed to connecting in person before we disconnected that night. I needed to see with my own two eyes if Anna was as impressive in person as she was in her online profile, and equally as important, I needed to see how I literally measured up to her.

Toward the end of our conversation, I decided to test the waters.

"Have you been to Manger yet?"

"Is that the new French restaurant at Fisherman's Wharf?"

"Yep," I responded. I considered going to a different spot, but, I was determined to completely put my nightmare evening with Claudia behind me once and for all, and just like being thrown off a horse and getting back on, I felt the only way would be to go right back to Manger and, this time, have the best dinner date of my life. I didn't feel the need to impress Anna by not telling her about my reservation connection, which I took to be a sign that I was with a different type of person than Claudia, and that I would likely enjoy my second visit to the restaurant much more than my first.

"No, I haven't, but doesn't it have a crazy-long waiting list for reservations?"

"My brother is friends with one of the chefs and told me that his buddy could hook me up with a reservation if I needed one. Would you like to check it out next weekend?" I said it so nonchalantly, it almost sounded like I had offered to get her a reservation so that she could have dinner with someone else.

Thankfully, Anna responded quickly with the right answer. "Sure, I'd love to."

As usual, I had little faith in my ability to continue our conversation without saying something stupid or offensive enough to make Anna change her mind about dinner and about me. So, without appearing too obvious, I ended our chat with a promise to call her once I confirmed our reservation time for dinner next Saturday. She sounded a little reluctant to hang up, but said she was already looking forward to meeting me in person, which left me in a very upbeat mood.

Practice What I Preach

Around half past ten the next day at work, I decided to go ahead and make the dinner reservations at Manger. Since it was still pretty early, I wasn't surprised when I got voicemail, and I left a message for Anton who called me back an hour later. "Hey, Ethan. I'm sorry, man, but we don't have any open slots next Saturday. We're booked solid from opening till closing."

That wasn't what I wanted to hear. I didn't want to give Anna the impression that I couldn't deliver on my promises, so Anton simply had to come through for me.

"Really? Isn't there anything you can do?" I pleaded.

I had the feeling that there was plenty Anton could do if he had the right financial incentive, but instead of feeding the chef's wallet, I was hoping that his ex-roommate would be more persuasive. Part of me dreaded asking Malcolm for another favor, but I was desperate and determined to take care of this ASAP, even if it meant incurring a few injuries from babysitting my lethal little nephews.

I called Malcolm's cell, but I couldn't reach him and had to leave a voicemail. "Hey, Mal. Thanks for helping me out with Mom last night. I guess things went okay since I didn't hear from either of you. And since I seem to have caught you in one of your rare favor moods, I thought I'd push my luck and ask you for one more. This is an easy one, but I'm ready to bribe you with babysitting if needed. Hit me back as soon as you can."

A half-hour later, my brother called me back, and after I promised to take care of his kids on two nights of his choosing, I had secured my reservation by the time I left the office. I thought about giving Anna a call as soon as I got home. With the reservation secured, I had a valid excuse to call her again, but it was still early, and since I was curious to get a sense of what she did on a typical Friday night, I decided to hold off and call her a little later.

While I had some free time, I decided to give Fritz a call. We hadn't spoken about doing anything to celebrate his birthday tomorrow, but I had a feeling that he was cooking up something that his mother wouldn't be too proud of.

"Hey, Fritz. What's goin' on?"

"Knox, my man, what's the plan? Are you down for gettin' into a little sumthin' sumthin' this weekend?"

"Something or someone?" If Fritz was involved, it was a question I had to ask.

"Hopefully both. I'm going to a church singles event tomorrow night and I think you should come check it out."

Fritz's parents were devout Christians and had brought him to church as often as possible as a kid. But as an adult, I was pretty certain that the only kneeling Fritz did was in a bedroom with at least one woman present.

"Since when did you start going to church?" I asked.

"I've always been a member of New Covenant, but I don't go every Sunday. Sometimes I like to just watch online."

"Fritz, did you forget who you're talking to? We both know that with the exception of porn, the only thing you watch on Sundays online is football. And don't forget, you told me long ago that you never had much luck with the women at your church, because most of them were too busy trying to get at the pastor, or as you put it, 'holla at the collar.' And this event is scheduled for a Saturday night, the night that you religiously reserve for committing as many sins as possible, so I'm kind of surprised we're even having this conversation!"

"Didn't I tell you a few weeks ago that you need to get out there more?"

"Yes, you did."

"Well I'm just trying to practice what I preach, pun intended."

"I guess that means you've already checked out the RSVP list for the event and are satisfied with what you saw?"

"You are correct, my friend," Fritz said proudly.

Something told me not to even ask how he got his hands on that list, so I moved on to my next question. "I'm guessing that the female-to-male ratio on the list is at least four to one."

"Right again! And now for the grand prize—can you tell me the name of the group activity?"

I immediately pictured Fritz escorting a shy young lady in tight jeans down a poorly lit bowling lane, and slipping his hands slightly below her waist at an opportune moment. While I often marveled at seeing Fritz "operate," and wouldn't mind bowling a game or two, I could feel myself getting more and more excited about my impending date with Anna, and I didn't think I had anything to gain by attending a singles event. However, I hadn't seen Fritz in a while, and I thought that this event would be a relatively safe and tame way to help him celebrate his birthday. After weighing the pros and cons for a few more seconds, I finally said, "I'll bring my bowling shoes."

"Bingo!" Fritz responded.

Too Many Beer Commercials

When I got off the phone with Fritz, I looked over at the clock on my oven, which read 8:13 P.M. Assuming that she had planned to come straight home after work, I suspected that Anna should have made it by now, and if she did have plans, it wouldn't take me long to tell her about our dinner reservation, and more importantly, find out what her Friday night plans were.

"Ethan! What a nice surprise! I wasn't expecting to hear back from you so soon."

"Hey, Anna—good news! I was able to get us a reservation at Manger for 7:30 P.M. next Saturday," I said.

"That's great! I guess your chef came through, huh?"

"Well, it wasn't easy, but he was able to work something out for us. Is that time okay for you?"

"Seven-thirty will be perfect. Do you want me to pick you up?"

I felt like someone had just slammed on the brakes somewhere inside my head. I had expected Anna to tell me that she would meet me there or possibly give me a chance to make an offer to pick her up. Never in my wildest dreams did I expect Anna to offer to pick me up. It wasn't in any dating script I had ever read and didn't sync at all with the dating pick-up dilemma that Mia had recently shared. So, for me, the tables had been turned. Instead of Anna having to worry about me putting her in an awkward position by offering to pick her up, she had me now thinking of potential answers and consequences.

Before I could respond, Anna laughed and said, "Bet you weren't expecting that!"

"No, I wasn't, but since you offered, you can pick me up at the local police station which is a few blocks

113

from my house. No offense, but we just started communicating and a guy can't be too careful these days."

Anna chuckled and said, "Let's just meet at the restaurant."

"Only if you agree to let me do the gentlemen thing and pick you up one day."

"Does 'the gentlemen thing' include opening car doors as well?" she asked.

"Yeah, *my* doors."

"Ethan!"

"Gotta start off with some baby steps," I joked.

The fact that we were even joking about future dates was cause for celebration in my mind.

"So, now that we've got the details for dinner taken care of, I've got to tell you that your phone call really surprised me," she said.

"Really? Why? I said I'd contact you once I set up the reservation."

"Yes, but, Ethan, it's Friday night, and I thought by now you'd be out... you know... doing your thing."

"And exactly what is my thing?"

"Well, if you're like most guys—hooking up with your boys and then going out to some spot."

Just like she did by offering to pick me up for our date, Anna had beaten me to the punch by trying to get a sense of how I spent my Friday nights.

"Anna, I think you've been watching too many beer commercials."

"What do you mean?"

"Despite what you see in all the beer commercials, not everyone has a 'crew' that they hook up with every weekend to watch ball games, eat wings, drink beer, and chase women. I've never had a 'crew' or any 'boys'—just a few good friends I occasionally meet up with individually. So, if I ever have a bachelor party, it's bound to be awkward as heck because most of the guys will be meeting for the first time."

"Okay, so no 'boys,' and no 'crew,' but that doesn't mean that you and a friend don't have plans to hang at some spot tonight."

"By 'spot' I'm guessing you mean somewhere like a club or meat market?" I asked.

"Not necessarily. I could picture you and a friend getting together for a Friday night cooking class." Apparently, I didn't have an enforceable patent on sarcasm.

"With all the wear and tear I've put my microwave through, just in the past few months, that's not a bad idea. But, tonight, I'm afraid it's just me and a John Grisham novel." As I described my rather boring plans for the evening, I wondered what Anna would say about my plans to attend an event for singles in less than twenty-four hours. Despite the fact that our first date was still a week away, I doubted that she would be too happy about it, or be satisfied with my reason for attending. So, before she could probe further and start asking me about my plans for the rest of the weekend, I decided to go on the offensive.

"Now that you know what I'm doing, it's time to turn the spotlight in your direction. Are you about to jump into a sexy dress when we get off the phone and head out with your girls to your own spot tonight?" I asked.

"Oh, my dress is already on and the girls are waiting for me in the car outside."

"I'm sure all your girlfriends love you, but I doubt seriously that any of them love you enough to wait patiently in the car while you chat on a Friday night with a guy you've never met, especially when they're all dressed up and ready to hit the town."

"No, most of them wouldn't even wait three minutes. But they're still my girls and I love them to death. I'm actually going out with them tomorrow night. What about you, Ethan? Any other plans for the weekend?"

"I promised a friend of mine that I'd go with him to a bowling night sponsored by his church."

"Oh, that sounds like fun! What's the name of the church?"

"New Covenant," I responded.

"Is that on International Boulevard?"

I wanted to say, "Yes, my friend has been hunting members there for years," but instead I said, "Yes, my friend has been a member there for years."

"Well, I hope you have a great time!"

I felt compelled to say something similar, but my preconceived notion of a good time for a group of women involved a group of men, which wouldn't include me. So, while I told her that I hoped she would have fun, my tone probably implied that I hoped she only had fun with her girls.

"Oh, Ethan, you just reminded me about something I wanted to mention about your profile."

I figured that sooner or later, Anna was going to address my height or our height disparity, and of the few things listed on my profile, it had to be the one thing that stuck out the most in her mind. I had hoped to hold off on this topic until we had gotten to know each other a little better, but it sounded like she had other ideas.

"Sure. What is it?" I said.

"I just wanted you to know how glad I was to see that you were a Christian and how happy I am to hear that you participate in church activities outside of Sunday services. There is nothing more important to me than my relationship with the Lord, and I couldn't date anyone who wasn't on the same page when it comes to my faith."

That was not what I was expecting and I wasn't sure how to respond. While I was thankful that she didn't start a height discussion, I was hoping that she wouldn't dive deeper into the subject of religion either, because whatever her standards were in that area, I knew that I wouldn't measure up well. Although I used to attend services on a semi-weekly basis, my attendance slipped drastically during football season, and if I were to drive into my church's parking lot these days, most of the members would think I was lost and needed directions.

"Have you always dated men who were Christians?" I asked.

"No, it's only been since I renewed my faith. In the past, because of my height, I tended to attract a lot of jocks, and ex-jocks whose only idea of worship was having women worship them 24/7. I've also dated guys who weren't as tall, but many of them just wanted to get with me to fulfill some sort of Amazon porn fantasy."

Since Anna was undoubtedly aware of my height from my profile, I didn't necessarily think it was a warning, but whatever the case, I made a mental note not to use the words "Amazon," "porn," or "fantasy" in her presence, at least not for a while.

Although she didn't come right out and say it, I came away from our conversation feeling that Anna, like me, felt that her height was hurting her ability to find a soulmate. Was it possible that we could "help" to solve each other's problems? I couldn't begin to predict what the future held, and I knew I was jumping the gun, but given how well our first two calls had gone, I started to entertain the thought of us having a future together.

Holy Rollin'

The following afternoon, I got a text from Fritz: *U still down for holy rollin' tonight?* I sent him a text back confirming that I would be there, even though I wasn't sure what I would accomplish other than fulfilling my promise to show up. While he had his share of opening lines to use on women, Fritz didn't need any at the lanes. Standing at 6'1", his bowling skills, his massive hands, and his fifteen-inch bowling shoes did all the talking for him. By the fifth frame, Fritz usually had carte blanche to personally "guide" the woman he had selected for the evening down the lane in the guise of a hands-on bowling lesson. While I'd witnessed it many times, this process always amazed me. After simply throwing two or three strikes in a row, Fritz was basically encouraged to feel up strangers in front of their friends.

The venue for the bowling event was a fairly new establishment owned by Fritz's brother-in-law, Nick. If I wanted to open an upscale bowling alley in a posh San Francisco suburb, the last name I'd pick would be "The Gutter." But, I guess that's why I've never been and will never be an entrepreneur. After its grand opening late last year, the place had been spewing money like a broken ATM for "Slick Nick" as Fritz called him. I was never quite sure if Fritz approved of his baby sister marrying Nick, a forty-three-year-old two-time divorcee from Argentina, but whatever reservations he may have had completely vanished after Nick opened The Gutter and offered us passes for free bowling whenever we showed up. While we didn't really abuse the privilege too much, our appearances were much more infrequent after Nick presented us both with a pair of gaudy bowling shoes that had our names sewn on the side in seventy-two-point font. Besides bowling, we also did our share of eating and drinking there, and I realized a while ago that any money Nick may have lost by not charging us for bowling was surely being offset by our average bar tab, which usually cracked the forty dollar mark before our second game. I guess Nick was pretty slick after all.

Neither Fritz nor I wanted to intimidate anyone by appearing like frequent bowlers at the church event, and an ill-timed, overly-friendly greeting from one of Nick's employees would certainly blow our cover. Our bowling balls and monogrammed bowling shoes would also be hard to explain, so we both agreed to leave them at home and planned to keep our distance from the staff as best we could.

"Hey, Ethan. Glad you could make it!" The mere fact that Fritz called me by my first name was a clear indicator that there was at least one Christian woman present whom he wanted to impress and eventually know biblically. The problem for me was that I had no idea what to call Fritz. He never went by Frederick, and he usually didn't bring out his nickname until he had already "sampled the goods," as he liked to say.

I decided to play it safe and not use anything. "Hey, what's up," I said as I quickly scanned the group. Standing near Fritz were five women who seemed disappointed that I hadn't brought at least three other male friends. Thanks to the heel limitations of their bowling shoes, most of the women seemed to be my height or shorter, prompting me to immediately add bowling to my mental list of potential activities for a future date with Anna.

After I made my introductions, one of them asked me if I had ever bowled before.

"I bowled a little when I was younger, but I don't do much bowling these days," I said.

Judging from her stare, she seemed to be evaluating more than my bowling skills before she said, "Well, if you can crack 100, you can be on my team."

"And if you can crack 100, you can be on *mine*," I quipped back.

She shook my hand as she said, "Okay, you've got yourself a deal."

As I walked away in search of a ball, I heard all sorts of whispering and giggling from my new teammate and her friends, reminding me of some of my painful interactions with girls in high school. I didn't know what they were saying about me, but all of a sudden, I felt like a scrawny, pimply-faced teenager who was too shy to find out.

By the time I returned, a few more people had shown up and they had already started bowling on the two lanes in our area. Including myself and Fritz, I counted three men and eight women. While the male to female ratio wasn't what Fritz had predicted, he had most of the women mesmerized as they watched him stride down the lane and throw his hard curving ball right into the pocket, before nonchalantly walking away as all the pins collided violently and finally surrendered to gravity. He ended with a score of 212 and could have possibly snagged the same number of phone numbers if there were enough women around. My solid game of 188 went practically unnoticed, which was all right with me. I had fulfilled my promise to show up and give Fritz a perfect opportunity to show off. My job was done, but before I could take off, I had one more thing to do.

"Hey, before I forget, I want to wish you a happy birthday," I said as I shook Fritz's sweaty hand.

"Thanks, Ethan, but my birthday isn't until tomorrow, so, as usual, you're a little premature."

Most of the people in attendance had probably never seen a Black man turn red before, but thanks to Fritz's untimely joke, they could now cross that off their bucket list, assuming they were looking in my direction.

A few members of our group were still snickering as I sulked my way toward the door, but before I could get too far, Fritz caught up with me. "Knox, where you goin'? Don't you see these babes drooling at you?"

"You mean laughing at me, thanks to your damn 'premature' joke. Thanks a lot, asshole."

"My bad, Knox, but I'm serious I bet you could pull any of them right now without even trying."

I knew that Fritz was shoveling a load of B.S. my way just to keep me from leaving. As much as he wanted all of the fine women to himself, he knew that he could only juggle a certain number of them before the rest would get frustrated, bored, and be ready to leave. Fritz also knew that he wouldn't get any help from the other guy in the group whose tremendous gut made it look like he had several bowling balls stuffed under his shirt.

Just then, the woman who had earlier invited me to be on her team approached me. "Are you leaving already?" she asked.

"Yeah, I'm afraid that I gotta get going before my Pinto turns back into a pumpkin."

"You mean your Mercedes," Fritz shouted over my shoulder.

I felt the sudden urge to throw one more ball, but it wouldn't be aimed at any pins. Sensing my anger, Fritz smartly stepped away.

"Well, that's too bad, but maybe I'll see you in church soon. What service do you go to?"

"I actually don't go to New Covenant. I occasionally go to a church in Fremont," I said.

"Oh, that's cool. By the way, my name is Sharon. I know you were hit with a lot of new names all at once when we were introduced the first time."

"Thanks, Sharon. And once again my name is…"

"Ethan… I remember," she said with a smile.

I had entered the bowling alley practically wearing blinders to minimize the chances of me noticing anyone that might distract me from Anna and our date next Saturday, but Sharon had completely knocked those blinders off. Standing at about 5'5", she had a solid hourglass figure and some irresistible freckles that were perfectly sprinkled across her cute nose. Part of me desperately wanted to continue our conversation and possibly exchange numbers, but I knew that it would make me less inclined to try my best with Anna. Still, the fact that she not only remembered my name, but made a point to tell me that she remembered it, seemed like an open invitation that would be hard to walk away from.

"And, why didn't you tell me you're such a good bowler, Ethan? You bowled a 188! I've never seen anyone bowl a game over 150 in my entire life!"

"My friend over there just bowled a 212 game," I said while pointing at Fritz.

Without even turning in his direction, she smiled and said, "I wasn't watching your friend." I didn't know how to respond, so I didn't. "So, what else are you good at, Ethan?"

The only think I could think to say was, "Presentations," which confirmed that I wasn't capable of doing much thinking at the moment.

"Really? Well, if you don't have any plans for the rest of the evening, I'd like to learn more about what kinds of things you 'present.'"

Her statement, and the way she looked at me when she said it, was just dripping with sexual innuendoes, and overall this exchange was proving to be much more difficult than I expected. Since this was a church event, I was intentionally trying to keep all of my conversations tame, and was very conscious of the topics I brought up and the responses I gave. Sharon, on the other hand, had become much more risqué now that we were away from everyone else, and apparently didn't have any problems talking about things that wouldn't be covered in any scripture reading. She was also close enough for me to get a better view of her ample breasts, and a dragon tattoo that was breathing fire down toward her left nipple. I wasn't a big fan of tattoos, but given their growing popularity, I had become more comfortable with some of the smaller, more conservative designs, especially the ones that weren't readily visible to the public. Sharon's obtrusive tattoo, however, didn't fall into any of those categories and was the type that would likely raise the eyebrow of a potential employer or mother-in-law. Though I tried to picture myself making an introduction, it just wasn't working. "Mom, this is Dragon Tits. Dragon Tits, this is Mom."

We talked for a few more minutes before someone told Sharon that it was her turn to bowl and that she was holding up the game. Before heading back to the lane, she seemingly hesitated to give me a chance to do whatever it was that I was going to do.

"Well, it was great talking to you, Sharon," I said, "and I'll try to check out a service at your church soon." Although it was the polite thing to say, I knew that I didn't sound too convincing and it clearly fell short of what she wanted to hear.

"If you do, I really hope to see you there," she said as she turned and walked slowly toward the lane.

I felt compelled to let Fritz know that I was leaving, even though he'd be perfectly willing to slip out without saying a word once he found a willing student. As usual, he was giving "personal" instructions to a very cute woman with natural hair and a form-fitting dress that she most likely wore as bait. But, Fritz had that look in his eye, which told me what was likely on tap for her later this evening. I waited until he escorted her down the lane and helped guide her second ball, which was thrown so poorly that it nearly went into the next lane. They both laughed it off and looked eager to participate in another physical activity that probably wasn't as foreign to her.

"Hey, I'm taking off."

Fritz rushed over to me and said, "Have you lost your fuckin' mind? Did you see all those other babes that showed up? There must be about twelve honeys here for just the two of us to share!"

"What about that other guy over there?" I asked.

"Who, Fat Albert? Please! The only woman who's talked to him all night is the waitress who's been taking his non-stop nacho orders."

I took a look at him and noticed that although he was overweight, he was still about 6'2". With his height, Anna couldn't see above him, but with his size, she couldn't see behind him either, and for a moment, I wondered which one of us was better off.

Not surprisingly, Fritz tried to use Sharon as a last ditch effort to get me to stay. "C'mon, Knox! I saw you talking to that babe over there. You can't tell me that you're just gonna walk away from that?"

Knowing how much tattoos, like everything else on a woman, turned Fritz on, I didn't want to tell him that hers had turned me off, but I did want to make it clear that I wasn't interested. "We talked for a sec, but I already told her that it was time for me to bounce."

"You're telling me that you already got her number?" he asked.

"I don't need it. I'm already going out with someone else." As the words came tumbling out of my mouth, I tried to suck them back in, but it was way too late. Telling Fritz that I was going out with someone I hadn't even met yet was a bonehead play, and I could tell by the way his eyes lit up that he was ready to start an interrogation that wouldn't end until I had absolutely no secrets left about Anna. Fortunately for me, the woman with the natural hair was calling Fritz over to help her bowl her next frame. Fritz looked at me and then looked back over at his new pupil.

"You know you're gonna have to give me all the juicy details on this, right?"

"I will, but you'd better get back to your student before your competition gets his greasy nacho hands on her," I said.

Fritz rolled his eyes and then headed back to the lanes.

Test Lab

When I got home, I wasn't tired at all, and for some reason, I was more excited about my upcoming date with Anna than I had ever been about a first date. I figured that Mia would be excited about it as well, and when I called, she answered on the second ring.

"Hey, Ethan, what are you doing at home on a Saturday night?"

"The same thing you are doing."

"Watching the Season Two DVD of *Scandal?*"

"Okay, maybe not. I just got back from an event, but I didn't stay too long."

"Really? What kind of event was it?"

"It was a singles event, sponsored by Fritz's church."

"Wait... did you say his name and 'church' in the same sentence?"

"Yes, you heard me correctly."

"Damn! He really is a slithering snake, isn't he?"

My natural reaction was to defend my friend, but deep down, I knew that some of his actions were simply indefensible.

I said, "I'm not sure if he'll be able to hit a home run at a church singles event, but even if he can't, you better believe he's going down swinging."

"Ethan, I'm not even a Christian and I feel the need to pray for the women who are still there."

"I'm sure he's taking good care of them," I said.

"Seriously, Ethan, I don't like his cavalier attitude toward women and I certainly don't want it to rub off on you. I'm sure that horny toad would be happy hopping from one bed to the next for the rest of his life until he finally realizes that he's old and alone. But I know you, Ethan, and I know that's not what you're about and not what you want. So, please don't let your buddy or anyone else keep you from finding Mrs. Anderson the right way."

Mia was sounding like a woman who had been burned by a man, but not just any man. She sounded like she may have had her own negative experiences with Fritz in the past, and judging by the fact that she couldn't even bring herself to say his name, I guessed it wasn't a good memory. I desperately wanted to confirm my suspicions, but decided that it was a topic for another day. Instead, I decided that it was finally the right time to tell Mia about Anna.

"Speaking of Mrs. Anderson, you'll be happy to know that I have a date next Saturday night."

"A date? That's great news!" she said. "So, who is she? Where did you meet her? Where is she from? You know the script by now, Ethan, so you might as well come clean."

"Well, her name is Anna and I met her on Match."

"What? You mean to tell me that my favorite mad scientist actually met a real live woman in his test lab?"

I figured that Mia would continue to milk my experiment for quite a while, and since I deserved it, I gave her a moment to laugh at her own joke before I responded. "I actually mentioned her before. She's the one that I had exchanged a few messages with back when you were first asking if anyone had contacted me."

"That's right! And I still can't believe that you actually responded to someone. What could she have possibly said in her message that motivated you to take some action?"

"It was a pretty brief hello, but after I didn't respond to her initial message, she sent me another one, which convinced me that she really wanted to connect."

I could picture Mia trying to desperately make sense out of what I was telling her. "Well, for you to respond at all, I'm guessing she looks like a supermodel, at least in her profile photos. Are you sure it's not a scam?"

"I'm not gonna lie," I said, "that was my first thought, too, especially since she listed her height as 5'11"."

"Oh… my… God! Did you just say that you're talking with a woman who is taller than you?"

"A lot taller, and according to her profile, she's open to going out with guys as short as 5'5"."

"Well, look who's finally growing up! Now, whatever you do, please don't let your fascination with her decision to go out with a shorter guy, prevent you from opening up and allowing her to get to know the real you. And for God's sake, try to have some fun. Who knows, you two may actually hit it off and end up having the time of your lives!"

"Okay, but if I open up too much, I won't have much to talk about on the second date."

"Look at you—already thinking about a second date!"

Big Date

My days and nights were packed during the week leading up to my date with Anna, which severely limited my contact with her or anyone else outside the office. Still, I was determined to make sure that our first experience together would be something special, and during lunch on Thursday, I even asked Alex for tips on relationships with taller women. Both of his two ex-wives were at least four inches taller than he was, and even though those marriages didn't have the type of fairytale ending that I was looking for, I assumed that they both had some decent beginnings.

"Sure, Ethan, I'll share some secrets from my big girl playbook, but first you gotta show me some pics," Alex said.

"Pictures? Really? What are you, some kinda psychic?"

"No pics, no advice."

"Look, Alex, I don't need you to read my fortune. I just need some advice."

"Oh, for cryin' out loud! Just humor me, will ya?"

I begrudgingly pulled up Anna's Match.com profile on my cell phone and handed it over to Alex.

"Damn she's fine! Wait a minute. I know her! She works at Sliders on Tuesdays and Thursdays from seven-thirty till closing!"

"Very funny, Alex."

"No, Ethan, I'm dead serious! Her stage name is Anna Bells! Don't believe me? Just take a look of this pic with my face smothered in your girl's boobs."

I sat there absolutely stunned for a moment, and then reluctantly reached out for the cell phone that Alex was thrusting at me. I couldn't understand how or why he could be smiling so smugly after he had delivered news that had completely torn my world apart in an instant. I resisted the urge to just smash his phone into little pieces before I took a look at his screen, hoping to see him with some other dancer that just resembled Anna. It wasn't. Staring me in the face was a selfie of Alex looking back as he mooned the world.

"That's what I get for listening to a sales rep," I said to myself.

When he finally stopped laughing, he did give me a bit of advice. "Seriously, Ethan, you should do what I used to do back when I was stupid enough to waste my money on dates. I just convinced myself that they were all at least two inches shorter than me and in my mind, that's how I always viewed them, regardless of how tall they really were. I know that sounds kind of weird, but it always helped me to forget about any height differences and allowed me to stay positive and in control throughout the entire date."

Alex's strange advice sounded somewhat profound the way he had said it, but since he was such a good sales rep, I shouldn't have been too surprised. Still, I doubted just how useful it would be. Picturing myself on a date with a 5'4" Anna didn't even feel right, especially since she was probably still in seventh grade at that height, and even in my mind, going out with a seventh grader wasn't a good look.

At about six o'clock on Saturday, I opened up my closet to decide what I should wear on our big date. I had no control over how Anna might react to my height once she saw me in person, but I had complete control over my attire and was determined that it, alone, wouldn't scare her off. I had an array of long and short-sleeved collared shirts, along with a few sweaters that I had relied on throughout the years for most occasions, and I was hoping that some combo of the clothes in my closet would help me make the right first impression. A suit would be too formal and would be a good indicator that I didn't go on too many dates, while jeans would be too casual and would suggest that I went on far too many dates. I finally decided on a dark V-neck sweater and some light slacks, which together seemed to say, "I'm a moderately experienced dater who is open to gaining more experience with you."

When I stepped into Manger, it was 7:18 P.M., and I felt an immediate chill up my spine when I looked over and saw the bar area. Remembering what happened last time, I was determined not to go anywhere near it. I knew that there was almost no chance of running into Stephanie again, but in my mind, the area was the equivalent of a gruesome crime scene and I felt the whole bar area should be covered up with police tape until a CSI team could solve the mystery of how she killed my chances with Claudia that night. I knew that if I continued to think about it, I'd eventually start to worry about a repeat of that disaster. So, in an attempt to quickly put it out of my mind, I walked toward the hostess stand and took a seat in the crowded welcome lobby as far away from the bar as possible.

Two minutes later, I got up and fought my way over to the hostess. When I told the young woman behind the stand my name and that I had a seven-thirty reservation, she gave me a noticeable double-take before telling me that the other person in my party had already arrived. I didn't really want the hostess or anyone else to know that I was on a blind date, so I looked around at the faces of all of the women in the waiting area. I did a full 360, and although I saw a couple of taller women, none of them looked anything like the Anna that I had agreed to meet. Instead of admitting defeat, I decided to put the onus back on to the hostess.

"I don't see her, but it's kind of crowded in here. Do you see her?"

"Hmmm? Let... me... see," she said.

We were now both scanning the female faces in the waiting area, and while she was hoping to find her, I was starting to hope that she wouldn't. Looking at these women a second time made me think that I had fallen for some sort of bait and switch. With my luck, Anna was probably a 4'8" sixty-two-year-old woman who was looking to get married within the next twenty-four hours in order become a U.S. citizen before her visa expired.

I was about to bolt for the door when I heard the hostess say, "There she is! She just came out of the restroom."

I turned toward the women's restroom and saw a tall, well-built woman with a cute bob haircut walking my way. It was Anna, and she looked even better in person than she did in her profile pictures. Despite the dim lighting near the hostess stand, her smooth complexion had a radiant glow that illuminated her warm brown eyes. She was wearing a black turtleneck sweater and a pair of jeans that seemed to be perfectly designed for her eye-opening curves. She gave me a warm smile, which immediately brought a big smile to my face, but before I could say anything, she walked right past me and asked the hostess if I had arrived yet. I forgot that she had no idea what I looked like, and before I could say anything, the hostess pointed to me and shouted, "There he is!" which made it fairly obvious to everyone in the crowded waiting area that they had a front row seat for Act I of our blind date.

I had been looking intently at Anna's facial expression when the hostess pointed me out, and from what I could tell, Anna didn't seem surprised or embarrassed at all. Instead, she just walked over to me without any hesitation, and simply said, "Hi, Ethan!" before giving me a very friendly hug. Thankfully, Anna wasn't wearing high heels, but she was still standing at about 6'1", and given the way she towered over me, I was sure that some of our audience members felt that she had gotten the short end of the stick in our arrangement.

"Hey, Anna. It's nice to finally see you in person," I said, and I definitely meant it. Although she chose to wear lipstick and a little color on her cheeks, Anna was naturally beautiful and, in my opinion, could easily get by without a drop of makeup.

"You too, Ethan, and I'm really looking forward to this. I've heard so many good things about this place!"

Out of the corner of my eye, I could see that the hostess was waiting to escort us to our table, so I said, "It looks like our table is ready if you are."

"Sounds good to me. Let's go!"

As we made our way through the maze of crowded tables, I was pleased to see that we were headed toward a row of booths that offered the level of privacy that I wanted. I always felt that attractive women turned heads wherever they went, but tall, attractive women stopped traffic, and this was certainly the case with Anna. She didn't seem to notice or care about all the attention from the waiters, chefs, and patrons, but I did, because she seemed to get taller with each step, while I seemed to be getting smaller. Based on the way I was feeling, I wouldn't have been too surprised to see a high-chair set up for me at our table. But once we were seated, I noticed that we were about the same height, which quickly put me at ease and gave me a new ray of hope. Knowing that our torsos were basically the same size meant that our relationship could possibly work, as long as we spent the majority of our time in a seated position.

"Ethan, this place is so nice! And did you see some of the dishes that they were serving? I can't wait to taste the food!" Before I could respond, Anna said, "Thank you again for taking a chance and agreeing to meet with me," as she gently squeezed my hands.

"I'd love to take the credit, but if you hadn't contacted me... twice, we wouldn't be here." I didn't mean to remind Anna that she had reached out to me on two different occasions, and I was afraid that I might have embarrassed her, but I had a feeling that, unlike me, she didn't embarrass easily.

A moment later, our waiter came by to introduce himself and show off his foodie skills as he proudly gave us way too many details about the life and times of the dishes that were available for our consumption. I used the opportunity to take a good look at Anna, who had been giving her full attention to the waiter. When I finally looked back at him, I realized that he was the same waiter I had the night I was here with Claudia, which sent a nervous shock through my system. I didn't know if he realized that I was here with a different woman, but if he made any reference to the last time I was here, I could picture the night unraveling quickly and leaving me with thoughts about dining with a mannequin again.

Fortunately, he was a professional and acted as though he had never seen me before. When he came back to take our dinner orders, Anna said that she would "need another minute," but suggested that I go first. Since I had seen the menu before, I knew that they had a beef tenderloin dish that I really wanted to try. Not knowing how Anna felt about red meat or people who ate red meat, though, I decided to play it safe and go with the sea bass.

"And for you, Madame?" the waiter asked Anna.

"I'll have the beef tenderloin with a side of creamed spinach" she said.

I laughed inwardly and wondered if Anna thought for even a second about whether or not I had an aversion to red meat.

After we passed our menus over to the waiter, Anna said, "I'm surprised you didn't get a steak! I remembered that you listed steak burritos as one of your true passions on your Match profile."

I had almost forgotten most of the things that I had listed on my profile, but I had a feeling that Anna had studied it intensely in preparation for this evening, and if tested on it, would get a much higher score than I would.

"I do love a good steak, but I prefer to have it wrapped in a tortilla and stuffed with rice, guac, sour cream, and all the other fattening stuff that keeps my gym in business."

"Well, don't worry, I'll give you a taste of mine, and maybe we can burn it off later."

I had no idea what that meant, but she said it with a smile that immediately caused a stir beneath my side of the table.

Throughout the rest of our meal, the conversation flowed so smoothly, I felt like I was talking to a childhood friend that I had known my entire life. Similar to our first real phone call, we broke every first date rule in the book as we shared intimate details about topics that were usually considered taboo for two people who had just been introduced by a hostess. We joked and laughed throughout the night as we swapped stories about ex-girlfriends, ex-boyfriends, ex-bosses, and others we wished could be "ex'd" out of our lives. I even told Anna about my experience with Sharon at the bowling alley, which led to me explaining my "Ink Jug Rule," forbidding me to go out with any woman who had more ink on her jugs than I did in my printer.

Over dessert, I learned about Anna's community involvement activities, including her current work as a mentor and tutor with a program designed to help disadvantaged kids. I felt a little guilty that I didn't have any accomplishments to share in those areas, and even guiltier because it had never been a priority for me. The desire was there, but I had convinced myself years ago that I needed to be at a certain place in my life before I could fully make a commitment to helping others through a formalized program. Although that "place" had been a moving target throughout the years, I got the sense from our conversation that Anna wanted to get me there, quickly.

"So, have you ever thought about becoming a mentor?" Anna asked.

"I have, but I don't know. Whenever I see kids in my neighborhood, I have a hard time figuring out how I could possibly bond with them in a meaningful way."

For a moment, I pictured myself walking down the street with a young mentee whose pants were hanging so far below his waist, I could see the unsettling skid marks toward the bottom of his white print boxers. I knew that I shouldn't have been stereotyping or judging a book by its cover, but I was having enough trouble picturing myself being completely comfortable in public with Anna. A mentee with his pants sagging too low would have needed to keep a distance of at least two blocks from me at all times.

"I think I'm a little too old to be a Big Brother. Do they have a Big Uncle program?" I asked.

Anna didn't even crack a smile. "Ethan, I'm serious. These young boys in our community desperately need role models like you who can show them that there is a world outside of the ten to fifteen blocks in which they spend most of their childhood. They need to be exposed to more men like you to see that they can make a good living with a legit job if they're willing to put in the work."

I was probably looking a little skeptical when Anna asked, "Even if you help just one kid escape the cycle of poverty that his family has experienced for generations, wouldn't it be well worth the effort?"

"Yeah, you're right."

I was suddenly overcome with a wave of guilt as I thought back on all the mentors and volunteers who had been instrumental at various times in my life. Thanks to them, there never had been a doubt that I was going to college after high school. They helped me prepare for SATs, complete college applications, apply for scholarships and financial aid, and get into several top universities, leaving me to do the easy part: select the school with the hottest-looking cheerleaders.

Although I was enjoying her company, I really wasn't ready for a deep discussion about how I could single-handedly save any or all of the *Boyz N the Hood*, and I was hoping that Anna would be satisfied with me just nibbling on her mentor hook tonight without trying to fully reel me in.

"Promise me that you'll at least think about it," she said.

"Okay, I'll give it some serious thought. I promise."

She gave me a skeptical look, but chose not to press me any further.

We had taken our time and continued to enjoy ourselves throughout the meal and by the time our waiter finally placed the bill on the table, the dinner crowd had thinned out.

Although I still wasn't in a hurry to leave, I quickly grabbed the check when I saw Anna reach for her purse. I smiled at her and playfully said, "Don't even think about it."

"That's really nice of you, Ethan, but c'mon. You don't have to do that."

"I insist," I said before she finally relented and thanked me again.

After our waiter ran my credit card and returned it with the portfolio, Anna made a suggestion. "I don't know about you, Ethan, but I'm really stuffed. Are you ready to go walk some of this food off?"

I wasn't ready for the night to end, but I would have been perfectly content to stay there for a little while longer and continue getting to know each other on our seated, level playing field. I couldn't have scripted out the start of our night any better and so far, just as Mia had predicted, I was having the time of my life. Out on the street, however, it could be a whole different ball game, and after seeing how much taller she was when we met, I wasn't sure if I was ready to take our act on the road just yet. But, the topic of our height disparity was bound to come up sooner or later, and a short walk together might enable us both to figure out how we honestly felt about it.

"That sounds good. I haven't walked down the Wharf in years," I said.

"Really? Well, it's time to bring back some good memories."

I was much more interested in starting some good memories tonight. I had heard many women throughout the years simply gush uncontrollably about how romantic they thought it was to walk down Fisherman's Wharf at night, and assuming Anna was as into the date as she appeared thus far, it was potentially the perfect next step. Personally, I remembered the Wharf to be one long tourist trap full of overpriced restaurants and shops, but when the sun went down, I knew the temperature in the area dropped substantially and often inspired couples to rely on each other for warmth.

When we were ready to leave, I opened the door for Anna, and was immediately slapped in the face with the cold damp mist from the fog that had rolled into the night sky while we were dining.

"Which way should we go?" she asked.

"I'd like to get away from all the crowds, so let's go this way." It only took a few steps for Anna to lock her arms in mine and snuggle closely to me, but instead of enjoying her closeness, my initial reaction was to look around and see if anyone had noticed us.

During our walk, Anna commented on some of the sights and sounds that caught her eye, but she soon realized that she didn't have my undivided attention. She finally turned to me and said, "Ethan, are you listening to me?"

"Why would you ask that?"

"Well, I don't think you've heard a word that I've said in the past five minutes and you seem to be really checking out everyone who passes by."

"I like to people watch, but I guess I haven't been too subtle tonight."

Anna smiled as she snuggled up to me again and said, "Well, I'm getting kind of jealous, so why don't you focus on me for a while?"

She was right. I was so concerned about other people and what they were thinking about us, that I almost forgot about the person at my side. I squeezed her tightly and promised to give her my full attention from here on out. That brought out another smile from Anna and the next thing I knew, she started leading me briskly down the Wharf. I asked her where we were going and she said, "You'll see."

Five minutes later, we were about a block away from Twist nightclub and I could already see a long line that wrapped around the outside of the club.

I pointed to the club and said, "Anna, is that where we're headed?"

"Yeah, it is. I didn't mention it during dinner, but I love to dance and I come here a lot. I hope you don't mind?"

Coming to the club was fine, but waiting hours outside in line to get in was not. I was about to suggest going somewhere else, when Anna grabbed my hand and headed to the front of the line. She walked right up to a big guy dressed in all black who was wearing a headset and holding a clip board. I couldn't help but notice the lone button that was trying mightily to hold his jacket together, and after Anna whispered something in his ear, he took a quick glance at his list before waving us inside.

After checking our coats, we rode the elevator up to the fourth floor where the DJ was playing a mix of reggae hits. I assumed that we'd make our way to the circular bar in the middle of the room and at least grab one drink to help us ease our quick transition from a quiet romantic stroll outside to the loud sea of grinding bodies inside. But Anna had other thoughts, and the next thing I knew, we were in the middle of the dance floor and her arms were gently wrapped around me. Instinctively, I reached around her waist and held on, but since this was our first date and our first dance, I didn't allow my hands to wander too low for fear of getting my first, and possibly my last, slap in the face.

After a few more songs, we finally made our way over to some empty seats at the end of the bar.

"So, were you surprised?" she asked.

"Shocked is more like it, but this is a much better way to burn off our dinner than a walk. I bet we'd still be outside in the freezing cold if it weren't for your hook up at the door." At least I would be freezing outside. There was no doubt in my mind that Anna had never spent a second waiting in line outside any club and never had to pay a dime to get in.

Even though we were no longer on the dance floor, Anna was clearly still feeling the music as she closed her eyes, tilted her head back, and started a sensual slow wind that made me jealous of her bar stool. When she finally snapped out of her trance, she turned to me and said, "Ethan, I want to introduce you to someone." And just like that, she grabbed my hand and led our expedition back through the jungles of the crowded dance floor.

She took us straight to the DJ, whose face lit up when she saw Anna, and she motioned for Anna to come into the booth as she prepared to mix in the next record. From behind the glass, I watched the DJ do her thing. I didn't know jack about her craft, but based on the speed at which she flipped and scratched records to smoothly transition into the next song, I could tell that she was a real pro. When she finally put her headphones down, Anna entered the booth and greeted her with a big hug. They chatted for a minute or two as I patiently waited outside the booth, not knowing if I should come in. I couldn't hear what they were saying, but when Anna turned and pointed my way, I smiled and waved at her friend. After another minute of inaudible girlfriend chat, Anna gave her friend another hug and backed her way out of the booth.

"That was Nina, my ex-college roommate. I wanted to thank her for putting us on her guest list. I was hoping to introduce you to her, but it's not a good time because she's in the middle of a mix-heavy set." I shook my head up and down in agreement, as if I knew what she was talking about.

"She's pretty good! How long has she been doing this?" I asked.

"Nina has been DJ'ing for as long as I can remember. I think she got started when her parents used to let her play music for some of their grown-up parties back in the day. She had no idea what the lyrics meant back then. All she knew was that the music she played made people feel good, and that made her feel good."

The image of a little six-year-old Nina playing Marvin Gaye's *Let's Get it On* in a crowded basement party full of adults made me smile.

"She said that she could meet up with us after her set, but she still has another hour or so to go."

Anna seemed to be searching my eyes to see if I could hang that long, but in my mind, the date had already been a success and I was almost ready to call it a night before things started going downhill. Still, it was a first date, and I certainly didn't want to give her the impression that I couldn't hang past eleven on a Saturday night.

I wasn't sure what to do next, but then I felt Anna grab my hand as we headed back to the dance floor. By the time we found a decent spot, her friend had mixed in a slower song, which didn't seem to catch Anna off guard as she put her arms around me and her head on my shoulder. I didn't know how comfortable Anna was while she was leaning on me, but if was up to me, Nina would have just repeated this record the rest of the night. She must have heard my silent prayer because she played two more reggae slow jams, and by the end of the third song, I was ready to elope.

We ended up dancing the night away and didn't leave until well after midnight, although we never caught up with Nina. By the time we left, it was too cold to walk back to the lot near Manger where we had parked, so we decided to catch a cab. After the driver dropped us off, I walked Anna toward her car, but I didn't want her to get in just yet.

"So, that was a great warm up, but are you ready to hit the next club?" I asked.

"Uh... I... uh..."

I laughed at the look of panic that was on Anna's face.

"Don't worry, I'm just playing. I barely have enough energy to crawl into bed."

Despite what I had just said, I knew that if I had met Anna a few years ago, I would have gladly pole vaulted into her bed on a first date, regardless of how much energy I had at the end of the night. Fortunately for both of us, I had grown up a little since then. I knew that I wasn't nearly ready for that step, and I doubted she was ready for me to take it.

Before we parted, I asked her to call me or give me a text to let me know that she made it home safely.

"Awww, that's sweet," she said. "I promise that I'll contact you... Dad."

I was about to walk away, but Anna wrapped her arms around me and surprised me with a type of sweetly soft kiss on my lips that I'm guessing she never shared with her father.

As I pulled into my garage, I heard a chirp from my phone indicating I had a text. *Made it home. Can't wait to see you again!* I was hoping to hear Anna's voice, so I was a little disappointed that she didn't call. Still, the date had gone much better than I expected and I was ready to see her again, and again, and again. I quickly sent her a short reply that properly summed up my feelings: *Me 2* ☺.

Beware of Boys

When I woke up the next morning, I saw that Malcolm had already sent me a text confirming our plans to have a late Sunday brunch with his family over at his place. He had invited me earlier in the week, but the reminder was a red flag that usually meant that he needed help with some sort of home improvement project that he couldn't handle himself. Regardless of his intentions, I was looking forward to seeing his kids, and finally giving Malcolm some good news about my social life.

As soon as I stepped through the door, my nephews, Zack and Jason, started charging toward me. It was normal for us to wrestle together, but when I saw that they were wearing their new peewee football uniforms, I knew immediately that I was out of my league. Several minutes later, after seeing me take one too many helmet shots to my ribs, Anita finally had pity on me and told her boys to take it easy on their uncle.

"Sorry about that, Ethan, but your brother should have warned you. Ever since they got those uniforms, they've been tackling everything and everyone around here. Our UPS driver won't even ring our doorbell anymore. He just drops our packages on the steps and takes off. He's got a good sense of humor, though, because last week, he taped a sign to our door that read: *Beware of Boys.*"

"As long as you promise me there won't be any helmets near the dinner table, I'll be fine."

"They know better than that," Anita said.

"Okay—good. Now where's that husband of yours?"

"He's in the garage, working on something that doesn't need fixing."

"Sounds like Malcolm," I said. "I'll go see what he's up to."

Just as Anita suspected, Malcolm was down in his junky garage, staring hopelessly at the open hood of his old Caprice Classic that had long since passed its prime. I walked over to him and said in an overly dramatic voice, "The patient is dead, Doctor, and he's not coming back. You did what you could, but you can't save them all."

Malcolm smiled and said, "Ethan, you know you haven't looked under the hood of a car in years, and if you did, you couldn't find the engine, even if the car was running."

"Well, I may not be much of a mechanic, but I know you need my help with something. I learned a long time ago that I gotta work for my meals in this house."

He laughed and said, "That's why you've gotta get me some nephews. In a couple years, you can just bring them over here, we'll let them wrestle with their cousins for a while, and then we can put them all to work while we 'supervise' with a beer in our hands."

"Sounds good to me, and you'll be happy to know that I've taken a big first step," I said.

"Really?"

"Yep. Remember that woman I met on Match?"

"Yeah—the tall one. What happened? Did you finally go out with her?

"As a matter of fact, we went out last night. If you lean in, you might still be able to smell her scent on me."

Malcolm gave a slight chuckle and said, "Shut up, fool, and just tell me what happened."

After I gave Malcolm a quick recap of my night with Anna, he said, "So what now?"

"What do you mean?"

"Ethan, what's your next move?"

"I hadn't really thought about it. I know I want to go out with her again."

"Well, you'd better move quickly because you need to keep your momentum going with this woman."

He was right. Assuming Anna had a good time, I needed to capitalize on the positive vibes she had about me while they were still fresh on her mind.

"Okay. I'll figure out something, but I know you invited me over for a reason. Now, what is it?"

"I need you to take a look at a quick paint job."

I let out a sigh because I knew that meant that he needed me to do a paint job by myself, and that there would be nothing "quick" about it. In my early teens, I had spent several summers with Fritz painting fences to earn extra spending money and, ever since then, I had somehow developed a reputation as an "expert painter" and was often called upon to help out my more frugal family members with all their painting-related projects.

We went out to the backyard and Malcolm pointed to a bedroom window on the second floor. The paint on most of the frame had peeled off and he was undoubtedly counting on me to make it look like new again. As we were looking up at what was a project that would take over an hour, I started to feel drops of water fall from the sky.

I smiled at Malcolm and said, "I guess my prayers have been answered."

He cursed and mumbled something about shitty timing as we went back inside just before the drops turned into a steady downpour.

Meals were always an adventure at my brother's house. My nephews played with their food, my brother did who knows what on his cell phone in between bites, and Anita made me feel like a captured spy as she mercilessly interrogated me about my love life. When she had first started doing it, I thought she might have been sizing me up for one of her girlfriends, but eventually I concluded that she just liked to see me squirm.

"So, Ethan, Malcolm tells me that you're doing the online dating thing," Anita said.

I glanced over at my big-mouthed brother who didn't bother looking up from his cell phone. "Well, I have a profile posted on Match, so technically, I guess I'm in the game."

"And have you met anyone special yet?" she asked.

"Every woman is special in her own way to me, Anita."

Zack laughed and started singing, "Uncle Ethan has a girlfriend! Uncle Ethan has a girlfriend!"

"Be quiet, Zack. I'm talking to your uncle." Anita turned back to me and said, "Seriously, Ethan, have you met anyone online yet?"

I was pretty certain that Malcolm had told her about Anna, but since she was playing dumb, I felt that I had a right to play even dumber. "Well, I've had a few bites." I could see that Anita was starting to get frustrated, but everyone else seemed to be enjoying our exchange, including my brother who was still staring at his cell phone and trying his best to pretend he wasn't listening.

"Uncle Ethan, I have a bite, too! It's here on my arm. Do you want to see it?"

Zack's mother gave him a sharp look and said, "My belt is gonna bite your butt if you don't stay out of our conversation!"

Anita then turned back to me and continued with her line of questioning. "Malcolm said that you've been exchanging emails with someone you met on Match.com."

I could tell that both Zack and Jason wanted to say something badly, but Anita gave them a look that told them they better not. Then, Anita gave me a look that told me that I better.

"Yes, I met someone on Match and our first date went well, so I think we're off to a good start."

I was pretty sure that Malcolm had also told Anita about our height disparity, and I figured that she was dying to bring it up.

"So, will we get a chance to meet her?" she asked.

I wanted to say, "Possibly at our wedding if you get an invitation," but instead, I told her that it was far too early to start introducing her to anyone. I continued to entertain Anita's questions without giving up too much information until I was ready to leave. I had spent time with my nephews, had a good meal, updated Malcolm on my date with Anna, and avoided his painting project. So for me, the visit was a complete success, and as I grabbed my jacket, I made a promise to my sister-in-law before I left.

"Listen, Anita, if things continue to go well with the woman I met on Match, I promise to bring her over so that you can conduct a proper interrogation, your husband can put her to work, and your rowdy kids can give her a concussion."

How Tall Is He?

Later that evening, I treated myself to a steak burrito at my favorite taqueria, and when I got home, I noticed that Fritz had left a message on my cell. I didn't need to check it in order to know that he was calling to either brag about how well his Christian single had been 'blessing' him since they met last weekend, or to get the scoop on my date with Anna. I wasn't sure which one was higher on his priority list and I didn't really care. Right now, I was more focused on Malcolm's suggestion to figure out a way to keep things moving in the right direction with Anna.

I had been weighing possible options for follow-up dates when my phone started ringing. I immediately answered when I saw Anna's name and number on the screen.

"Hi, Ethan!"

"Hey, Anna! How's it going?"

"Good! I just called to see what you were up to."

"You... you mean right now?" I asked.

"Yeah. What are you doing right now?"

"Well... I... ugh... I'm not really doing anything. I just got home from visiting my brother and his family."

Anna said, "Are you sure I'm not interrupting anything?"

"Unless there's a game on, things are fairly slow Sunday nights at my place, and even on game night, all of the action is on the TV screen." I wanted to kick myself for sounding so boring and providing her with way too much detail.

"Well, I hope you're ready for a little action tonight. Would you like to meet me at High Tide for a drink?"

I did a poor job of hiding my enthusiasm and blurted out, "Sure!" long before Anna even finished asking her question.

High Tide was the name of a fairly popular bar in the Jack London Square district of Oakland. I had been there before, but from what I remembered, the atmosphere was pretty tame and the patrons were fairly "seasoned." So, unless it was just going to be our starting point, I couldn't picture too much action taking place this evening.

We had scheduled to meet at eight o'clock. Anna hadn't said anything about dinner, and since the place wasn't known for any food beyond its free bowls of mini pretzels, I decided to scarf down a small microwave chicken dish before heading out. Due to an accident on the freeway, which slowed traffic to a crawl for a while, I got to the bar about ten minutes late. I had called Anna while I was on the road to give her a heads-up that I'd be delayed, and I expected her to already be there when I arrived. When I stepped through the front door, I looked around, but didn't see her on any of the stools or at any of the small tables near the bar. I was about to pull out my cell phone to find out where she was, when I heard a familiar voice calling my name.

"Hey, Ethan!" I turned around and saw Anna standing in front of the pool table, which was located in a connected room. "I forgot to tell you that I'd be at the pool table when you got here. Do you play?"

She was casually dressed in a bright gold Cal sweatshirt and a pair of slightly faded jeans. After finally realizing that she had asked me a question, I turned and looked at the pool table as if it were a long lost friend. Fritz had a pool table at his house when we were growing up, and given the number of hours that we spent on it each day, it turned out to be the best babysitter we ever had.

"I played when I was younger, but since you apparently hang out at bars on Sunday nights to shoot, I'm guessing that you're about to give me some lessons that I'll never forget."

"We'll see."

Anna reached over to a pool stick that was leaning against the wall and tossed it my way as she added, "Let's see what you got." She then walked confidently over to the ball rack and quickly arranged the pool balls like someone who could do it in her sleep. "You can break," she said.

From the look in her eye, I could tell that this wouldn't be a relaxing, playful game. She clearly had a competitive streak. I wasn't sure how well it would mesh with my laid-back attitude toward most things, but I was looking forward to finding out.

Before lining up for my break, I applied some chalk to the tip of my cue and sprinkled some powder on the area between my thumb and my index finger, where the stick would rest on my hand. This modest bit of preparation might have given Anna the impression that I may have played a little more than I had let on earlier. As I made my way around the table to position myself for my break, I took a good look at her again. Even though her loose-fitting clothing did a decent job of concealing her assets, without even looking up, I could feel that she had already gained the full attention of the other male patrons in the bar.

I pulled the stick back and hit the cue ball hard, but none of the balls fell into a pocket, giving Anna an open table and an opportunity to strut her stuff. She proceeded to drop four balls in a row using a combination of spin and bank shots, which made me glad we weren't playing for money. The only thing that saved me was the fact that her remaining balls were surrounded by mine, forcing her to try a seemingly impossible fifth shot, which she almost made. By now, we had a sizable male audience that was solely focused on my opponent, even while I was shooting.

After I sunk my second ball in a row, someone put a stack of quarters on the inside ledge of the table, indicating that he wanted to have Anna all to himself. This move seemed to break the ice, as three other men positioned their stack of quarters in the same line. It looked like everyone wanted a piece of Anna and assumed that my time with her was running out. Their total lack of respect stirred something inside of me that I didn't even know existed, and when Anna was unable to make a difficult shot on the six ball, I was determined not to let her back on the table. After sinking a ball on the far end of the table, I hit three shots in a row before sinking the eight ball on a delicate bank shot that momentarily silenced the crowd.

"Great shooting!" Anna said as she placed her stick back into the holder hanging on the wall. Not surprisingly, most of the guys picked up their stacks of quarters and headed back to their barstools. They obviously weren't interested in me, and I wasn't interested in them either.

I turned to Anna and said, "Let's go."

"Aren't you going to play the next man up?"

"I didn't come here to spend time with them," I said. A wide smile came across her face as she leaned over to give me a peck on the cheek.

After we left the bar, we decided to go to a nearby Thai restaurant. As we walked hand in hand down the street, I noticed a group of young guys hanging out near the corner on our side of the street. Even at a distance, I could tell that three of them had bottles in their hands, and it smelled like they had also been testing out the limits of California's marijuana laws. Fearing what might slip out of their mouths at any moment, I could feel my body tense up as it became clear that we'd have to walk right through them. As we got closer, I could see that there were five guys in either their late teens or early twenties.

As we walked briskly through the pack, someone looked at Anna and said, "Damn! He gonna need a ladder for that one."

Then, one of his friends quickly chimed in, "Nah, man. He gonna need a step ladder to even get on the ladder."

I turned back and saw them laughing and sharing fist pounds at my expense. I could feel the anger swelling up inside and preparing me to do something that I might live to regret. Fortunately, Anna diffused the situation by gently squeezing my hand as if to say, "Don't worry about those idiots."

The restaurant was usually pretty empty and had historically survived by feeding off the overflow of people who got tired of waiting for the more popular restaurant next door, which didn't take reservations. Since only one table was occupied, the hostess allowed us to seat ourselves and we settled for a table on a raised platform near the window.

"So, here we are having dinner again. That's two dates in two nights. How do you feel about that?" Anna asked.

Up until a few minutes ago, I was feeling great. I was really enjoying my time with Anna and felt that we were continuing our momentum from the night before. But that crack about the step ladder had brought me back down to earth and had put me right back to square one in my attempt to get over our height disparity.

"I feel great because it means that you're not sick of me yet," I said.

She chuckled and said, "Not yet, but if you keep beating me in pool, I won't be around much longer!"

"Well, now that my pool career is officially over, I did want to talk to you about something."

Anna had a puzzled look on her face when she said, "Sounds kind of serious. What's up?"

Given what had just happened, this seemed like a perfect opportunity to have a height discussion, but I realized that up until this point, I had been so focused on how I felt about the difference in our altitudes that I hadn't really thought much about how Anna felt. I decided to take the same sort of roundabout route that I imagined a seasoned psychiatrist would use and hoped she would feel comfortable enough to fully open up to me. "Anna, what was it like growing up as a taller kid?"

She looked at me with a raised eyebrow and asked, "Where did that come from?"

"I don't know. I guess it's a question that I've wanted to ask you earlier, but I just wasn't comfortable approaching the subject."

Anna paused briefly before responding. "You really want to know?"

"I do," I said.

"I'm not going to lie to you, my childhood was tough. Until I reached eighth grade, I was much taller than all of the girls and almost all of the boys in my class, and I was also taller than most of the kids in my neighborhood."

"It sounds like you were literally an easy target," I said.

"You got that right! Imagine being teased all day at school, and then hearing the same hurtful remarks after school from the kids on your block. I was in tears all the time and it didn't take me long to develop a real introverted personality, which led to even more teasing."

I could already see the pain from those years in Anna's face, and it was clear that I had taken her back to a place that she had never wanted to revisit. I didn't want this night to end on a downer, so I had to figure out a way to quickly bring her back from her difficult past and into a positive present.

"Did it get any better in high school?" I asked.

"It did. It actually did." Anna seemed to be staring into space as she answered, and for a moment, I wasn't sure if she had planned to elaborate on her answer. "I was still one of the taller girls on campus, but at least I wasn't alone and I could kind of blend in with the other taller students. I also did well in sports, which helped a lot. You don't look too cool teasing the MVP of the volleyball team about her height. I also took up tae kwon do my sophomore year, and even though I had no clue what I was doing, I quickly developed a rep as someone you didn't want to mess with."

"What about dating? Was that hard?"

"Ethan, dating was, is, and will always be hard for me, and what makes it especially difficult is the fact that so many people in my life are completely fixated on my height." She said it with a sense of frustration that I hadn't seen before, and even though she didn't directly accuse me of anything, I was pretty sure that she now considered me to be a card-carrying member of her height fixation club. "I eventually stopped saying anything to my mom and sister about my dates, because as soon as I mentioned anyone, the first question out of their mouth was, 'How tall is he?' as if his height alone would determine whether or not he would turn out to be the right guy for me."

It was kind of ironic how that same question posed by Claudia's friend had set us both off for different reasons. In the end, I guess we were just two people who didn't want to be solely judged by our height, or in my case, a lack thereof.

Now that I had brought up the topic of height, there was a good chance that Anna would start asking me some questions that, for now, I was hoping to avoid. Fortunately, I was able to transition us into a fun recap of our favorite moments from our previous night out and a brainstorming discussion of activities for future dates.

"What about bowling?"

"I look hideous in bowling shoes," she said.

"They're hideous for security reasons."

"What are you talking about?"

"Would you ever steal some bowling shoes?"

"No way!"

"Well, that's why they make 'em look so hideous."
I had no idea if I was right, but it sounded reasonable
enough to me.

Anna smiled at me and said, "Sounds like
something you just made up."

I laughed and teased, "And it sounds like
something you almost fell for."

"Hmmm? I don't know, Ethan, something tells
me that you're a good bowler. Are you? 'Cause I'm not
ready for another beat down like the one you gave me
tonight."

"I bowled a little when I was younger, and I was
pretty good, but I don't bowl too often these days."

"Okay, we'll put bowling down on our 'maybe'
list, right below one-on-one volleyball," she said with a
smile.

Just like the night before, I didn't want this one to
end, but neither one of us wanted to be half-asleep at work
the next day. So, after we walked back to where we had
parked our cars, we decided to call it a night. The heels of
Anna's shoes looked only to be two inches, but they were
high enough to keep me from easily reaching her lips, and
given the way that we ended last night, giving her a
passionate kiss on the throat or not giving her one at all
would have been anticlimactic. Fortunately for me, when I
reached out to give her a good night hug, she leaned back
against the side of her car, which made it much easier for
my lips to go where they wanted to go and do what they
wanted to do.

Wherever the Wind Takes Us

Anna spent the next week in Los Angeles on a business trip to her company headquarters. Although we spoke as often as possible, it wasn't enough for me and after several days, I was already starting to miss her. I was thinking about her so much that I finally broke down and told Fritz about her over lunch.

"She's what?"

"She's 5'11", which means without heels, she's five inches taller than me."

"Since when did you start wearing heels?"

I ignored Fritz's joke and continued, "We've gone out twice and I think we've hit it off pretty good so far."

"Really? And how well have you hit it off in the bedroom?" Since this was, more than likely, the only detail Fritz really cared about, it wasn't too surprising that it was the first question to tumble out of his mouth.

"You'd have to ask one of her ex-boyfriends, because we haven't gone there yet."

"Haven't gone there? How long are you planning to wait? If she's as fine as your last woman, guys are hollerin' at her every day, and unless you close the deal soon, she's gonna start looking at other offers. Before you know it, you'll be paying for her dinners while she's giving another guy her dessert behind your back."

I let Fritz ramble on with his doom and gloom lecture for a few more minutes, before I made up an excuse to get back to the office. I hated to admit it, but I felt that we were growing further apart with each conversation. I guess I had felt that way for a while, but those feelings were accelerating now that his advice was directly clashing with the direction I wanted to take my budding relationship with Anna.

Before we went our separate ways, Fritz asked me one last question. "So, when are you going to introduce me to Big Babe?"

"As soon as you get neutered," I replied as I turned my back on him and headed toward the office.

Anna got back into town on Friday and before she returned, we had made plans to get together on Saturday night. After a surprising amount of coaxing, Anna said that I could pick her up at her place, as long as I was okay with not coming in. She promised me that she didn't have anything to hide, but since she would just be coming home from a business trip, she wouldn't have time to clean up her place. I was fine with the arrangement and I looked forward to spending time with her again.

Since traffic was light, I arrived at her place a little early. Anna lived in a condo located in the Jack London Square district of Oakland, not too far from High Tide, which explained why she suggested meeting up there last Sunday. Her neighborhood bordered the waters of the San Francisco Bay and had tremendous views of San Francisco. It had an eclectic mix of apartments, condos, and warehouses, with just enough retail stores sprinkled in to allow the locals to stay local for most of their basic needs. If it hadn't been for the eardrum-shattering horns of the trains coming into the Amtrak station seemingly every two minutes, I could have pictured living there… with the right person.

Anna came through the gate of her building wearing a light green dress that showed off her well-defined legs and her speed bump behind, which was bound to force every man in her vicinity to slow down. I was already parked in front of her building and had planned to simply get out of the car and open the door for her when she came out. Little did I know that she had no intention of getting into the car until she used her lips to show and tell me how much she had missed me.

"Okay, where to?" she said.

I smiled and said, "Like I told you before, we're just going to play it by ear tonight and go wherever the wind takes us." A look of confusion and uncertainty came over Anna's face before she shrugged her shoulders and jumped into my car.

Although I was being purposefully vague, I did have a plan for the evening. I had already decided that the quickest way for me to finally get over my lingering issues regarding our height disparity was to spend as much time in public with Anna as possible. In particular, there was an area in Oakland that was densely populated with a lot of popular bars and restaurants, all located within a few blocks of each other on Broadway Street, that I felt would be a great starting point. I wasn't sure how many places we'd actually make it to, but regardless, my goal was to make it through the night feeling much more comfortable about our height difference, no matter what looks, laughs, or comments might come my way.

Our first stop was the Team Cafe, a popular sports bar that was located at the bottom floor of a sprawling apartment complex. The place was packed, primarily with a mix of people in their twenties and thirties who had come to watch two of the top five college football teams in the country square off in a late-night contest. As we squeezed our way through the crowd, Anna spotted a couple leaving their table in the bar area, and we immediately pounced on their seats.

"You're probably wondering if I actually have something planned for us tonight, aren't you?" I asked.

"I must admit that I'm kind of curious. 'Wherever the wind takes us' doesn't tell me much, and you have no idea how hard it is for a woman to get dressed when she doesn't know where she's going. Do I look okay?"

I had told her to dress as if she were going out for drinks with her girlfriends, and looking at her outfit, it was clear that I needed to be a part of her girls nights going forward.

"Let me put it this way, I don't think you'll embarrass me based on what you currently have on."

"But, I am capable of embarrassing you?"

I couldn't tell if this was Anna's roundabout way of asking me if I was embarrassed about our height disparity, but if so, she would need to be more blatant, because I had no plans for a serious height discussion tonight.

"Possibly."

"And how might I do that, Mr. Anderson?"

"Let me look at my list of dating no-no's and see what might embarrass me the most." I looked down at my hand and pretended to read off a list that was written on the inside palm of my hand. "Let's see—ordering a pint of beer, swigging it down in one gulp, and letting out a loud belch like a proud Viking would be embarrassing. Telling the waiter that you didn't want to order any appetizers, but you'd need a plate and some cocktail sauce, as you started pulling out pieces of fried calamari from your purse would be embarrassing. Going over to the bar and asking the bartender if he could turn the channel on the big screen TV over there from the football game to *The Real Housewives of Brooklyn* would be embarrassing…"

"The Real Housewives of Brooklyn, Ethan?"

I wasn't sure why she was laughing, but I wanted to know. "What?"

"That's not a real show."

"Maybe not, but from what I can tell, they're running out of cities. So, trust me, it's just a matter of time."

"Oh, really? Okay, I think I have an idea of the types of things I need to stay away from." She then got up from her side of the table and slid on to the couch close to me as she whispered, "But, I didn't hear your name on that list." As I felt the weight of her body leaning into mine and the heat of her breath on my neck, I had to admit that I wasn't embarrassed at all.

After a drink and a couple of appetizers, we were off to Fine Vine, a new wine bar in the area that greatly benefitted from its location, as well as its large selection of unique wines. While I didn't consider myself much of a wine guy, I was hoping that Anna would like the place. As soon as we walked in, I saw a group of guys whose faces lit up, which was a sight that I was now getting used to.

"Hey, Anna!" shouted a guy from across the room. Anna's face lit up as well, as she and three guys came together for a group hug in the middle of the floor.

Anna turned to introduce me immediately. "Hey, Ethan, these are my friends from business school. This is James, Eric, and Devon. Guys, this is my friend, Ethan."

I was never big on labels, but I had to admit that I was disappointed to hear Anna refer to me as her "friend" instead of her "date," and I wondered if she was trying to let her grad school friends know that she was still fair game.

"Hi, Ethan. It's nice to meet you!" Devon said with a handshake that lingered on a little longer than I was expecting. The other two guys were further away, so they just gave me half-hearted waves, which worked for me.

After the intros, Devon turned back to Anna and said, "We're just hanging out. Do you and Ethan want to join us for a drink?"

I was hoping that Anna would say, "No." A quick drink might not be too bad, but there was something about the look in Devon's eye that made me uneasy. I couldn't tell if it was an "I used to have sex with your date" look or an "I want to have sex with your date" look, but there certainly was some kind of sexual implication that I didn't like.

Fortunately, Anna and I were on the same page. "Thanks, guys, but I want this one all to myself tonight," she said with a wink.

I heard Devon whisper, "I hear you, girlfriend, and I don't blame you at all! But let me know if things don't work out."

As we walked away, I saw Devon licking his lips at me while his buddies laughed at the shocked look on my face, and I heard another burst of laughter from the group after Devon said something about me being small, dark, and handsome.

A few minutes later, we found a table against the window on the opposite end of the bar, but it still wasn't far enough away from Anna's college buddies for me. Anna gently teased me about how long it took me to figure out which of us Devon wanted, and while I was still a little disturbed about the incident, I was very relieved to know that he and I weren't interested in the same person.

Having a Family

We spent the next few minutes talking about football, but then I got us on the topic of kids. Anna had listed "yes" to the question about wanting kids on her profile, but I figured there were additional thoughts and feelings behind that answer that could only be expressed in a live discussion.

"So, did you have fun taking care of your niece while your sister was away?" I asked.

"I always do! Her name is Amber and I miss her already. We had a blast together and when my sister came by to pick her up, Amber actually pushed her away and said, 'Mommy, you and daddy can stay on vacation because I'm not ready to leave Auntie Anna yet.' Ethan, you should have heard her. She was *so* cute!"

"Sounds like you're ready for some Ambers of your own."

"I think that part of me has been ready for a while, and I've seriously thought about adopting one, but I really don't want to raise a child by myself. My grandparents were together for thirty-six years before my grandfather passed away, and I want to be able to provide the same type of stable, loving environment for my kids throughout their childhood that my grandparents provided for my mother and her siblings. Don't get me wrong, I have plenty of female friends and relatives who are single parents and do a remarkable job of providing happy and healthy homes for their children, but that's not what I want for mine. I'm not going to lie, though, my body seems to be screaming for a child, and every baby I pass by or see on TV looks so damn cute." My body couldn't relate so I just kept my mouth shut and let her continue. "I know that I need to be patient and wait for my wedding day, but at the rate I'm going, I don't know when or even if I'll ever get married. What about you, Ethan? Do you want kids one day?"

"Me? Well, I actually adopted a little Black girl not too long ago, but I had to send her back because I couldn't figure out what to do with her hair."

"Come on, Ethan, I'm serious. How do you feel about having a family?"

I felt like I had suddenly been dropped into a field of land mines. Our relationship was just getting off the ground and was already in danger of exploding right in my face if I gave the wrong response. However, I had brought up the topic and had no one else to blame.

"When I was younger, I felt that my life would be incomplete if I didn't have the experience of raising at least one child, but now that I'm older, and now that I've already watched my brother raise his kids, I'm not as obsessed with it as I once was. I still want to have a family, but as I get older, I realize that parenthood may not be in the cards for me, and if it's not, I can live with it. Does that make sense?"

Anna nodded and said, "I hear you and it makes perfect sense, but if you really want a wife, kids, or anything else in life, I'd suggest that you don't wait too long to put your plans in motion. If there's one thing I've learned, it's that windows of opportunity are small and close really fast."

I couldn't tell if she was indirectly saying something about the pace of our relationship or simply giving me some sort of self-help advice, but either way, I was glad that Anna had shared her views about having a family, and even happier that her views were in-line with my own.

Sounds Like Samba

After spending over an hour at Fine Vine and getting a little too deep into some current event discussions that were rapidly off-setting the relaxing effects of my wine, I suggested that we head out to our next stop. Sounds Like Samba was a nearby establishment that was known for its authentic Brazilian food, drinks, and music. The restaurant was only open until 11:00 P.M. on the weekends, and soon after they closed the kitchen for the night, the place transformed into a Brazilian nightclub with live samba dancers and Brazilian bands that sometimes played until 3:00 A.M.

As soon as Anna heard the music from down the street, she started dancing her way to the front door. When the burly doorman saw Anna heading his way, he took full advantage of the opportunity and engaged her in a few samba steps right there on the sidewalk, including a spin, which seemed to catch her off guard. The sour look on my face caught the doorman off guard, and he quickly apologized once he realized that Anna already had a capable dance partner for the evening.

The inside looked like a renovated warehouse that was dimly lit, and the walls were lined with portraits of people who were probably legends to most Brazilians, but complete unknowns to most Americans. The busboys were frantically clearing the tables to make way for the swelling crowd of people waiting impatiently near the stage. I had a sneaky suspicion that, unlike me, Anna had been here several times before. She was clearly in her element and she moved rhythmically to the songs the DJ was using to warm up the crowd. When we went over to the bar, Anna ordered caipirinhas for both of us. We had stuck with wine throughout the night, so I was a little hesitant to introduce a different type of alcohol into my system. But, even if it resulted in some volcanic eruptions in my stomach, there was no doubt that I had to "man up" in front of Anna, at least for one drink.

Various couples quickly started staking claim to their territory on the dance floor even before all of the tables had been removed. As we nursed our drinks and lingered near the bar, Anna said something to me, but between the music, the people shouting their orders at the bartender, and the bartender shouting back, it was nearly impossible for me to hear her, even though we were standing side by side. So, for a moment, we just silently watched the place come alive.

I turned around to put my drink on the bar, and before I could turn back, I felt Anna holding onto my waist and grinding her crotch into my behind. It was a surprisingly bold move for her and it wasn't necessarily how I drew that play up on my chalkboard. When I turned around, I was shocked to see another woman behind me. Anna had apparently been holding in her laughter for as long as she could, and was now keeled over and cracking up uncontrollably. To make matters worse, before I could do or say anything, the mystery lady grabbed my hand and pulled me deep into the sea of bodies on the dance floor.

From a distance, Anna's eyes met mine and I gave her a sincere "help me" look, which she didn't seem to pick up on. My mystery dance partner quickly got my full attention again as she probed the front of my pants with her backside like she was searching for loose change. I was never one of those guys who felt that dancing had to be a full-contact sport, especially not with someone I didn't know, and given the amount of lower-body contact we were making, I felt like I should have been wearing protection. I politely tried to back away, but with a crowd of sweaty bodies smashed behind me, there was only so far I could go. My partner, whom I had now nicknamed Ass Attack, was clearly getting frustrated by my attempts to avoid the collision of our jeans when she finally looked over her shoulder to see who I had been looking at.

I stopped dancing and screamed in her ear, "I'm sorry, but I'm here with someone and I really should get back to her."

Without saying a word, she waved me off in disgust and proudly jiggled off in the opposite direction. As I watched Ms. Attack leave, I realized that I hadn't sized her up immediately, something I had done with women for as long as I could remember. In fact, even though she had been close enough to accurately count my nose hairs, I hadn't given her height a second thought.

I was about to go find Anna when another woman snuck up to me from behind. As she wrapped her arms around my waist, I could feel her soft breasts gently pressed up against my shoulder blades. Fortunately, I quickly recognized Anna's perfume and the familiar scent brought a big smile to my face.

"I was starting to get a little jealous watching you two and I was all set to cut in, but she took off right before I got here. What did you say to her?"

"I just told her that I was a male prostitute and that I charged twenty dollars a song for dances. I also said that if she wanted to keep dancing, we should move to the corner so that we could avoid you, my jealous pimp."

"Is that so?" asked Anna.

"There's more!"

"How am I not surprised?"

"I also told her that you were on the U.S. Olympic boxing team while you were in college and that seemed to get her moving a little quicker."

"Well, are you ready to go a few rounds with me on the dance floor?"

My big grin answered Anna's question and we started moving and sweating to the non-stop Brazilian beats. Around half past midnight, I noticed that the crowd was getting younger, which made me feel older. I could tell

Anna was becoming more uncomfortable too, as the dancers around us were getting much more flamboyant and aggressive. Sensing that it was time to go, I grabbed Anna's hand, pulling her off the dance floor and out of harm's way.

"Wow! It's getting kind of crazy out there!" she said.

"Yeah, it looks like the late shift has arrived and they're taking no prisoners tonight. I think we escaped just in the nick of time!" I took one last look at the dance floor and saw kids doing some grinding moves that were probably outlawed in Brazil and in most other parts of the world. At the rate they were going, the place was going to sound a lot more like sex than samba by the end of the night.

While I once again wasn't ready for the night to end, I was feeling pretty good about what I had accomplished. We had been out in public all night in various environments, and with the exception of the brief encounter with Anna's Cal buddies, I had thoroughly enjoyed our date and had been completely oblivious to anything that, in the past, might have kept me from doing so.

Her Place

As we approached Anna's condo building, I started to think about what Mia had said about this potentially awkward end-of-night scenario. I wasn't planning to put any pressure on Anna to invite me up, especially since I had already promised her that I would simply drop her off, but I was open to an invite if she changed her mind. Despite my obvious attraction to her, my interest in being invited up was being driven more out of curiosity to see her place than my desire to test out the springs in her mattress. The fact remained that this was only our third night out, and I realized that we needed to know a lot more about each other and spend much more time together before we went anywhere near the bedroom. Most of the guys I knew would think I was crazy if they knew how I really felt, but making other guys proud had never been on my list of priorities.

To show Anna that I was planning to keep my promise, I double-parked in the street when we reached the front of her building. I certainly wasn't in a rush to let her go, so I turned off the engine and put my hazard lights on.

"You know there are some parking spaces around the corner," Anna said.

When I realized what she had innocently suggested, I don't think that Dale Earnhardt, Jr. could have spun the car around the corner and parked any faster than I did.

"Whoa! I guess you really wanted to park, didn't you?"

In an effort to save face, I said, "Yeah... well, you'd be surprised at how many accidents involve cars that are double-parked. It's a lot more dangerous than you think."

Anna tried to keep a straight face when she said, "Is that so?" She then pointed to one of the condos above and said, "Well, the space you picked just happens to be directly below my balcony."

"Really? I wonder what the view looks like from up there," I said in a hopeful tone before I caught myself.

To my surprise, Anna looked at me and said, "Let's go find out."

Her building seemed fairly new, but it had a retro feel to it, including a big freight-style elevator, which must have made the building a favorite among the movers who frequented buildings in the area. Unlike the larger buildings in the area, it only had twelve units, and Anna had a third-floor penthouse with a great view of San Francisco and the Bay Bridge. Thanks to the triple-paned glass, the constant horns emanating from the nearby Amtrak trains were barely audible inside Anna's condo. She excused herself to use the restroom as soon as we got inside, and I used the opportunity to quickly check out all of her visible pictures, especially the ones that contained other men. In the midst of my exploration, one picture froze me in my tracks. I couldn't tell for sure, but it looked like a picture of a younger Anna with her arm around a younger Fritz. I suddenly felt all of the evening's appetizers rising up inside my stomach and was hoping that Anna had a second bathroom.

"Are you okay? Is something wrong?"

I spun around and saw Anna with a concerned look on her face. "Oh… I'll be all right. I think my head is still spinning from the drinks and all the dancing we did tonight." I'm not sure if she bought my explanation, but I didn't give her much time to think about it before I tried to get to the bottom of my sudden discomfort. "Hey, you look like you were still in college in this picture. How long ago was it taken?" I asked.

"Well, my ego thanks you, even though I know you're full of it. I took that picture with my cousin,

Maurice, about five years ago. He's in the army, but he was on leave at the time after being stationed somewhere overseas for a few years."

Thankfully, Anna didn't seem to hear my exhale or notice the color come back to my face when she explained that the guy, who looked a heck of a lot like Fritz, was never a real threat. Instead, she walked over to a frame near her fireplace and said, "Now here's what I looked like in college." It was a picture of Anna and two other drop-dead gorgeous women, and they were all wearing skimpy University of Texas cheerleading outfits. Apparently, I had chosen the wrong college.

I caught Anna trying to subtly arrange a stack of magazines on her coffee table, which reminded me that she hadn't expected me to be here. I glanced outside through her floor-to-ceiling windows and saw my car staring at me from directly below, as if it were impatiently waiting for me to drive it back home. It had been a long night, but before I left, I wanted to finally ask a question that I'd been holding onto since we first connected.

"Anna, why do you date shorter guys? Wait... that's not what I meant. What I meant to ask is... why are you open to dating shorter guys? Most women I've come across only seem to want guys that are at least as tall as they are in their highest heels."

She chuckled and said, "I guess I should just start expecting at least one 'out of the blue' question per night with you, huh?"

"Hey, I'm sorry... we can talk about something else."

"No. It's fine."

She turned to me and slightly exhaled, as if she were gearing herself up for the difficult task of trying to explain the Pythagorean Theorem to a child who was still slobbering on his Legos.

"Part of it is simply a numbers game. About ninety percent of the men in this country are 5'10" or shorter. So, if I refused to date anyone shorter than me, I've already wiped out the vast majority of the available male population. But, for me, it's more than that. I know that some women love the feeling of a bigger man wrapping their arms around them and giving them a sense of comfort and security, but I can get those same feelings from the right man, regardless of his height. What he says to me, what he says about me, and his actions are the things that I value the most, and to me, they'll always be much more important than his height."

I thought back to my eleventh commandment again and my belief that taller women didn't want anything to do with me. Her admission confirmed that she truly was an exception to my rule, and while I had to concede that she probably wasn't the only one, she was the only one I cared about.

Since I had been asking most of the questions, I was starting to feel like a paid professional listening intently to his patient, but I wasn't. I was on a date with a woman who was becoming more attractive to me by the minute. We had covered some important territory in our discussion, but I felt the night was finally coming to an end. We spent the next few minutes going through the rest of the pictures scattered throughout Anna's apartment, with the exception of the ones that were presumably in her bedroom. As we moved from picture to picture, I did my best to gently tease her about hairstyles, braces, and glasses. She was a good sport about it and even laughed right along with me on a couple of occasions. I wondered how many men had gone through this same process with her, but stopped myself when I admitted that I didn't really want to know.

When we finally ran out of pictures, Anna brought out a bottle of wine from her fridge. She then grabbed two glasses and said, "Would you like to join me?"

At this point, I was feeling pretty sober, but I knew that a late night glass or two of wine might tempt me to use my steering wheel as a pillow on my drive back home. Part of me wanted Anna to offer up her couch for the night, but if I were in her shoes, I wasn't sure that I would have been comfortable with that arrangement.

"I'd love to, but I'd also love to get home safely, so I'd better pass this time."

"Oh! I'm sorry, Ethan! Are you sure you're okay to drive home tonight?"

"Yeah, I'll be fine," I said as I grabbed my jacket and headed slowly to the door.

"Okay, but will you at least send me a text when you make it home?"

I gave her a big smile and said, "I will."

I couldn't tell by the look on Anna's face if she was disappointed or relieved that I didn't take her up on what I thought was her implied offer to spend the night, but when she wrapped her arms around my waist and pressed her lips against mine, it was clear that she wasn't ready for me to go just yet.

A few minutes later, I opened my car door and headed back to my place. I smiled at the thought of how close our goodnight kiss came to becoming a good morning kiss, despite my best efforts to control my emotions, and I hoped that my patience hadn't gone unnoticed. I was trying to strike a delicate balance. On one hand, I didn't want her to feel any pressure to do anything she wasn't ready to do in order to keep me interested. On the other hand, I wanted her fully aware of my physical attraction to her and my ultimate desire to have an intimate, fulfilling relationship that would also be my last.

As I was pulling into my garage, my cell phone vibrated. My face lit up when I saw Anna's name and number on the screen.

"Hi, Ethan. Where are you?"

"I just made it home. Weren't you supposed to wait for my text?"

"I know what I said, but I was a little worried. When you turned down the wine, I got concerned and felt guilty about letting you drive home."

Something told me that no man had ever turned down an offer for a nightcap from Anna and, given my growing feelings for her, I doubted that I could ever do it again.

The List

Earlier in the week, I had decided to surprise Mom with a weekend visit, but by late Sunday morning, I was still groggy from my late night out with Anna, and was seriously thinking about pushing it off until the following weekend. I was sitting on my bed when I turned and took a good look at the picture of my mother, which I kept on my nightstand. She seemed to be staring at me and asking me how I could possibly be satisfied with only seeing her in a five-by-seven frame. I couldn't any longer, so I picked up my car keys and headed out the door.

When I arrived, Mom was outside on her hands and knees, furiously doing something to a plant in her front lawn. She didn't notice me pull up, and after I parked, I crept toward her. "I thought mouth-to-mouth only worked on people. Do you really think you can breathe life back into that dead thing?"

Mom turned around and started brushing dirt off her pants before giving me a much-needed hug. "Well, this is a pleasant surprise! How's my boy doing? Is something wrong?"

I've learned from experience that whether it's on the phone or in person, whenever a loved one goes from excitement to concern in no time flat upon hearing your voice, it's a sure sign that they haven't been hearing it enough.

"Believe it or not, I just stopped by to see you. Nothing's wrong and I don't need anything."

"Well, you don't look too good. Are you sure you're okay?"

"I was out late last night and I'm still a little tired, but other than that, I'm fine."

"Where did you go? Did you have a date?"

I could feel my mother's interest swell as she reacted to the whiff of a potential daughter-in-law like a shark reacts to blood. I reluctantly replied, "Yes, I had a date."

"That's wonderful! Who did you go out with?"

The theme from *Jaws* seemed to be getting louder and louder in my mind.

"Her name is Anna and we met through Match.com. She works in finance for a pharmaceutical company. She did her undergrad at the University of Texas and she has an MBA from Cal. She's originally from the Bay Area and lives in the Jack London Square district of Oakland. She's thirty-four and has no children. We've gone out three times so far and things seem to be progressing well. Did I miss anything?"

When Mom didn't say anything, I started to feel a little guilty. Here she was just expressing some natural curiosity about her son's recent date and I had just unloaded on her. I was about to apologize when I realized that the small wireless earpiece she was wearing had diverted her attention.

"Hey, Clara. How are you doing? Are you feeling any better? That's good. Listen, Ethan stopped by. Yes, I'm as shocked as you are, but I have to get off the phone before he disappears for another three months. I don't think he'll stay too long, but I'll call you back as soon as he leaves." She pressed a button on her device and looked back at me. "Sorry, Ethan. Your Aunt Clara has been ill the past few days, so I had to take her call. Now, what is her name?"

"Three months? I was just here a few weeks ago!"

"Well, it feels like I haven't seen you in three months. Now, who was this date with?"

I spent the next few minutes repeating the same information that I had just shared with no one at all while Mom had been talking to my aunt. My tone was much more respectful this time and, not surprisingly, Mom reacted as if my budding relationship with Anna was already a done deal.

"Well, that's great news! I'm so glad that you finally found someone who makes you happy. I've been praying for you, Ethan. Maybe you can bring her to the family reunion we're having this summer!"

I tried my best to hide my disappointment. "Another one? Whose idea was that?"

Even before I asked, I had a good idea. Mom lived for planning challenging events like family reunions, which took all of her time, energy, and patience. When I was a child, she insisted on throwing big birthday parties for me and my brother, often inviting other kids we had never seen before, and in some cases, never saw again. I don't know if I had ever witnessed my mom so down as the day when Malcolm told her that he and Anita would handle all of their own wedding arrangements. To help pick up her spirits, I promised that she could be involved in my wedding plans, and ever since, it seemed that she had been hell-bent on getting me to the altar with anyone who had a decent pulse and could say, "I do," preferably in English.

"It was a group idea. Your Uncle Ray, Aunt Leslie, and I started talking about it last week, and after we checked dates and found a location that we thought would work for everyone, we started sharing the idea with the family."

"Mom, we've only been out a few times, so it's a little too early to be thinking about reunions or ordering the wedding cake." Despite my growing excitement about my prospects with Anna, I didn't want her to jump the gun because she was capable of taking things to a whole different level that often went far beyond my control.

"Can't I be happy for my son?"

"Sure, but can you wait until I give you something to really be happy about?" I asked.

"Okay, but I have a good feeling about this one." The last time I heard my mom say that she had a good feeling about something, she was referring to her lottery numbers for a $375 million drawing, and I was hoping that the odds of things working out with Anna were a little better. "Ethan, promise me that you'll at least think about bringing her to the reunion."

Mom's family, which Malcolm and I nicknamed "the circus" many years ago, had a long history of having disastrous reunions that were often painful to watch. Inevitably, someone would cuss someone out, a fight would break out, and then someone would fire a warning shot in the air to "calm things down." Why she thought I wanted Anna to be a part of that madness was beyond me.

"Mom, you've got to admit that the quickest way to scare off a woman would be to expose her to your... I mean our family prematurely."

"Now, Ethan, you can't tell me that she doesn't have any relatives in her family that she's not too proud of."

"I'm sure she does, but I'm also sure that she plans to keep them as far away from me as possible, for as long as possible."

"Okay, let's forget about the reunion for now. Tell me more about this woman. I'm guessing that she's shorter than you?"

"As a matter of fact, she's five inches taller."

"Wow! She's a whopper!"

"Mom, if that was a compliment, and assuming I introduce you to her one day, I'd strongly suggest leading off with a different one."

"Ethan, after listening to you complain for years about women not giving you a chance because of your height, you can't blame me for being surprised when you tell me that you're dating someone so tall."

"That's fair," I said.

"And how do you feel about it?"

"Feel about what?"

"Your height difference."

"Honestly, I had almost forgotten about it until you brought it up, which, given my prior bad experiences with taller women, is a very good sign."

"So it's not an issue?"

"I wouldn't say that. The truth is that I'm not completely comfortable with it yet, but I don't want my discomfort to be the thing that ultimately keeps us from moving forward."

I expected her to say something about how silly I was being, but Mom just stared at me as if she was trying to figure out where she went wrong with her youngest son.

"Ethan, I love you and although it may seem, at times, like I'm obsessed with getting you married, the truth is, I just want you to be happy, and I know you. I know that you won't be truly happy until you have someone special in your life. Now, I don't know if you have an ideal height in mind for the woman you want to spend the rest of your life with, but believe me, eventually, her height won't matter at all."

"I don't know."

"Don't just take my word for it, Ethan. You can prove it to yourself."

"How?"

"Well, don't you want your relationship with whomever you marry to last like mine did with your father?"

"Of course!"

"Then, try looking at things from a long-term perspective. Try creating a list of important characteristics, criteria, traits, or whatever for your partner that you think will still be important to you at my age. If you're honest with yourself, I'm pretty certain that height won't be anywhere on the list when you're done."

I stayed at my mom's place for an early dinner, but as soon as I made it back home, I picked up a pen and notepad. I wasn't sold on her advice, but I tried to fast forward to what I wanted my life to look like at Mom's age. By that time, I wanted to have great memories of many years spent with someone special, and following her suggestion, I made a list of the characteristics that person would need to possess. It didn't take long for me to decide that I simply needed someone who was loving, intelligent, compassionate, fun, and honest. As my mom had predicted, height didn't make the cut.

Decoys

I got back home from my mom's place early that afternoon, but I still had some restless energy that had me thinking about getting back out of the house. I decided to go to the gym to get in a workout. I rarely went there late on Sundays, and by the looks of things, I wasn't the only member who could make this claim. The rows of aerobic machines, which were normally in use, were mostly dormant, and the person who seemed to be burning the most calories was the cleaning lady who was laboring to move some randomly-scattered weights as she tried to vacuum the carpeted area. I was just about to jump on an elliptical machine when my cell phone buzzed.

Mia had sent me a text: *U free?*

I got off the machine and typed in a response. *At the gym.*

Okay. Not urgent, but call me later.
Will do.

After burning a sufficient number of calories on various aerobic machines, I went back home and gave Mia a call.

"Hey, Mia, what's up?"

"How was your workout?"

"It was short, but necessary. I had some alcohol that I needed to sweat out of my system."

"Something tells me that I shouldn't ask how that alcohol got into your system in the first place."

"It was just another Saturday night out on the town," I said rather nonchalantly.

"Who did you go out with? The bride you created in your recent lab experiment?" Apparently, Mia wasn't going to let that go and was planning to tease me about it until they closed my casket.

"I told you that her name is Anna, and in case you're wondering, it was one of the best dates I've had in years."

"Really! Well, you know you can't just tease me like that. I need some details."

I proceeded to give Mia most of the highlights about last night's date, but unlike most of our recent calls, I was determined to make sure that this one wasn't one-sided.

"So, what's up with you?" I asked.

Mia's hesitation got me thinking that it was going to be something heavy, and that she wasn't certain if she should share it with me. "I need a favor."

"Sure! Do you need an escort for a boring work function or something?"

"Please. No offense, but I'd rather go alone or not go at all than to bring a pretend date to something like that. I just want you to help me and a few of my girlfriends check out a new guy that Paula has been dating. She's really starting to feel him, but before she goes any further, she wants to get some more opinions, and we also wanted to have some other guys with us to make him feel more comfortable."

My mind wandered back to past invitations from other women I had known to "hang out" with their girlfriends and someone's new guy. Similar to Mia, most of them were quick to point out that "other guys" would be there, and now I understood our role: decoys. I knew that most women wanted their girlfriends to meet and approve of their significant others before they became too significant, but I doubted that a decoy's opinion carried much weight, assuming it was even needed. But, Mia rarely asked me for favors, and given the number of times she had come through for me, there was only one answer.

"Okay, count me in."

By the way things were steadily progressing with Anna, I hoped that I'd eventually be meeting her friends.

If so, I figured that I could use this as a learning opportunity to get a preview of how I might be picked apart, from head to toe.

"Thanks, cuz! We're getting together next Thursday for drinks after work at Tap City downtown. Have you been there before?"

"I haven't been inside, but I know where it is," I said.

"Okay, we're planning to meet up between six and six-thirty, and if you want to bring your new friend, that's fine with me."

I thought about it for a moment, but given the purpose of the get-together, and because I didn't have a good sense of who would be there other than Mia and Paula, I decided to hold off on inviting Anna.

"Oh, and I almost forgot to tell you that Claudia called me yesterday."

"Claudia? What the hell did she want?"

"Believe it or not, she actually wanted to apologize for walking out on you at the restaurant. She feels awful about it, but was still too ashamed to speak with you directly. She didn't get into it, but, as I told you before, I still think that she had some unresolved issues from her situation with Tony, and I doubt she was ready to start dating anyone when you two went out."

I thought about the list that I had created based on my mom's suggestion, and judging from the limited interactions I had with Claudia, I had to admit that she was intelligent and fun, but I never saw the loving or honest sides of her, and had a hard time seeing compassionate as a bullet point on her resume. Fortunately, I didn't have to spend too much time thinking about Claudia, because I had long since moved on, and was now focused on someone who seemed to have everything I was looking for.

IPO

Throughout the week, Anna and I weren't able to get together much, and instead had to rely on a combination of phone calls, video chats, IMs, texts, and emails to keep our fire burning. Since our offices were only twenty minutes apart, we were also able to sneak in a few quick lunches and coffee breaks, but they were no substitute for the type of quality time that I wanted and needed to spend with her. During a late lunch date on a Tuesday afternoon, we were trying to make plans to see each other, when Anna made a suggestion about getting together on Thursday, Mia's happy hour night.

"What about Thursday? My last meeting ends at 6:00 P.M., so maybe we can meet up for drinks and then do an early dinner?"

"I'm... uh... I'm kind of tied up on Thursday." Before she could ask any questions that I didn't want to answer, I threw out some alternatives. "What about Friday or Saturday?"

"I was hoping that we wouldn't have to go the whole week without spending an evening together, but I guess I can wait. So, who's the lucky girl you're seeing on Thursday?"

Although she said it in a half-joking kind of manner, I knew that Anna wanted some details about what must've appeared to her as my mysterious plans for Thursday night.

"It's my cousin, Mia. She asked me to do a favor for her and I promised that I would."

"You know, Ethan, you talk so much about Mia that I feel like I know her better than most of my own cousins, and I haven't even met her yet!"

"You will, I promise."

"Why don't you invite her out to dinner with us this weekend?" Anna asked.

Up until this point, I felt like I had perfectly orchestrated Anna's gradual integration into my world, while successfully fending off requests from her, my friends, and my family for introductions that I wasn't ready to make. Apparently, Anna had now decided that the time had come for us to take our relationship public, regardless of whether or not I was ready for our IPO.

"Okay, I'll check with her and see what she says. I think that Saturday will be better for her since she likes to just come home and collapse on Fridays."

Anna laughed and said, "I hear that! Okay, let's shoot for this Saturday."

Before Anna could dive back into her line of questioning about my Thursday night plans, I told her that I needed to get back to work and promised to catch up with her the next day. When I got home that evening, I called Mia to see if she was free to join us for dinner on Saturday.

"This must be serious if you plan to finally introduce me to the big lab rat!"

"So, will Saturday night work?"

"Saturday's perfect and I can't wait to meet her! And don't worry, I won't make any references to your little lab experiment, I won't make any rat jokes, I won't make any cheese jokes, and I'll try not to say or do anything that might mess things up between you two."

I wasn't even thinking about the possibility until Mia brought it up, but now I was a little concerned. Since I knew they were dying to meet each other, I expected Anna and my cousin to get along like two long lost sisters who were separated at birth. But Mia's last comment reminded me that her big mouth would be an uncontrollable variable, whose impact I might live to regret.

The Right Woman

My last conference call on Thursday ran a little long, but I was still able to make it to Tap City by 6:25 P.M. Other than Paula, Mia, and Paula's man, I didn't know who else was coming, but from what I could tell, I was the first one to arrive. I didn't know how long it would take everyone to show up, so instead of trying to save the open table in the corner which could fit at least six people, I plopped down on an empty bar stool.

With a name like Tap City, I assumed there was a large selection of tasty beers available, and I was right. After listening to the bartender ramble on for far too long about the boring history of the place and some unwanted details about a few of the beers on tap, I decided to just get a pint of my trusty Sierra Nevada Pale Ale. A few sips into my beer, I saw Mia enter the bar area. Even though we were related, I still got a kick out of how she was usually able to turn a few heads and light up the room with her presence. She always claimed not to notice, but I noticed it every time.

"Hey, cuz," she said as we hugged. "Are you the first one here?"

"I don't know. I haven't seen Paula and I don't know what her man looks like. Who else is coming besides them?"

Mia checked her cell phone and said, "Kendra is in the parking lot now and she'll be here in a sec. I don't know if you remember, but you met her at the party."

I vaguely remembered the name, but was curious as to why Mia didn't mention any men. "I thought you said that you wanted to have some other guys check him out?"

"We tried, but Kendra doesn't have a man and we couldn't get anyone else. So I guess you'll be responsible for giving us the male perspective on this guy."

I wasn't surprised that they hadn't been able to convince any other fellas to show up. I couldn't think of any guys who would willingly spend time checking out and evaluating another guy, and unless Paula's dude showed up wearing an orange prison jumpsuit or a probation ankle bracelet, I wouldn't say anything to throw salt in his game.

"Hey, there's Kendra! By the way, she only agreed to come after I told her that you would be here," Mia said.

"You what?"

I turned around and saw a woman wearing a massive weave that seemed to be in the process of swallowing up her pin-sized head. She still had her sunglasses on even though she was now about fifteen steps inside the bar and well away from the "glare" of gray skies outside. She was wearing a skin-tight dress, which highlighted her rolls of body flesh, indicating that she had gone home to change, assuming she didn't work on her back for a living. As she got closer, it was clear that Ronald McDonald had inspired her makeup selections, and while I sat back to take it all in, I suddenly wished that I had ordered a stronger drink.

Kendra and Mia greeted each other with hugs and kisses, but when she came over to greet me, I felt my whole body tense up as she proceeded to squeeze the life out of me. She turned her cheek in expectation of a kiss, but instead, got introduced to my cheek, which clumsily smashed into hers. It was already clear that I was in for a long night.

Just when I thought the situation couldn't get any worse, it did. I only vaguely remembered what Paula looked like, but I definitely recognized her man as they entered the bar and headed our way. Paula was grinning from ear to ear as she confidently held hands with Devon, the man who, just a few days ago, expressed his interest in holding my hand and God only knows what else.

When he saw my face, Devon's smile disappeared for a quick second, although I doubt that anyone else noticed. For a moment, I thought back to the way that he tried to embarrass me in front of Anna, knowing full well we were on a date, and I realized that tonight had plenty of potential for payback. As he got closer, I could tell that Devon was already pleading with his eyes for me to play along with his charade. Paula introduced him to all of us before I spoke.

"Hi, Devon, it's nice to meet you," I said with a knowing smile. He knew that I had him by the balls and ironically, he didn't like it at all. Fortunately for him, I didn't care enough to do anything about it.

Within a few minutes, the table for six that I had scoped earlier opened up. It was only in the low sixties outside and not much warmer inside, but Paula's man was already sweating. Devon immediately jumped into a seat in the far corner, most likely to stay far away from me. Coming into the evening, I had planned to pretty much be a silent participant, and since I wanted nothing to do with Devon, I was fine sitting as far away from him as possible. Unfortunately for both of us, Kendra positioned her body so that I was cut off from the other seats and had to sit directly across from Paula's man. Right after I sat down, Kendra squeezed into the chair next to me, and proceeded to rest her left breast on the side of my elbow as soon as she sat down. In fact, the whole left side of her body was smashed against mine, and for the moment, it felt like we could have fit together in the same pair of Spanx.

Paula was sitting on the opposite side of the table next to Devon, and Mia was sitting next to Kendra. We ordered some drinks and appetizers, and after they arrived, Mia started things off by lobbing some softball questions to Devon about his background and career. Just based on his background, Devon seemed to have it all together professionally. He was originally from Atlanta, and had moved out to California in order to go to college. He eventually received an engineering degree from San Francisco State University and an MBA from CAL, which helped him to land a good gig as an architect at a large firm headquartered in downtown San Francisco.

Kendra looked at Devon and said, "So, Devon, how long have you two been going out?"

Devon smiled at Paula and put his arms around her as he proudly said, "Tomorrow will be our three-month anniversary."

I quickly did the math and realized that they were already dating when I first met Paula.

Kendra then raised her glass and said, "Well, here's to your first three months and many more."

After clinking glasses with everyone at the table, Paula caught me off guard. "So, Ethan, you've been rather quiet so far. Don't you have anything to say, or do you and Devon just want to go off somewhere without us and talk about sports the rest of the night?"

I took a quick look at Devon, who was trying to suppress the look of panic on his face, which was the same one that I had.

"Sorry, I'm not good at conducting interviews with a beer in my hand."

Mia said, "Ethan, this isn't an interview."

To my surprise, Devon looked at me and said, "No, it's cool. Go ahead."

"Okay... well, let's see. Have you ever been married before?" It was the first question that came to mind. Paula almost gagged on her drink and I could even feel Kendra giving me a "where are you going with this?" kind of look. I was certain that Mia would've kicked me under the table, but she would have had to make it around Kendra's thighs, which wasn't happening.

"Uh... no, I haven't been married yet, because I've been holding out for the right person," Devon said.

"You mean the right *woman*, right?"

Devon looked me dead in the eye as he stabbed a stuffed mushroom with his fork.

"Yeah, the right woman, of course."

In an effort to ease the tension that had quickly built up at the table, Paula pointed to her empty glass and asked, "Does anyone else need a refill?"

Mia said, "I do, but I was thinking about getting a bottle of wine for the table. And speaking of wine, has anyone been to that wine bar called Fine Vine on Broadway?"

"I've been there," I said.

By now, Devon's smiles were few and far between, and even though I wasn't, he must've thought I was on the verge of revealing his secret right in front everyone.

Paula said, "One of my girlfriends went there a couple of weeks ago, but she said that the crowd has sort of changed since it first opened."

"Really? Changed how?" Mia asked.

"She said that she used to go in there to check out the selection of wine and the selection of men, but now, she's noticed that most of the men come there to do the exact same thing!"

Mia laughed and said, "So, Ethan, do you have a secret you want to share with us tonight?"

I knew that she was joking but apparently Kendra wasn't so sure, because for the first time all night, I felt that there was finally enough separation between us to fit a single sheet of copy paper between our thighs.

"No, sorry to disappoint you, but I was there on a date not too long ago with my friend, Anna."

As soon as I said "date," it felt like a phone book could fit in between me and the woman who had been practically glued to my side ever since we sat down. I wanted to change the subject, but before I could, Devon started coughing violently, and excused himself before making a mad dash to the restroom. After about ten minutes, Paula started getting worried. Up until now, she had coerced her man into taking pictures throughout the night of what she expected to be a joyous occasion, but there wasn't a trace of joy on her face when she finally begged me to go check on him.

As soon as I entered the restroom, Devon approached me and started shouting in my face. "What kinda fucked up shit was that?"

"Back up and calm down!"

"All that stuff about marriage with 'the right woman,' and why the fuck did you bring up Fine Vine?"

Prior to meeting Anna, I would've made this the most uncomfortable night of Devon's life, and might have tried to embarrass the hell out of him just as he had embarrassed me in front of Anna and his friends. But he didn't matter to me, and even though Anna wasn't here physically, I wanted to handle the situation in a manner that would make her proud of the man who was trying to become as indispensable to her as she had become to him.

"Devon, I'm sorry for the marriage comment and the 'right woman' comment too, but I didn't bring up Fine Vine, Mia did. I just said that I went there, remember? If I really wanted everyone to know I saw you there, I had plenty of chances, and even though I think Paula deserves to know whatever you're not telling her, it's none of my business, so I'm staying out of it."

He gave me a skeptical look before he said, "Cool." Then he reached out his fist to give me a pound, but I just couldn't do it. As I headed out the door, I heard him say, "You may not believe it, but I really care for Paula and I want things to work out," which left me wondering how many other people he cared for, and how many other situations was he hoping to 'work out.'

When I got back to the table, Paula had a worried look on her face.

"How is he? Is he okay?"

"He's fine. I don't want to get into any of the details, but he's feeling much better and I think he should be out soon. But I'm actually going to head back to the office to finish preparing for a presentation."

The presentation wasn't urgent, but the fact that I'd rather go back to the office and work on it after hours than hang out at a lively bar was a clear indicator of just how painful the night had been. I pulled out enough cash to cover my drinks and started heading toward the door. On my way out, I faintly heard Paula suggest that we all get together again real soon, but from the looks on everyone's faces, it was clear that no one, including Paula, really wanted it to ever happen again.

Silence

The next day at work flew by quickly, and I spent most of the day in a training class to learn about all the new bells and whistles on the latest version of our company's software product. Because I had a role in the product development process, I was already familiar with most of the new features covered in the training, leaving me free to daydream about Anna. It had now been just over a month since I received her initial email, and while I thought that our long-term prospects were looking better and better each day, I was interested in getting Mia's take on Anna, and counting on her to help me avoid any unwanted surprises down the road, like the one that was undoubtedly in Paula's future.

I met Anna at her place the next evening, and after allowing me to drive most nights we had gotten together, she insisted on driving us to the restaurant. I had suggested that we meet up with Mia at Zachary's, a legendary pizza place in the Rockridge area of Oakland. Mia had already put her name on their long waiting list when we got there and, as I had expected, right after I introduced them for the first time, they hugged and carried on like they had known each other for years.

"Finally we get to meet! Ethan talks about his favorite cousin all the time!" Anna said.

"Really? Well, he's notoriously secretive about his personal life, so when he started talking about you and suggested that we actually meet up, I knew that you had to be something special!"

They were obviously enjoying the moment, but it all sounded like some polite and unnecessary butt-kissing to me. The same intro for two guys would've been over in three words: "Hey—what's up."

I let the ladies pick out a pizza for the table, and after we placed our order, Mia started her informal interview.

"So, Anna, Ethan tells me that you met online. I think that's great!"

Anna looked into my eyes, possibly for some sort of approval before she responded. "Well, I haven't had too much luck in online or offline dating for the past few months, but there was something about Ethan's profile that just got me curious."

"Well, as you may have discovered already, my cousin is a curious individual, so that kinda makes sense," Mia responded without looking at me.

"Ladies, I'm right here! If you're going to talk about me, can you at least wait until I'm in the bathroom or something?"

Mia smiled at me and said, "Ethan, you didn't tell me that you were into online dating?"

Even though Mia promised me earlier that she wouldn't bring up my Match research project, she didn't promise that she wouldn't make me squirm.

"Well, I was pretty late to the game compared to most online daters, but I have nothing against using technology to enhance my social life. From the looks of things, I'd say that it's working out just fine." I then gave Anna a big fat smile, who returned the favor.

While we were waiting for our pizza, Mia and Anna dominated the conversation, and traded questions and more information about their backgrounds, jobs, and interests. I was embarrassed to admit that I learned almost as much about Anna in those thirty minutes as I had learned in the entire time we'd been dating, which told me that either I wasn't a good listener, or that most of our conversations had been far too shallow. By the time our pizza arrived, Mia and Anna had exchanged numbers and were already making plans to get together without me.

"Anna, you are hilarious! You remind me a lot of my friend, Paula. We just went out with her and her new man after work this past Thursday."

As soon as Mia mentioned Paula's name, I felt like I was in the front passenger seat of a car, skidding helplessly downhill on an icy street toward an imminent disaster.

Before I could take any preemptive measures, Mia turned to me and asked, "Now why didn't you invite Anna to drinks with us?"

I tried to open my mouth, but nothing came out, which was probably best because I didn't know what to say. After what had happened that night, I thought my decision not to bring Anna into that awkward situation was a good one, yet, just two days later, it was already coming back to bite me.

Sensing that I was at a loss for words, Anna said, "I was working on a big project at work this week, so I couldn't make it." For the first time all night, there was an uncomfortable silence at the table. I was pissed at Mia for asking her question about Thursday, and Anna was obviously pissed at me for not answering it.

Not seeing an easy way out, I said the only thing that I could think of to change the topic "Does anyone want this last slice?"

Mia could probably sense that the mood at the table had changed for the worse, and in hopes of ending the evening on a high note, she suggested that Anna and I get together for a picture. I reached over and put my arm around Anna's chair in preparation for some seated shots, but when Anna decided to stand up, I stood up as well and cautiously put my arm around her waist. We took two pictures together, and then our waiter took one of the three of us with Anna in the middle standing out like a hot dog that was too long for its bun. I felt that the fact that I was even able to inwardly joke about our height disparity was a sign that I was feeling much better about it, but the frosty look I got from Anna as we said our goodbyes told me that there would be another issue that I'd have to overcome at some point tonight.

Based on her non-verbal signals (like silence), Anna was undoubtedly upset on the ride back and clearly wanted me to know it. My car was parked on the street outside her building. As we approached it, she didn't say a word, and barely slowed down long enough for me to dive out onto the street before she headed into her parking garage.

I knew that the worst thing I could do was to not acknowledge the fact that she was upset and to let her go to sleep pissed off at me. So, I got in my car and gave her some time to cool down as I headed south on Highway 880. Fifteen minutes into my drive, I was about to give Anna a call when I changed my mind. I knew what I wanted to say, but I wasn't confident in my ability to get it all out in a manner that sounded the way I wanted it to sound. Instead, as soon as I got home, I pulled out my laptop and sent her an email.

Hi Anna—

I know you're upset that I didn't invite you to join us on Thursday, but I honestly didn't know what to expect. It was Mia's group of friends. Other than Mia and Paula, I didn't know who else was coming, and I didn't get the warm and fuzzies from Paula the one time that I met her. It would have been different if it was a bunch of my friends, but since I wasn't certain what I was walking into, I didn't want to risk inviting you to something that neither one of us would enjoy. I know that I should have given you the option, and next time I will, but this time I didn't, and for that I'm sorry. Please forgive me.

Ethan

I considered adding something about Devon, but that would have opened up a whole other can of worms that I wasn't ready to deal with. After giving it a final look, I was somewhat concerned about how sappy I sounded. But knowing that I'd much rather be sappy with Anna in my life than be a "real man" on my own, I hit the send button. Just to make sure Anna wouldn't go to bed without knowing that I had reached out to her, I sent her a text which read: *Please read my email apology.*

I stayed up to hear something from Anna, but the only person who contacted me was Alex, and I wasn't surprised at all about where he was and what he wanted.

"Hey, Ethan, my man! Guess where I am."

"At a Strippers Anonymous meeting?"

"Nope."

"Visiting your kids in Toronto?"

"Close! I'm visiting someone else's 'kids' at Sliders, and some of them were asking about you."

"I'm sure they were."

"They want you to hurry up and get your ass down here."

"I'm sure they do."

"Wait... I think one of them wants to talk to you."

Over some blaring background music, I heard Alex tell someone that "his name is Ethan" as he was handing over the phone.

"Hi, Ethan! This is Candy. Whatcha doing?" She sounded like she was fifteen and I already felt that I was committing a crime by just listening to her voice.

"I'm at home hoping that a friend will contact me soon," I said.

"Well, I want to be your friend, and if you come down here to see me, I'll show you just how friendly I can be. How does that sound?"

Since I had no intention of ever stepping into Sliders again, I didn't mind being blunt.

"It sounds like I'd be walking into an FBI predator sting operation, so I'll pass. But, take good care of Alex and enjoy the rest of your evening, Candy."

She hung up before I could, but instead of putting the phone down, I just held it in my hand and stared at it for a good two minutes, hoping that it would ring and Anna's name would appear. It never did, but before I stuffed it back into my jeans, I decided that from then on, Alex and I would no longer be mixing business and pleasure.

Her Good Side

The next morning, I got a call from Mia, who I guessed was eager to share her thoughts about the woman who wasn't speaking to me.

"Hey, Ethan, can you talk or is Anna still with you?"

"Mia, I'm at home alone in my bed and I'm guessing that Anna is still alone in hers."

"Okay, okay! You don't have to jump down my throat about it and I hope you didn't miss out on any lovin' because of me."

"What are you talking about?" I asked.

"Oh, come on, Ethan! Despite that B.S. excuse she made to cover for you, I could tell she was clearly pissed off that you didn't invite her to Tap City on Thursday. And she doesn't seem like the type to easily go off on anyone, so I'm guessing it was a rather quiet ride back home last night."

"She was a little upset, but I sent her an apology and—"

Mia cut me off. "Wait, you *sent* her an apology? Like a stupid email or a text?"

"Email."

"Ethan, why didn't you just call her?"

"I was going to, but I was worried that the words wouldn't come out quite right."

"Well, how did she react?"

"She hasn't yet."

"I'm not surprised. If you don't hear from her soon, I'd suggest calling her because I really like her and I think you guys have some good chemistry. I should tell you, though, that I think that she's way more into you than you realize. So, you better straighten things out quickly, because a woman like that isn't going to wait around too long, even for a catch like you, cuz."

It was nice to hear Mia say that she thought Anna was really into me, but unless I could quickly make things right, those feelings could start to fade fast.

"I'll call her as soon as we get off the phone."

"Sounds good, but before I forget, what happened between you and Devon?"

"What do you mean? Did he say anything after I left?" I asked.

"Now that's funny. He was supposedly sick in the bathroom doing whatever, but when he finally came out, all he was worried about was what you had said to us. Now what the hell is going on, Ethan? What really happened between you two in that bathroom?"

I didn't want to answer her question because I didn't want to get involved, but I certainly wasn't going to lie to Mia in order to protect someone who had no role in my life whatsoever.

"Mia, I think he's gay... I mean, I think he's bisexual."

"How do you know?"

"I didn't mention it when I said that I had been to Fine Vine, but I saw him there with a few of his... buddies the night I was there with Anna."

"So, that's why he looked so weird once we started talking about that place!"

"You don't sound surprised at all about the bisexual part," I said.

"I'm not. I didn't walk away with a good feeling about Devon that night, and the look on his face when Paula mentioned the changing crowd at Fine Vine got me thinking that he might be much more familiar with that place than he was letting on."

"Well, in case you're wondering, I didn't think it was my place to tell her and that's what I told him in the bathroom before I left."

Mia said, "I guess he didn't believe you because he was trying desperately to find out what you had said before you left."

"Yeah, I'm sure he was scared to death. But, now that you know what happened, what are you going to do?"

"I'm going to tell Paula, of course! That's my girl and even though it's going to be a tough conversation, this is something she needs to know… don't you agree?"

I didn't have a dog in the fight, so I didn't want to give an opinion at all. Still, I reluctantly answered Mia's question. "I agree that Paula needs to know, but I think that Devon should be the one to tell her, even though I doubt that's going to happen."

"No, I don't think Devon's going to do a damn thing."

When Mia and I finally hung up, my thoughts turned to Anna. I still hadn't heard from her since last night and was concerned that I was now deep inside her doghouse with little to no chance of escaping for a while. My call rolled over to voicemail.

"Hi, Anna, this is Ethan. I don't know if you checked out the email I sent last night, but regardless, I just wanted to apologize for not inviting you to happy hour with Mia and her friends the other night. I meant what I said in the email. I didn't feel comfortable bringing you into a situation that I wasn't comfortable coming into myself, but I still should have let you make that decision. Please call me."

Twenty minutes later, Anna called me back.

"Anna?"

"Hi, Ethan."

"It's good to hear your voice. Did you get my messages?"

"I did, and I that's why I called… Ethan, I told you early on that one of the most important things to me is honesty, and I don't think you were honest with me about the happy hour last Thursday. I understand your

201

reasoning, but like you said in your email, you should have just explained the situation and then let me decide whether or not I wanted to go. Keeping information from me, whether you lie about it or just decide on your own not to share it, is equally dishonest."

Honesty was on the list that I had created after speaking with my mother. It was good to hear that Anna found it to be equally important, but it wasn't good to hear her question my abilities in that area, even though she had every right to.

"Okay, fine. I had planned a surprise birthday party for you, but since you need to know everything, make sure you wear something nice and act surprised when we go out next Tuesday."

"Ethan, my birthday is three months away."

"Then, I guess it will be a surprise for everyone!"

Hearing Anna's light laughter was music to my ears. "Ethan, you're so silly sometimes."

If I had to occasionally sound silly to get back on her good side, then that was exactly what I would do, and now that I was there, I was determined not to leave.

Holding Pattern

According to Fritz, over the next few months, Anna and I had turned into "a boring old married couple," which was fine with me. Our schedules had become a little more predictable, enabling us to fall into some comfortable routines. Most evenings, we gave each other a blow-by-blow description of our day, including all the highs and lows. If I were an outsider looking in, I would've thought it was a pretty lame ritual, but I wasn't an outsider, and I enjoyed every minute of it.

Thanks to Anna, I had come a long way since we first connected. Early on, she shot down my assumption about women I wanted not being interested in shorter guys, and from the beginning, it was clear that she never had a problem with my height or our height disparity, which eventually helped to make it a non-issue for me. In addition, all of the time that we had spent in public these past few months had helped me to forget about how other people perceived us, and instead, focus on how we could build a future together as a couple.

When I first took my mom's advice and created a list of must-haves for my soulmate, I didn't know Anna well enough to determine how she stacked up against it, but now it was clear that she was everything that I had ever wanted. Even before I met her, I could tell that she was extremely intelligent, simply based on the information I found about her online, including the papers she had written, the presentations she had delivered, and the steady progress she had made throughout her career. Our many conversations, about a wide range of topics, simply confirmed her smarts in my book. Her strong desire to improve the lives of kids in her community was clear evidence of how compassionate she could be, and even though she had covered for me at Zachary's with Mia, she had always been honest with me, and never gave me a reason to doubt her. I could also tell that she was a very loving person by the way that she treated her niece and mentees, and more importantly, by the way that she treated me. Overall, I was happier than I had been in years, and when I told Mia that I had recorded the 49ers' first playoff game so that Anna and I could attend church together, she knew that something really special was happening between us.

Despite all the progress we had made in our relationship, I felt there was still plenty of progress to be made in one key area: the bedroom. Fritz seemed more frustrated about it than I was, and at lunch one day, he proceeded to let me know it.

"You mean you still haven't smashed that? What are you waiting for, the second coming? I warned you months ago that she wasn't going to wait forever. And don't get it twisted. Just because you two are still going out, doesn't mean that she's still waiting on you."

My brother was just as bad, but at least I knew that his heart was in the right place. Deep down, he wanted me to be happy and to find the right woman, but even he couldn't resist the urge to tease me mercilessly while my balls continued to turn bluer each day.

"Hey, Ethan, I thought you should know that the guys at work started a pool about your currently nonexistent sex life. The over-and-under for your next session is eight months, and don't hate me, but I took the over." Malcolm had referenced a type of wager that enabled betting above or below a certain number. Based on our few trips to casinos in the past, I knew that he had terrible luck, and I was really hoping that it wouldn't turn around for quite a while.

"That's real funny. Did you guys do an over-and-under on how long I'd last, too?" I said sarcastically.

"Actually, we did. It's set at three minutes, and trust me, you don't want to know which side I took."

Malcolm had no way of knowing, but he was in serious jeopardy of losing his bet about my next encounter. I was scheduled to attend a four-day industry conference in Las Vegas, and I was planning to invite Anna to join me. Based on the rather light agenda, I knew that I'd have ample time to hang with her while we were there, and more importantly, there was only one room, and only one bed, which, in my mind, could lead to only one thing.

I brought it up with her at lunch on Monday, three weeks before the start of the conference.

"Guess where I'm going in a few weeks?"

"Judging from that gleam in your eye and the excitement in your voice, I'd have to guess that you're leaving the country," she said.

"No, but I am going to a different kind of place… I'm going to Vegas!"

"Vegas? You never struck me as a Vegas kind of guy."

"What does that mean?"

"Well, you know—someone who's into excess gambling, drinking, and partying. I'm not saying that you need that kind of release all the time, but I've heard stories about what kind of things happen in Vegas."

I needed a release all right, but it wasn't going to happen without her cooperation. "Well, I'm not that kind of guy in Vegas or anywhere else, but the only way that you'll know for sure is to come with me."

"Come with you? Ethan, I can't just up and go off to Vegas at a moment's notice."

"You've got three weeks to make arrangements, and you've told me before that you need to start using your vacation days before you max out and start losing them. And don't worry about the cost, because I've already got a room for us at the Mandalay Bay."

"I appreciate the invite, Ethan, but I've never been interested in Sin City. It's just not my kind of place."

Without Anna along for the ride, Vegas just wasn't my kind of place either, and it turned out to be the longest four-day conference of my life. Fortunately, soon after I returned, she gave me a legitimate opening. We were finishing up our dinner at a new Mediterranean restaurant on a Saturday evening, and while we looked over the dessert menu, Anna suggested that I come over to her place to "hang out and relax a little." Something about the way she said it was music to my ears, and upon hearing her suggestion, I immediately closed my menu and asked the waiter to hurry up with the check.

"Ethan, how do you know that I don't want any dessert?"

"You never order your own dessert! Every time I ask you about dessert at a restaurant, you always tell me that you'll just have SOY."

SOY stood for "Some of Yours," and as I thought about it in a purely sexual context, I was hoping that we would both be having SOY very soon.

Once we got inside her place, she turned on the TV, presumably out of habit, and said those words that I had been longing to hear for months.

"Ethan, I'm going to change into something a little more comfortable. So, be a good boy and wait here." On her way to the bedroom, she abruptly turned around, winked at me, and said, "I'll be right back."

I was foaming at the mouth by the time she continued her sexy stroll to the bedroom, but as long as my breath was minty fresh, I didn't care. I tried to guess what color her lingerie would be and eventually decided that it really wouldn't matter since I didn't plan for her to be wearing it too long.

"Okay, I'm back. I guess I'm getting real comfortable with you now that I'm letting you see me in something like this!"

My jaw dropped to the ground as I stared at her in a fluffy full-length robe tied around her flannel matching

Hello Kitty top and bottom pajamas, along with a pair of floppy-ear, pink bunny slippers on her feet.

"You... uh... do look comfortable, I'll give you that."

Sensing that her G-rated outfit was going to set the tone for what would, most likely, be a very tame night, I lowered my expectations just in time for Anna to put a big barrier-type blanket between us, and eventually fall asleep on my shoulder, trapping me on her couch in front of an agonizing, commercial-filled chick flick for the next two and a half hours.

I looked down at her and noticed that she literally and figuratively seemed perfectly content with where we were at the moment. But, I was not. I suppose that I had been waiting for the perfect opportunity or a clear sign to move forward, like Anna giving me a thumbs up and directing me into her bedroom the way an airplane marshal would safely guide a jet into its gate. Instead, I seemed to be stuck in an inexplicable holding pattern far away from my desired destination, and had no sense of when or even if the situation would change before I completely ran out of gas.

The Fire We Make

The following week, while I was having drinks and appetizers at a happy hour with Mia on Thursday, Anna sent me a text to see if I was interested in coming over to her place for a last-minute dinner the next day. Mia had once confided in me that, on those rare occasions when she was finally ready to allow a man into her bedroom for the first time, she typically invited him over for a romantic dinner in order to get things going. This was the first time Anna had offered to cook for me. So despite my recent string of disappointments, I translated her text to mean, "I'm finally ready to have sex with you if you're interested." Before I knew it, my fingers fired off a rapid response: *Can't wait!*

As excited as I was about the possibility of my first night together with Anna, I was also a little nervous because I had no idea whether or not I was any good in bed. My only real barometer was the indirect feedback I received in the form of repeat invitations from women I had dated, which, in the past, came often enough to satisfy my fragile ego. My initial sex education came from my days working in a video store with Fritz our senior year in high school. On slow days when our shifts overlapped, one of us would cover for the other while we went to a back room and sampled the store's seemingly endless collection of adult films. I studied the moves and techniques of the male porn stars like they were going to be part of an upcoming SAT exam, and paid special attention to the things that made women scream the loudest. Eventually, through a little trial and a lot of error, I realized that most of the action in adult films wasn't designed to please the women or even the men who were having sex on screen. It was designed to please the guys who came into our store on a regular basis and paid $5.99 per rental, which pleased the store owner even more.

Friday was, by far, the slowest work day I had ever experienced in my life. I was supposed to develop the first draft of a new product data sheet, but I spent most of the day checking my watch, the clock on my computer, the clock on my cell, and the giant clock on the wall directly above my boss' office. Throughout the day, they all seemed to be in a weird sort of backwards race to see which one could move the slowest. By four o'clock, I had completely run out of patience and simply ignored the curious looks of my coworkers as I packed up my stuff and swiftly headed out the door.

When I got home, I took a quick shower and opened my closet to pick out an outfit. I wanted to wear something that would be easy to remove when the time was right and I wondered what Anna would say if I showed up wearing a sweat suit. I finally settled on some black jeans and a polo shirt. Before heading over to Anna's place, I stopped by Wine-O, the aptly named neighborhood liquor store. As usual, scattered outside the entrance was a collection of old military vets who, at 6:30 P.M., had already started their all-night shifts. The guy closest to me was too drunk to even ask me for some change, but it wasn't hard to interpret his grunts and hand gestures, and I promised to hook him up when I came back out.

The owner of Wine-O had spent a great deal of money on the interior of his store, which was designed to resemble the fields of a winery. Strands of authentic-looking grapes were intricately woven into the store shelves that contained an overwhelming array of wine bottles from vintners throughout the world. I had already jotted down the name of a wine that Anna seemed to like the most when we were at Fine Vine, but I wasn't sure where I could find it. I went up and down one aisle after another in search of anyone who looked like an employee.

I finally found a name tag pinned to a bald man in his forties who could have opened a jewelry store right there in aisle three, given all the rings he had pierced through his body. At first, I tried to compete with the deafening music that was blasting through his ear buds by raising my voice, but when it was clear that he wasn't taking them off to deal with a nuisance like me or any other customers, I just pointed at the name of the wine I had written down, and then he pointed me in the direction where I could find it. After paying for the bottle, I stepped back outside in search of my soldier friend. I didn't have to go far because he was now passed out on his urban battlefield on the side of the store, and after slipping a couple of dollars into his coat pocket, I jumped into my car and sped toward Anna's place.

When I arrived, Anna opened the door and greeted me with a smile and a soft kiss that immediately made me forget about dinner. She was wearing a casual black dress that was spotted with white polka dots.

"Sorry about the late notice, but I'm really glad you could make it," she said.

I didn't think any advance notice was necessary, given what we both had in mind. So, I looked at Anna and said, "Nothing could keep me away from you tonight."

She froze and looked for a moment like she wasn't quite sure what to do with that statement, but she played it off nicely by turning her attention to my contribution to our dinner. "Wow! How did you remember the name of the wine I liked at Fine Vine?"

"I didn't, but I remembered to write it down while we were there."

"Awww. Thank you so much," she said before giving me another disorienting kiss. "I hope you're hungry, because I made quite a bit of food."

The scents from the kitchen were fantastic, and the food looked as good as it smelled. The biggest pot on the stove was full of spaghetti which was one of the few things that I could cook myself, but when I saw a pan filled with a wide variety of seafood, I realized that at least half of this meal was way beyond my skill set.

"Well, I am hungry, but judging from the amount of food you made, I'm guessing you invited everyone in your building."

Anna looked slightly embarrassed when she said, "I'm so used to cooking for myself that I guess I went a little overboard."

We started off with a glass of Italian wine from the bottle I had purchased earlier that, prior to Anna's brief history lesson on it, I had simply referred to as "red." Then she brought out some warm, delicious focaccia bread which I finally stopped eating when I realized that I had almost downed half a loaf by myself. After the bread, she brought out a caprese salad that was arranged so nicely, I was hesitant to even take out the first tomato. I had already spotted the main course on the stove, which turned out to be a tasty dish called Frutti di Mare. By the end of our meal, Anna had confirmed my suspicion that she was a fabulous cook. When she asked me if I had room for dessert, I was somehow able to resist blurting out the carnal response that I was undoubtedly giving her with my eyes.

I started thinking about how I could turn up the romance and begin our inevitable transition into Anna's bedroom. I suggested that we move over to the couch so that we could get more comfortable, and was pleased that Anna eagerly followed my lead. Before I sat down, I noticed something in a picture that I hadn't noticed before. It was a group shot of Anna and a bunch of her friends at a ski resort, but one of her friends appeared to be friendlier with her than the others, which had me wondering if this guy or any of her exes had ever tried to get her to the altar. If so, I wanted to know exactly where they went wrong because I didn't want to make the same mistake.

"Anna, I know we've talked a lot about our dating history and our exes, but I never asked you if anyone has ever proposed to you."

"That's it, Ethan. From now on, your nickname is 'Left Field.'"

"Why 'Left Field?'"

"Because at some point during the night, I can count on you to ask me a question from…"

"Left field, I get it. But it was a serious question."

"Actually, I've been proposed to twice."

"Twice! A lot of women go their whole lives without ever receiving one proposal. Can I ask what happened?"

Anna grabbed the bottle of wine and said, "I'll tell you, but I think we're both going to need a refill first." She poured each glass to the halfway point. Given the sizes of our enormous glasses, I felt it was further confirmation that I wouldn't be driving home that night.

Anna tilted her head back and took a small sip of wine before she looked directly at me. "The first guy who proposed to me was Marcus Powell, my high school sweetheart. I think I told you a little about him before. We were young and in love, but neither one of us was ready for marriage. We both knew it, but he really didn't want me going away to college and thought that if we got married, I wouldn't be going anywhere."

As she often did, Anna was kind of staring off into space as she told the story, almost as if she had transported herself back into time… her time with Marcus.

"Do you ever regret leaving him and not getting married?" I asked.

That seemed to snap her back into the present.

"No, I don't. He just wanted things to stay the same as they were in high school. He didn't do well with change and he did everything in his power to fight it. That wasn't the man for me then and it never will be. I need a partner who understands that our world is constantly evolving, and that different aspects of our lives are changing at different paces for different reasons. We both need to be able to adapt as a team, sometimes on the fly, in order to make it together through all of life's ups and downs."

I had always been fascinated by how the same types and amounts of alcohol could have vastly different impacts on people, even taking into consideration differences in body mass. I guessed that Anna and I had consumed about the same amount of wine, and while she was getting deeper into our conversation, I had a growing urge to get deep into her thighs. I wasn't sure just how I could shift us toward her bedroom at this point, especially given the non-sexual discussions that we were currently having, but quickly finishing up the stories about her previous pretenders would be a step in the right direction.

"So, what about the second guy?" I asked.

Before she responded, Anna looked at the ski resort picture that I had noticed earlier. "The other man who proposed to me was Steve Cannon."

"The porn star?"

"There's a famous porn star who goes by that name?"

"I don't know, but it just sounds like one. Doesn't it?"

"*I* wouldn't know. Anyway, Steve was a great guy, and some of my girlfriends to this day still think that he was the one who got away," she said.

"And what do you think?" I asked nervously as I glanced back at her ski resort picture with Steve.

"I think that he was much more driven by money and power than he'd ever admit, and the more time that he spent chasing them, the less time he spent with me. Don't get me wrong, I have nothing against ambitious and career-driven people. I've been told that I'm one myself. But if I stayed with him, I could see a lot of lonely nights, and me possibly trying to raise a family with a part-time father who would occasionally drop in or phone in from somewhere halfway around the world. I'm fine with some business travel, but when it starts having a negative impact on our family, then it becomes a problem that I can do without."

"Whatever happened to him?"

"Oh, we're still friends, and he's proposed to me a few more times since then, but I know that I'd never find happiness with him."

I was glad to hear that she had mentally closed the book on this guy, but I was still a little concerned that an ex, who was capable of proposing at any moment, still had an open line of communication.

"What about you?" she asked.

"What about me?"

"Your Match profile says that you've never been married, but have you ever proposed to anyone?"

I smiled at Anna and said, "No, I haven't proposed to anyone yet, but I think my time will come... someday soon."

We looked at each other in silence for a moment as if we were both trying to master the art of mind reading at exactly the same time. Despite my best effort, I had no clue about what Anna was thinking, but all this talk about marriage and being together, combined with the wine that had been steadily working its way in my system, got me thinking about making a move.

I got up from the table and walked slowly toward her stereo, which was connected to an iPod. "So, who's your favorite artist?" I asked.

I was sure that Anna was trying to figure out what I was up to, before she responded. "Hmmm? That's a tough question, but if I had to choose one, it would have to be Maxwell."

I expected Anna to ask me the same question, but before she could say anything, I found a playlist entitled Slow Jam Faves and noticed a duet by Alicia Keys and

Maxwell called "The Fire We Make." It seemed appropriate for the mood that I hoped to quickly create, so I hit "play." From the first note, I could tell that I liked the song. When I turned and saw Anna with her eyes closed and gently swaying to the music, I could tell that I was not alone. I just stood and admired her for a moment before I gently tapped her on the shoulder. She opened her eyes and saw me holding out my hand as an invitation to join me on our makeshift dance floor. When she got up from the couch, she came toward me and then wrapped her arms and body around mine as we quietly danced to what was about to become my favorite song of all time.

If this were a movie, my character would have started to slowly unzip Anna's dress, which then would have gently fallen to the floor before I picked her up off her feet and confidently carried her to the bedroom. Unfortunately, from my vantage point, the fastener at the back of her dress was so complex, it might as well have been a deadbolt. And even if I could have somehow picked the lock, given our size differences, Anna would have had a better chance of carrying me into the bedroom than me carrying her. Figuring that I should still do something, I started gently kissing her neck, which, besides her arms, was the only bare part of her body that I could easily reach. After a few soft kisses on each side, I felt some heavy breathing coming from her body and heard some light moans coming from her lips. I took this as a sign that I was on to something that required further exploration. I started to slowly slide my hands up from her waist in search of her breasts.

Suddenly, Anna grabbed both of my arms and almost apologetically said, "No! No, Ethan. We... we can't do this. We have to stop! We have to stop right now!"

"Why? What's wrong? Is it a... uh... 'Mother Nature' thing?"

Anna put her hand over her mouth presumably to either keep her from laughing in my face, laughing too loud, or both. "No. It's not a Mother Nature thing. It's a Christian thing."

"A what?"

I had a sinking feeling that I knew what she meant, and I could already feel the cobwebs rapidly forming in my underwear. When she asked me to "please sit down," I knew for certain that I wouldn't need the lone condom that had made an embarrassing imprint on my left front pants pocket.

"Ethan, here's the thing. For thirty-four years, I've tried to do things my way and it hasn't gotten me anywhere. So now I've decided to try it God's way, which means the next time that I make love to someone, it will be with my new husband."

Anna looked at me for a reaction, but I just stood there frozen like one of those movie characters who had been turned into stone by Medusa.

"Ethan? Ethan? Aren't you going to say something?" asked Anna. It was the same question I was asking myself.

When I finally remembered how to work my mouth and lips I said, "Soooo, when did you make this decision?"

"A few months before we started dating, and it's totally my fault for not being brave enough to come out and tell you very clearly when we first connected. I told you how important my faith is to me, and I told you that it was very important to me that you were also Christian. But, I know that not everyone who calls themselves a Christian actually practices Christianity in the same way."

I wanted to be offended by that comment, but the bulging condom in my pocket was a reminder that I couldn't.

"I also told you about my struggle to be patient and wait for my wedding day, but looking back, I realize that I was talking about sex in the context of starting a family and since it probably wasn't clear, I shouldn't have expected you to know that I had decided to totally abstain from sex until marriage... Look Ethan, I know that I had plenty of chances to say something early on, but deep down, I guess I was afraid of scaring you away before we even had a chance to get to know each other."

Anna's hands were slightly trembling, and for the very first time, I witnessed a vulnerable side of her that I hadn't known existed. She was acting like someone who was desperate to hold onto a relationship, which was making me feel guilty, because, from the moment I had stepped through the door, the only thing I had been thinking about holding onto was her naked body.

As she stepped toward me and grabbed both of my hands, I could see that Anna now had a few tears streaming down the corners of her eyes, making her mascara run.

"Ethan, I'm sorry if I misled you, but I honestly think this could be something really special and... and I'd hate to see it end without us giving it our best shot. I know that we're still learning more about each other, but you've already shown me that you have a lot of the qualities that I want in a husband and in a father for my children." I was tempted to say something about how we should at least practice the baby-making process if she really wanted children, but I knew that it wouldn't change her mind and would, instead, come off as a poorly-timed joke. So instead, I just listened. "Ethan, this wasn't an easy decision and I thought long and hard before I finally made it. I don't want you to think that I'm not attracted to you, because I really am, which makes this even more difficult. But honestly, my desire to abide by my commitment to God and his plan for my life is a lot stronger than my desire for anything or anyone else."

I couldn't help but think about my own relationship with God, and even though I had always called myself a Christian, the thought of abstinence rarely crossed my mind. Several times a year, the pastor of my church would touch on the subject and point to references of "sexual immorality" in the Bible to back up his stance on abstaining until marriage. But the term always seemed too vague, which left it open to very liberal and very conservative interpretations, and given all of the rumors throughout the years about the pastor's struggles with his own sexual immorality, he didn't have too much cred on the topic in my book. In theory, I suppose I could have done my own research or sought out other church elders to discuss it further, but I admittedly wasn't in a rush to find proof of something that I honestly didn't want proven.

Coming into the evening, I had expected that by now, Anna would be wearing nothing but her birthday suit and that I'd have a spectacular view of her kicking her heels to the heavens, but instead, our relationship had reached an unexpected inflection point. At least it was unexpected for me. Anna had to know that once she admitted that she'd been wearing a chastity belt the entire time we had been together, and had no plans to take it off before someone walked her down the aisle, it would surely impact our relationship one way or another. The part of me that had swelled in anticipation of a passionate session in her bed had now shriveled up and was completely disinterested.

I was feeling numb by the time I heard Anna say, "Ethan, please talk to me!"

"Well, I didn't see this coming, that's for sure. And I've never even considered the possibility of being in a sex-less relationship. So, I guess what I'm saying is that I'm going to need some time to let this sink in before I'm ready to talk about it."

"That's fair, but, Ethan, please let me know as soon as you're ready."

I picked up my jacket and turned around to see Anna looking into my eyes. Through her expression, she seemed to be pleading for a goodnight kiss, possibly as a sign that everything was going to be okay, but this sudden turn of events had prevented me from making that promise. I decided to at least give her a hug, and when I wrapped my arms around her, she said, "Ethan, I know we had a lot of wine tonight and despite what happened, I would feel much better if you spent the night here."

By this time, I was stone sober and in no mood for another frustrating night of floppy pajamas and boring chick flick movies on her couch. "Thanks Anna, but I'll be fine. And, I'll contact you to let you know that I've made it back safely."

Before I left, she gave me a soft kiss, and although I willingly pressed my lips against hers, it was clear that I wasn't fully committed.

As promised, I sent Anna a quick text to let her know that I made it safely, but I was too amped up from our evening to sleep. Up until now, I felt that our relationship had been progressing at a nice, steady pace without any major bumps in the road. Although I knew we'd eventually hit some, I didn't expect to run head-on into a brick wall less than six months into it. After Anna sprung her surprise, I used the phrase "sexless" on purpose to see if she would drop any hints about other things we could do in the bedroom. When she didn't bite, I realized that while Anna might eventually prove to be the "woman of my dreams," in my dreams was the only place that I was going to "have her" for quite a while.

Dump Her

I knew that I needed some serious help to work out this situation with Anna, and at least to start, I needed to get a male perspective from someone who would give a damn and would be willing to talk on a Friday night, leaving my brother as my only viable option. Knowing that Malcolm would still be up doing whatever he did on the web late at night, I sent him a brief email:

Hey Malcolm—Give me a call (and yes, it's about a woman).

Two minutes later, my phone rang. "Dump her," he said.

"Come on, Malcolm. You don't even know who I'm talking about or what's going on!"

"Call it a feeling."

"Can I at least give you some details first?" I asked.

"I'm just messing around. What's up?"

I spent the next few minutes walking Malcolm through my evening with Anna and ended with her big revelation and my reaction. "And that's where we left off," I said.

"So, let me get this straight… The two of you have been dating for over five months, and in that time, you've barely gotten to first base and haven't even tried to round the corner toward second, neither one of you has mentioned the L word yet, and the last time I checked, it sounded like you weren't even comfortable with your height difference."

"That's not an issue anymore," I protested.

"Sure it isn't."

"Seriously, Mal, I'm not embarrassed when I'm with her in public, I don't even notice any stares or petty jokes from strangers, and I don't even size other women up immediately when I meet them. I know it's a cliché', but for the first time in my life, I'm comfortable with the skin I'm in."

"Well it's about time," Malcolm responded, "but, if you're asking me whether you should stash your junk away for the unforeseeable future in hopes of one day using it with a woman who you may or may not want to marry, and who may or may not want to marry you, I'd say: hell no."

Malcolm's reasoning made it sound like a simple equation with only one possible answer. I supposed that it would be different if I was deeply in love with Anna, but I wasn't there yet, and tonight's revelation would require me to take a good, hard look at my feelings in order to figure out what to do next.

Before I got off the phone with my little big brother, I had a question that I had been dying to ask. "I'm just curious, how long did Anita make you wait?"

He chuckled and said, "She didn't. We went through three condoms on our first date."

I suddenly got hit with an unwanted image that made me sick to my stomach. I didn't know if Malcolm was joking or not, but I wished I hadn't asked. Even though she was now a victim of my male double standard, I didn't quite know how I'd ever be able to look at my freaky sister-in-law with a straight face again.

A Strange Way of Showing It

Around quarter to nine on Saturday evening, I realized that for the first time in a few months, I hadn't communicated with Anna at any point during the day. I was tempted to reach out to her, but any communication we had from here on out was bound to be pretty hollow until I made a final decision about whether I wanted to continue with our relationship.

Since I had already talked to Malcolm about my situation with Anna, I felt it was time to get a female perspective. Thankfully, Mia was available.

"M-I-A, whatcha say?"

"Hey, Ethan, what's going on?"

I didn't want to hit her with the news about Anna's celibacy immediately, even though it was the only thing that seemed to be "going on" in my world right now.

"Not much. What about you?" I said.

"Well, I just got off the phone with Paula, and we had a long talk about Devon."

I had almost forgotten about her friend's soap opera drama that I had somehow been dragged into several months ago. "Oh, yeah! I thought you were going to have that talk with her a few months ago."

"Trust me, I tried, but she wouldn't listen to me back then. She got into this weird state of denial and even accused me of being jealous, before she just stopped answering my calls altogether. But, when I recently heard from a mutual friend that they were getting more serious, I started thinking about Paula and wondered whether Devon had ever told her the truth. I had to find out, so, I started calling again and finally caught up with her today."

"Did she believe you this time?"

"Yeah, she did. As it turns out, he hadn't said a thing, but she admitted that she had been trying for a while to ignore some warning signs that were getting harder and harder to overlook."

"Is she going to confront him in person?"

"No. She never wants to see him again, and I suspect she's breaking up with him over the phone right now."

Just then, I remembered why I had called her in the first place.

"Well, on a different note, it's time for me to share some interesting news of my own."

"Interesting news? Is it about Anna? Ethan, what did you do?"

"It's nothing I did; it's something she said."

"She told you she's pregnant?"

"No, she *definitely* didn't tell me that!"

"She broke up with you?"

"No, she didn't break up with me, and why are all your guesses so extreme?"

"Ethan, just tell me what happened!"

"She told me that she's celibate and plans to stay that way until she gets married," I said.

"Really? That's interesting."

"Yeah, she fooled me, too."

"Well, what did you say?" Mia asked.

"I told her that I needed some time to think about it. That was last night and we haven't spoken since. We're supposed to get together for dinner at Yoshi's on Wednesday and a show afterward." Yoshi's was a well-known Japanese restaurant with an intimate jazz club that routinely showcased some of the world's top musical artists.

Mia laughed and said, "Oh, there's going to be a show, and depending upon what you say, it may be at your dinner table." When Mia stopped laughing she said, "Sorry about that, cuz, but seriously, what are you going to do?"

"I was hoping you had some advice."

"Well, how do you feel about her? Do you love her?" she asked.

"No, but I was clearly heading in that direction."

"What does that mean?"

"It means that I look forward to hearing her voice and seeing her face every day, to the point that I don't just want her in my life, I need her in my life. I have a hard time picturing a future without her, and quite frankly, I don't want to. I'm more comfortable opening up to her than anyone I've ever known, and you've seen first-hand how proud I've become of our relationship, and how she's helped me to get past my height issues. I was even going to introduce her to Mom soon, but now, I'm not so sure. I guess I'm concerned that we won't be able to develop the type of bond or level of closeness that I've only been able to develop with an intimate partner."

"But, Ethan, you just said that you're more comfortable opening up with Anna than with anyone else, which means that you two have been able to develop a level of intimacy with your clothes on that you haven't been able to match with any woman who's seen you naked."

"Yeah, but when there's no sex, it's just… different. I can't really explain it."

"Okay, forget about sex for a second. How do you think she feels about you?" Mia asked.

"She says that she wants a future with me, but I'm not convinced she's necessarily in love. She's said that she sees me as the type of man she would want as a husband and as a father for her children, but she's never come out and used the L word."

Although I couldn't see her face, I could sense the wheels turning in Mia's head, and I was hoping that she was about to come up with some words of wisdom that made perfect sense and would somehow lead to a happy ending.

"Well, between you and me, I think she's in love with you," Mia said.

"If she is, she sure has a strange way of showing it. Did she say something to you?"

"No, but believe it or not, a woman can fall in love with a man without sleeping with him first, although I guess it rarely works both ways."

"So, now you can see my problem. I can't make a life-long commitment to someone I'm not even in love with yet, and I'd have a hard time falling in love with someone until our relationship has progressed to an intimate level."

"Well, you may have your mind stuck in the gutter, but every day there are newlyweds on their honeymoon who are getting their rocks off for the first time with their new spouses. So, it can be done. Did you know that before your parents got married, your father may have gotten a total of thirty kisses from your mother in the twenty-one months they were dating? That's *all* he got while dating the same woman for almost two years, and that was the start of a forty-one-year marriage! If your father was alive today, don't you think he'd tell you that your mother was worth the wait?"

"Of course, but who told you about this?"

"Your mother."

"How come she never told me this story?"

"If you had a daughter, would you feel comfortable talking to her about your sex life?

I knew that I wouldn't, even though there wouldn't be much to tell. I had tried not to dwell on it, but Mia's comment reminded me that I hadn't had sex since I broke up with Stephanie over a year ago, and at the rate I was going, there was no doubt that I was destined to shatter the family record that my father had apparently set.

"Okay, it obviously worked out for my parents, but you know as well as I do that these are different times. So, what would you do if you were in my shoes?" As soon as I said it, I knew that I had responded with a weak argument, and I was hoping Mia wouldn't challenge me on it, and instead just focus on my question.

"If you are falling for her and really do see her as a potential soulmate, then I'd at least stick it out for a while and see which way your feelings go. If your relationship continues to grow and you fall in love, you should go ring shopping. If not, you should just go your separate ways."

Away in a Crate

On Monday, Fritz insisted that we meet up for lunch in the Embarcadero area of downtown San Francisco. Our buildings were nearby and we both liked sitting outside on warm, sunny days. I liked to take in all the fresh air and Fritz liked to take in all the "fresh meat," his endearing term for unfamiliar women with potential. We had both purchased our to-go lunches from one of the many local restaurants that thrived off the lunchtime business crowd, and after we found a place to sit in the spacious Embarcadero square, it was time to find out what Fritz had on his mind. I was almost certain it was Anna. Since he hadn't mentioned her in a while, I thought he had determined that I wasn't going to be sharing any details about all the great sex he assumed I'd been having with her, until he confronted me, face to face.

Right after he updated me on his prospects with this year's crop of summer interns at his company, Fritz went straight for the kill.

"So, give me an update on Big Babe. What's the latest with you two?" he asked.

"Her name is Anna."

"Okay. What's up with you and big Anna?"

"Well, we've been going out for a while."

"Oh, yeah? I've never banged a taller chick before. God, it must be insane when she's got her giant thighs wrapped around you."

"I'm sure it is," I said rather indifferently.

Fritz was about to bite into his sandwich, but almost dropped it down on his lap in disbelief when he realized what I had said.

"Knox, for the love of God—*please* tell me you've hit that!"

"You mean with a bat or something?"

227

"No, with something much, much, much smaller," he said while purposefully squinting at my crotch.

"I can't. She just told me that she's saving herself until marriage," I said.

Fritz laughed hard and said, "You mean, keeping herself *from* marriage!"

"Seriously, she doesn't want to have sex."

Fritz paused for a moment and looked at me as if I was too dumb to even spell I.Q. "You mean she doesn't want to have sex with *you*," he said. "Knox, I've only seen you with fine chicks, so I know that Big Babe must be top notch, and with her height, she's getting hit on every day by every baller and wanna-be-baller in the city. Do you really think that a woman like that, in her sexual prime, is gonna risk scaring off all those other dudes with that abstinence nonsense?"

I wanted to ask Fritz what ages defined a woman's sexual prime, because something told me that the span of his range would terrify most people, but before I could open my mouth, he answered his rhetorical question.

"Hell no! She's just gonna use it on suckas like you once she's squeezed out as many lobster entrees, plays, concerts, and movies as she can without giving up the goods."

After a brief pause, Fritz looked at me and said, "So, what are you gonna do?"

While it may have sounded like Fritz was asking me if I was going to consider staying celibate with Anna, I was pretty certain that he didn't even view that as a legitimate option.

"What can I do?" I asked.

"Well, you can either keep it moving, or keep her hanging around while you spend more of your time and money with women who know how to take care of their men and act like they want to keep them. I bet you babes like Sharon from the bowling alley and that other one you mentioned a while ago—what's her name?"

"Claudia."

"I bet Sharon and Claudia could take good care of you, and unlike Big Babe, they'd only make you wait long enough for you to slip on a condom."

Although I hadn't had many girlfriends, I never cheated on any of them, and certainly wasn't about to start at age thirty-seven. Fritz's chick-on-the-side suggestion wasn't even a remote possibility. Before I could respond, he went on.

"Now I hope you see why I like to smash, or at least try to smash, on the first date. If she's not with it, I can just move on. If she's not ready, I'll start my timer and give her a date or two to get ready."

It was times like these that I was glad that Fritz didn't have any sons, mentees, or any other impressionable young men around him on a regular basis.

"Knox, another thing to think about is what will actually go down in your bedroom if you do stick it out and eventually get married. I don't know about you, but I wouldn't want to be in a situation where I find out on my wedding night that I'm stuck with a wife who doesn't do 'certain things' or won't do certain positions."

For some reason, I wasn't worried about the possibility of Anna being a prude in the bedroom, but I had to admit that I'd been burned plenty of times before by making assumptions. I supposed we could have some kind of sex talk soon to make sure that we were compatible, but there would be no guarantee that either of our post-nuptial actions would sync with our pre-marital words.

I was still picturing this uncomfortable conversation with Anna while Fritz kept on. "Here's one more thing to think about, Knox. Let's just say that she isn't having sex with anyone behind your back. I don't believe it, but even if she isn't, if she makes you wait months or years for sex, she's already proven to you that she's perfectly capable of going quite a while without it.

So, if you do eventually get married, don't be surprised if you go through long droughts in the bedroom whenever and for whatever reason she chooses."

Sensing that I had enough to chew on for a while, Fritz briefly changed the subject and talked about the 49ers for the last few minutes, but before he left, Fritz had one more question for me. "Look, Knox, I know what a sentimental soft shit you can be sometimes with women, so it wouldn't surprise me one bit if you let this chick lock your dick away in a crate until you and a pastor try to pry it open at an altar somewhere down the line. But let me ask you something. If you would've known when she first reached out to you that she was gonna drop this bomb several months down the line, would you have still replied to her first email?"

It was a great question, and I thought about it for a moment before I responded.

"Maybe not, but I'm glad I did."

"Oh, please!"

"No, wait. Just hear me out for a second… I'll admit that I wasn't looking to get into a celibate relationship back when she first contacted me, and I'll admit that I'm not happy about the celibacy part now, but you don't know Anna like I do. She's the real deal, and even though I don't know what the future holds, I know we've got a shot at making it, which is something that we wouldn't have had if I never replied to her in the first place."

Thou Shalt Not Have Sex

I grew up across the street from a kid named Seymour Money. His name might have been well-suited for a life on Wall Street like his father had envisioned for his only son when he picked out his name, but didn't work too well for the life he chose behind a pulpit. His parishioners knew him as Pastor Seymour, but I remembered him as a foul-mouthed kid who spent almost as much time in the principal's office as the principal herself.

Three years ago, I bumped into Seymour at a grocery store, and he invited me to stop by his church after he handed me his business card. I hadn't felt the need to take him up on his offer before, but Anna's recent revelation had changed my thinking. Before entering any agreement to completely give up sex for God only knows how long, I needed someone to show me clear cut, biblical proof that it was what God wanted me to do. Thanks primarily to my spotty attendance, I had never developed a close relationship with any of the leaders in my church, so instead of going to any of them, I thought I'd be more comfortable having a conversation with Mr. Money.

I went through my collection of business cards and finally found Seymour's. On it was a simple image of a glowing cross, along with contact info for his church, A Better Way. I thought about giving him a call, but the chances of getting caught up in a few days of phone tag were high, and my patience was running low. I needed to make a final decision about Anna and our relationship quickly, so that we could either move forward, or move on.

According to the church's website, Seymour was scheduled to lead a "Monday Night of Prayer," from 7:00-9:00 P.M. At around quarter after nine, I slipped into one of the pews in the back of his church in time to see him ending a conversation at the front with one of the few remaining attendees who were still milling about. After he shook the person's hand, I got up and started heading toward the altar.

Seymour's eyes lit up when he saw me. "Hey, Ethan! It's been a long time!"

"What's up, Money Man! How's the flock?"

His hesitation told me that greeting Seymour with an old nickname that he had probably been trying to escape most of his life wasn't the best way to start off, and I made a mental note to myself not to use it again.

"God is good, Ethan, and He's continually blessing our church with new members each day. We'll be opening up a second location in the Bay Area soon, but I'm still waiting for you to bless us with an appearance during one of our services here. You know, His door is always open for you, Ethan."

"I know that, Seymour, and I just may take you up on your offer soon, but tonight, I came by to talk to you about something that God has apparently closed for me, at least until marriage."

"Oh!... I see."

"Do you have a few minutes to talk?"

"For you? Of course, Ethan."

I looked around and didn't see anyone else in the church.

"Well, without getting into too much detail, I've been dating a Christian woman for the past five months or so, and it's starting to get serious. But, I recently found out that she's celibate and plans to remain that way until marriage."

"I take it that her celibacy is a problem for you?"

"I'm kind of torn. I respect her commitment, but it's not my preference and, to be honest, I've never been convinced that it's something that's spelled out in the Bible as a requirement."

"Ethan, I can point to plenty of instances in the Word that make it clear that sex is a benefit reserved only for marriage, and that any sexual activity outside of marriage is considered immoral in God's eyes, but I have a feeling that you're looking for an eleventh commandment."

"Actually, I already had one, and I'm glad I broke it."

"I'm afraid I'm not following you," he said.

"Long story—don't worry about it."

"Well, as I was saying, it sounds like you're looking for a passage in the Bible that says, 'Thou shalt not have sex until you are married,' and I hate to disappoint you, Ethan, but as far as I know, that explicit phrase is simply not there."

"So, there's no proof?" I asked.

"Not the kind of proof that would convince you, I'm afraid."

"Then what should I do?"

"Forget about the Bible," he said.

"Excuse me… *Pastor* Seymour?"

"Yes, you heard me, Ethan. For a moment, I want you to forget about the Bible and just focus on this woman."

"Uh… okay."

"Are you convinced that she's committed to abstinence?"

"There's absolutely no doubt in my mind that her chastity belt is locked tighter than a—"

"Okay, Ethan, there's no need to elaborate. I believe you, but if you want to keep this thing going, you're going to need to abide by her rules which, in this instance, line up quite nicely with God's will for your life. Now, I don't know this woman, but from what you've told me, it sounds like she's walking down the right path and headed in the right direction. The only question now is, are you going to join her, or let her reach her destination without you, and possibly, with someone else?"

Stepping Into the Ring

With less than twenty-four hours to go before my big dinner with Anna, I spent several hours on Tuesday night preparing. I practiced what I was going to say as though I was prepping for a major presentation. We hadn't spoken since our dinner on Saturday, and I didn't know whether there would be the equivalent of a Q&A session after I revealed my decision, but it was a possibility that I wanted to be ready for. I was still feeling a little uneasy about her suggestion to meet up at Yoshi's instead of letting me pick her up, especially since it was so close to her place, but I decided not to dwell on it, and continued with my prep work.

I didn't see Anna when I entered the restaurant, and after taking a quick peek in the lounge area, I grabbed a seat on the couch in the entryway near the hostess stand. Just as I sat down, Anna walked in. She was wearing a fire engine red dress that exuded much more anger than sexiness, and at the bottom of her feet were heels that I imagined were high enough to get her a tryout at Sliders. Before I could stand up, she walked right in front of me and I literally had to tilt my head back as far as it would go in order to see her face, which was noticeably missing her usual warm smile. She mumbled something that sounded like my name and then told the hostess that we were ready for our table. I got up and started walking briskly behind the hostess and Anna who seemed to be trying to get as far away from me as possible.

As soon as she sat down, Anna attempted to order a cocktail from the hostess who said that she would send our waitress right over. She hadn't said a word to me yet and she was clearly upset. My first thought was that she probably felt that it shouldn't have taken me this long to make a decision, if I truly wanted us to have a future together.

"Okay, what's wrong?" I asked.

Anna looked directly at me for the first time since she had entered the restaurant. "What makes you think anything is wrong?"

"Just a wild guess."

"Well, why don't you tell me what's wrong, Ethan? And this time, let's hear the truth!"

I didn't know what "truth" she was talking about, but I had a feeling that it had nothing to do with me making a quicker decision about our future together. She seemed to be mad about something else I had done. I just wished I knew what it was.

"Well, I'm not sure what I did or said, but whatever it was, it's clearly got you upset, and for that, I apologize. Now, can we start enjoying our evening?"

"Nice try, Ethan, but you can't apologize or truly be sorry if you don't even know what you did." Anna had obviously brought her boxing gloves tonight and was ready to go a few rounds with me, even though I had no intention of even stepping into the ring.

"Okay—you're right. Please tell me why you're upset." I knew that I sounded a little patronizing, but I was hoping that she would overlook it.

"I got a call from Devon yesterday," she said.

After Mia told me about her breakthrough with Paula, I had hoped that I would never hear that man's name again. But, I should've known that it wouldn't work out as smoothly has I had hoped.

"What did he say?"

"He told me what you should have told me a long time ago."

"Which is?"

"He told me the truth! He told me the real reason that you didn't invite me to Mia's get-together a few months ago."

I raised an eyebrow and said, "And what would that be?"

"Ethan, don't play dumb with me. You didn't invite me because you already had some bitch there!"

"What are you talking about?"

"I'm talking about your little girlfriend, Kendra, who you were cuddled up with that night!"

I could feel far too many sets of eyeballs on our table, and it looked like our server was about to come over in hopes of lightening up the mood, until Anna dared her with a "make my day" look that would've petrified Clint Eastwood.

"Devon said I was there with Kendra, and you believed him?" I asked.

"Ethan, he even showed me pictures!"

Anna pulled out her cell phone, which contained several pictures that bastard must've taken while I wasn't looking. In most of them, I was next to Kendra and looking past her at Mia, but in one shot, Kendra was leaning into me as she had been most of the night. Thanks to her low-cut top, her breasts were on full display and were comfortably resting on the side of my elbow. I remembered how Paula had begged Devon to take pictures throughout the night, and at some point, he must have realized that these incriminating shots of me and Kendra might come in handy one day. I had to admit that the pictures made it look as though Kendra and I were used to having our bodies smashed together, with or without clothing, and coupled with Devon's lies, even the top notch attorneys on *Law & Order* would have a hard time clearing me of any wrong-doing. Fortunately, I had the truth on my side, and I was hoping that it would "set me free."

"And, Ethan, what makes it even worse is that Mia knew about it, and both of you had no problem going to dinner with me just two days later, knowing full well that you had this slut on the side." Anna's eyes started tearing up when she said, "Is that why you haven't attacked me yet?"

"What? Attacked you? What are you talking about?"

"One of my girlfriends, who knows I'm celibate, said there was no way that you weren't having sex with another woman all this time, but I defended you, Ethan. I said you were different and I told her that you would never do that to me!"

I wanted to put my arms around her and help to stop her tears before I started sharing some ugly truths about Devon that she obviously wasn't aware of and might not take too well. Unfortunately, we were at a table with two chairs, so, logistically, that wasn't going to work. Instead, I reached across the table and grabbed her hands.

"Anna, Anna... listen to me for a second."

She didn't pull her hands away, which was the first positive thing that had happened all night.

"I know that Kendra's got her breasts all over me in some of these pictures, but if you look at it again, you'll see that I'm not all over her."

She picked up the camera and started to slowly scroll through the misleading evidence that she had thrust into my face only moments ago.

"In fact, I'm not even paying attention to her. I had no idea she was even coming. She's a friend of Mia's who, apparently, was into me. I'm not dating her, I'm not sleeping with her or anyone else, and I don't care if I ever see her again. The reason Mia didn't say anything is because there was nothing to tell you. She knows that I don't have any feelings for Kendra, and more importantly, she knows about my feelings for you. And by the way, those feelings include an intense physical attraction that, as you'll remember, I was trying to act on at your place last Friday night. So, if it makes you feel any better, I have tried to 'attack' you."

As I reminded Anna about my feeble attempt to make a move on her, I had a slight smile on my face, but her expression didn't change, and if anything looked even more pained than before.

"But, Ethan, why would Devon lie?" she asked.

"Don't you believe me? Anna, don't you believe what I just told you?"

She looked at me and asked again, "Why would he lie? Ethan, tell me why would he lie?"

We had both posed questions, wanted answers, and were getting more and more frustrated with each other for not responding. I never wanted to be the one to tell anyone about Devon's dirt, especially not Anna. I just wanted her to believe me, but since all this back and forth was getting us nowhere, I finally decided to give in.

"Anna, Devon lied because he is a liar, and from what I can see, he's been living a lie for a while." I spent the next ten minutes going through the details of last Thursday night, including my final encounter with Devon in the bathroom and my conversation with Mia about him. "So my guess is that when Paula confronted him, he thought that I had ratted him out, and he decided to pay me back by trying to end our relationship."

Anna looked like someone had just punched her in the gut, and I wasn't sure if she would blame me or Devon for the blow. She looked to be in a daze of disbelief when she said, "I've known Devon for years, but I had absolutely no clue that he was even the slightest bit interested in women."

"I'm sure that Paula was surprised, too."

After finally exposing her friend for the jerk that he was, I felt a sense of relief and was ready to tell Anna about my big decision. But just when I thought I had safely navigated us through a treacherous start to our evening, I found out that Anna wasn't ready to move on.

"Ethan, why didn't you just tell me about Devon when all this went down?"

"I honestly felt that Paula should be the first to know, and I felt that he should be the one to tell her. Unfortunately for him, he waited too long."

"So, were you ever going to tell me?" Anna asked.

"I didn't think it was any of my business."

Based on the way things were going, I wasn't expecting to see the inside of Yoshi's jazz club tonight, and I had a strong suspicion that we wouldn't even make it past an appetizer.

"Ethan, I told you that withholding information is just as dishonest as lying about it. You knew that Devon was a friend of mine, so, didn't you think I'd want to know?"

"And didn't you think I'd want to know up-front that you were celibate?"

Anna slapped down on our table hard with her open hand, causing all of the silverware and glasses on it to jump before she said, "Dammit, Ethan, we talked about this and I already apologized!"

Even before she reacted, I knew I had made a big mistake. She had already poured her heart out last Friday in an effort to explain why she didn't tell me about her celibacy immediately, which made me feel guilty about bringing it up again. We had spent far too much time talking about Devon and I didn't want to talk about him ever again. It was time to move on and talk about my decision, a discussion that I felt much better prepared for than the one we had been stuck in from the moment we sat down.

"You're right. I shouldn't have brought that up again, but unless you tell me that you actually planned to run into Devon and his boys at Fine Vine, I assume that you two aren't as tight as you used to be. And if that's the case, I'm guessing that what he does in his personal life, and who he does it with, doesn't have a big impact on your world."

"But, Ethan, that's not the point! I'll admit that we haven't been as close since our days at Cal, but the fact that you chose not to tell me about him is part of a pattern of dishonesty that's making me rethink our whole relationship."

"Pattern? What kind of pattern are you talking about?"

While she wasn't crying yet, Anna's tearing eyes were an ominous sign, like dark clouds forming overhead before a thunderstorm. "Ethan, you've developed a pattern of keeping things from me, which has me concerned, and it's been going on for a while."

"Keeping things from you? Like what?"

"Well for starters, you didn't tell me about the happy hour get-together."

I jumped in quickly. "I already explained why and I apologized for that!" I said.

"Yes, I know, but the fact remains that you didn't give me a chance to decide whether or not I wanted to go. Then, you also decided that I didn't need to know about Devon."

"And I just explained my reasoning for that, too," I said. "What else?"

"I'm not just talking about Devon's secret. I'm also talking about the fact that he was with you guys in the first place."

"But, Anna, how in the world could I have told you that I saw him there without revealing that he was there with a woman? I would have been withholding information and, by your definition, lying."

"So you choose a different way to lie about it? And it also sounds like you have a problem with my definition of lying? Do you?"

"No, but I'm having a problem with you accusing me of being a pathological liar and not having much evidence to back up that claim."

"All right. What about your family reunion? Is there a reason why you chose not to tell me about that?"

My jaw dropped helplessly as I tried to figure out how the heck she had heard about an event that I was trying my best to forget about.

"Mia asked me if I was going when we got together for drinks last week."

The growth of Anna's friendship with Mia over the past few months seemed to parallel the growth in my relationship with Anna, and up until now, I thought it was a good sign.

"What did you tell her?" I asked.

"I told her that I hadn't made a decision… even though it was clear that, once again, you had already made one for me."

"Anna, I hadn't even decided if I was going to the reunion and I still don't know. So, how could you expect me to invite you to something that I might not attend myself?"

"I don't know? Maybe we could have done something radical like make a joint decision, but I'm sure that possibility didn't even cross your mind, did it?"

I didn't respond, but her comment got me thinking. In my mind, joint decisions were made by two people who considered themselves to be an official couple, and while I didn't recall either one of us ever labeling our relationship, I took this to be clear evidence of how Anna felt, or had felt before Devon called her.

"And what about how we met?" she asked.

"How can you be mad about that? You're the one who contacted me, remember?"

"Of course I remember, but I only contacted you *after* you checked out my profile. I was hoping that was a sign that you might be interested in me, but little did I know you were only interested in my height preferences."

I was momentarily stunned into silence. I immediately threw my cousin into my mental doghouse and locked the door.

"And don't blame Mia. All this came out after we had a few too many drinks last week, but you're the one who decided to conduct your stupid experiment and start playing with people's lives."

"So, are you saying that you wish I had never responded to your initial email?"

"I don't know, Ethan, because I'm not sure if you're the man for me after all. The man for me would be proud to have me at his side whenever possible, but you want to pick and choose those moments yourself. The man for me is honest and open, but as I've pointed out, you want to decide what I should and should not know, which I consider to be dishonest. And, the man for me would willingly join me in my commitment to remain celibate until our wedding day."

It wasn't going to be as planned, but I finally had a chance to tell her that I was ready to make that commitment.

"Anna, I—"

She cut me off and said, "And it wouldn't take him four or five days to make that decision."

I felt like I was back on my first date at Manger with an upset Claudia preparing to exit my life for good, even before we could order our appetizers.

"Ethan, I don't know if you had come here prepared to tell me that you had finally made a decision about our relationship, but it's a moot point now, because I don't think you've asked yourself the right question. Now that I've clearly spelled out what kind of man I need in my life, you need to honestly ask yourself if you really are that man, because as I've told you, I'm having some serious doubts."

The tears that Anna had tried to hold back earlier had taken full control of her eyes and were now flowing freely down her cheeks, but after taking a tissue out of her purse to wipe them away, she got up from the table.

"And one last thing, Ethan: There's no need to ever call me again until you can answer 'yes' to that question."

I supposed Anna knew that this night could turn ugly, which was why she insisted on meeting up at Yoshi's instead of meeting up first at her place. Even though it would have only been a few blocks, getting into a car together, even to just drop her off, would've been the longest ride of my life after what had just happened. Instead, I was alone again at a restaurant after yet another upset woman had walked out on me. I was getting too good at losing them and wondered if I'd ever figure out how to keep one.

On my way out, I spotted an elderly couple at the bar holding hands. Looking at their wedding rings, I imagined that they had spent many years together. I was happy for them, but I was also jealous. They were where I wanted to be, and I had no idea how to get there. I walked over to where they were seated, placed the tickets for the 7:30 show on their table, and told them to enjoy it.

Scarred Him for Life

When I got home, I didn't feel like doing anything. I didn't want to talk to anyone, I didn't want to go anywhere, and I didn't want to check out anything on TV or online. The only thing I wanted to do was to turn back the clock and undo the mistakes I had made with Anna. Since that wasn't going to happen, I settled in for a long, boring night alone. After a few hours of just staring into space, I started to doze off on my couch when I heard a few beeps from my phone indicating that someone had sent me a text.

How'd it go with Big Babe?

I forgot that I had told Fritz about my big night with Anna, but I wasn't in the mood for a long back and forth text session, so I just gave him a call.

"Whadup, Knox. I guess you got my text?"

"Yeah, I did, but what's up with your voice? You sound half-asleep."

"It's all the drugs they pumped into me."

"Who's *they* and what kind of drugs are you talking about? Fritz, are you in the hospital?"

Fritz coughed and laughed at the same time. "Sounds like Detective Anderson has solved another tough case."

"What happened?"

"I'll tell you everything, but first I need you to pick me up if your date's over. They said I can go, but they won't let me leave on my own. Someone has to take me home."

"Yeah, it's over."

After he gave me the name of the hospital, I told Fritz I'd be there as soon as I could. Thirty-five minutes later, I saw him sprawled out in the emergency waiting room. His right arm was in a sling, his ribs were bandaged, and he had a serious black eye, which, combined, made it look like he had been in a fight that didn't go his way.

When he looked up and saw me, the first words out of Fritz's mouth were, "'Bout time!"

"Sorry, bad traffic. You ready?"

Fritz's look said it all.

"Never mind, dumb question," I said.

At this time of night, the drive to Fritz's place in San Leandro took about twenty minutes, which was more than enough time to find out what happened.

As soon as we got in the car, I asked, "How do you feel?"

"I feel like I look, Knox. Now are you going to ask at least one intelligent question tonight? Because if you're not, you can just take me back to the hospital and I'll get someone else to drive me home."

I doubted Fritz could get anyone to drive him who wasn't driving a yellow car with a running meter, but I wasn't nearly done asking questions.

"Okay, what happened to you?"

"I had a date and I got into a little scuffle."

"Who was your date with, Floyd Mayweather?"

"I'm glad you're not funny, Knox, because laughing would make my ribs hurt more than they do already."

"Seriously, did a woman do this to you?" I asked.

"No, but her boyfriend did."

"Fritz, why in the hell would you go out with someone when you knew she had a boyfriend? I thought that was a big 'no-no' for you."

"Knox, I'm not stupid. I don't mess with women in relationships."

"Well, did she just lie about hers?"

"Technically, no. She just never brought him up until she heard him opening the door to her apartment."

Fritz was still talking, but his voice was now in the background of my mind, and all I could think about was what Anna had said about my dishonesty. Although the circumstances between my situation with Anna and Fritz's recent encounter were vastly different, we were both now suffering as a result of a deception. In his current state, Fritz also served as poster child for abstinence, and as I glanced at his injuries and thought about my conversation with Seymour, I wondered if Someone above was trying to send me a message.

When we got to his place, Fritz suggested that I come up for a beer, and after he popped the top off my bottle, he asked me the question that he had asked me a few hours ago.

"Forget about me. I want to know how things went with Big Babe."

"Not so well."

"Really? What happened?"

"She got upset and walked out."

"Well, screw her. Don't worry, Knox. Once I heal up, I got a few new spots that we can start hitting up."

The fact that my supposed best friend responded to the news of my troubles with Anna with a simple "screw her" as he tried to quickly move me on to greener pastures completely pissed me off, and without thinking, I grabbed Fritz tightly by his shoulders and started shaking him violently.

"Dammit Fritz, what's wrong with you?"

"Owww!"

His shriek reminded me of his current condition, and after I released my grip, Fritz stared at me as if I had completely lost my mind.

"What's wrong with *me*? I'm not the one attacking handicapped people fresh out the fuckin' hospital! What the hell's wrong with you, Knox?"

"I'm just tired of you disrespecting Anna. 'Screw her,' is not the kind of advice I need from someone who claims to be my best friend, and the last thing in the world I want to do is go hunting with you at any new spots. I've already found what I'm looking for." This wasn't the first time Fritz had alarmed me with his vengeful attitude toward women and I decided that it was finally time to get to the bottom of it. "Fritz, what do you have against women?"

"Now, what makes you think I have anything against women? I love women and in fact, I've spent most of my life trying to love as many of them as possible."

"Come on, Fritz. You didn't always treat women like they should all be speeding down a conveyor belt headed straight to your bedroom. I remember you were crazy about that girl you were dating after college, and I'm guessing that something happened with her because you've been on the prowl ever since. Now, are you gonna tell me what went down?"

"Knox, you've known me for well over thirty years, but in some areas, you still don't know shit about me. I know it may seem to you that all I care about is bonin' as many babes as I can, and I must admit that I do enjoy the challenge, but I bet you can't find one woman who would complain about the way that I've treated her."

I scoffed at his answer and said, "Since you're done with most of them in less than twenty-four hours, you're probably right."

"Seriously, Knox, I'm very upfront and honest with women. They know what I'm about and what I'm looking for, and as I told you, if they're not with my program, I just move on to the next one—no questions asked."

I wanted to feel sorry for Fritz, but it sounded like he was more than happy with his lifestyle. "Sounds like an empty and lonely life to me, but I guess it works for you," I said.

"Lonely? I've boned five different women in the past two weeks. What have you been up to, Desert Dick?"

Trying to keep the focus on him, I said, "Fritz, you can have all the sex you want with all the women you want and still be lonely as hell."

"Oh, yeah? How would you know, Knox?"

I didn't, but I wasn't going to let him off without telling me what got him started on his 24/7 panty patrol. "All I know is that you seemed a lot happier when you were all up in love with that girl you were dating for a few years after college, and to this day, you never told me what happened with her."

After a long pause, he finally responded, "Her name was Tracy."

"That's right, I knew it started with a 'T'," I said.

"We met in college but we didn't seriously start dating until a couple of years later. I don't know if you remember, Knox, but I started working with IBM as a sales rep while I was still an undergrad."

"Yeah, I remember going out to celebrate with you the first day you got your company car."

"Yeah, that was a good night and those were some good times. By the time Tracy and I got serious, I was making good money, I had my own apartment, and I was even saving up for my first house. Your cousin, Mia, was actually one of Tracy's friends back then, and you may not know this, but Mia is the one who introduced me to Tracy."

I wasn't sure why Mia never told me that she knew Fritz back then, but I was definitely going to ask her about it.

"Anyway, here I was, head over heels in love with this woman and making plans for us to spend the rest of our lives together when she calls me up one day and tells me she's pregnant."

"What did you do?"

"I'll admit that I was stunned at first, but once it sunk in, I was happy as hell, and I made damn sure that Tracy knew it, too. And keep in mind that I was head over heels in love with her, so I figured that our baby was just another sign that we were supposed to be together forever."

The fact that Fritz had been spending more time with Tracy back then meant that we spent less time together, and it was one of the reasons why we lost touch for a while.

"Well, what happened? Because when you and I reconnected a couple years later, Tracy was long gone and had been replaced by Stacy, Trina, Cheryl, Tamika, Connie…"

"You wanna know what happened? I'll tell you what happened! The day after she told me that she was pregnant, I went out and bought an engagement ring because no kid of mine was coming into this world without two legally married parents. Later that same day, I started sharing the news and showing off the ring to my family and a few close friends."

I guess I didn't make the "close friend" cut back then, and based on the way we had been steadily growing apart, I doubted that we'd ever be close again.

"As happy as I was, the fact that I wasn't able to reach Tracy the next day seemed a little odd, and by the end of the week, when I still couldn't reach her, I was in total panic mode. I called her apartment and her job at least three times a day that week. The people at her office kept saying that she was out sick and didn't know when she would return, and all of my calls to her apartment just went to voicemail. I even went to her place late at night a couple of times, but her evil roommate kept saying that she wasn't there and she wouldn't let me in. When Tracy's parents stopped answering my calls, I knew something was up, so I hired a PI who found her one week later. She had been staying with her aunt in LA, and while she was there, she decided to have an abortion."

"An abortion! She had an abortion without even talking to you about it first?" I said.

"She sure as hell did, and as soon as I found out, I drove straight down to her aunt's place. When I showed up, Tracy was still there recuperating, and before I could go off on her, she told me, with almost no emotion in her face, that the baby wasn't mine."

"What?"

"You heard me. After treating this woman like a queen and doing everything that I could for her, I come to find out that she was her giving her body to someone else behind my back."

A wave of questions flooded my mind, but I wasn't quite sure what to ask next. "Wait! If she was planning to have an abortion, why did she tell you that she was pregnant in the first place?"

"I asked her that same question. She said that when she first found out she was pregnant, she wanted to keep the baby and thought that they'd be much better off with the life I was building than whatever she had going with that other muthafucker. I think it was her aunt who made her realize that the truth about the baby's father was eventually going to come out and I think she convinced Tracy to go ahead with the abortion."

Even though Fritz had brought it up before, I couldn't really picture Anna having sex with someone else while we were dating, and I tried my best to completely erase the thought from my mind.

"And don't ask me how long she was bonin' that dude behind my back, Knox, because I never asked and didn't want to know. I just knew that it was never, ever, ever, ever going to happen to me again." Fritz paused for a second and said, "And by the way, to this day, a lot of the people who knew us at the time, including Mia, still think that I forced Tracy to have an abortion after she told me that she was pregnant."

"But, why didn't you just tell everyone the truth?"

"At first, I was completely pissed when I heard the rumor, but then I decided that I'd much rather have people think I was a giant asshole than a giant sucker. So I never told anyone the truth and I don't think Tracy ever did either."

For the first time in a long time, I was beginning to understand Fritz. His lifestyle, his treatment of women, and his jacked up relationship advice were all connected to this traumatic episode with a woman who broke his heart and apparently scarred him for life. As a friend, I felt for him, but marriage and a family obviously weren't on Fritz's radar any longer, and it was now painfully clear that we had to go our separate ways before I allowed him to take me back to a place that I didn't want to be: alone.

400 Miles Longer

Before I left, Fritz made me promise not to tell anyone about what went down with Tracy, especially not Mia, and while I wanted her to know that he wasn't the type of guy to force his pregnant girlfriend to have an abortion, I focused our discussion on my situation with Anna when Mia and I met up for coffee the next morning.

"Ethan, this is all my fault!"

"No, it's not. I'm the one who didn't invite her to the happy hour. I'm the one who didn't tell her about Devon. I'm the one who didn't tell her about our family reunion, and I'm the one who didn't tell her about my experiment. These are decisions that I made, and now I've got to deal with the consequences."

"So, you let her leave the restaurant, just like that?" Mia asked.

"No, I did the primitive caveman thing and chased her down before I hit her over the head with my club and dragged her by her hair back to the restaurant."

I always knew that Mia wasn't a big fan of my sarcasm, and if I had any doubts, the look on her face confirmed it. "Well, someone should've hit you over the head for just letting her go without saying anything," she said.

"What was I supposed to say?"

"How about saying something that would give her a reason to stay, and not just in the restaurant, but a reason to stay in your relationship?"

"She made it perfectly clear that she felt I had been dishonest, and at that point, I doubted that she would have believed anything that came out of my mouth."

Mia looked like she wanted to remove the coffee cup lid so she could throw the coffee in my face, just to wake me up.

"So, that's it? You're just gonna give up and move on?"

"Mia, didn't you hear what I said? She doesn't trust me anymore."

"Don't you want to regain her trust?"

"Of course I do!"

"Well, it can be done, but it's going to take time. Unfortunately, you might not have that much time to work with."

"What do you mean?"

"She didn't tell you?"

"Tell me what?"

"Ethan, she got promoted to VP a few days ago and they want her to move down to LA ASAP."

"What?"

"She didn't want me to tell you because she wanted to talk it over with you during dinner last night."

"She didn't say anything to me about it!"

Mia said, "I guess she changed her mind about telling you after Devon sent her those pictures."

I was feeling sick to my stomach, but it had nothing to do with the Grande Caramel Macchiato that I had been sipping on. The possibility of Anna moving to Los Angeles hit me like a ton of bricks, but if our road to happiness was now 400 miles longer, then I would need to make up the distance somehow, before it was too late.

Something Personal

By the time I got back to the office, I had devised a plan. First I called Malcolm, and when I got back into the office, I stopped by Alex's desk and spoke to him briefly before opening my laptop and checking my boss' calendar. I could see that his schedule was open for the next ninety minutes, so, I quickly walked down the hall and knocked on his door. When Charles looked up from his computer and saw me staring at him through his glass door, he waved me inside.

"Hey, Ethan! Come on in."

"Thanks, Charles. Say, do you have a quick second?"

"Sure! What's up?"

"I'm just going to get right to the point."

In an instant, the pleasant smile that was on Charles' face when I stepped into his office vanished from his face and was replaced by a concerned look of a man who was bracing himself for some bad news.

"Ethan, please don't tell me you're leaving. Aren't you happy here? Did you come to talk about a raise? Did you get an offer from II, too?"

"II" stood for Inventory Innovations which was our closest competitor and home to a growing number of our company alumni.

"Charles, I could always use a raise, but I'm not planning on leaving the company anytime soon."

"Thank God!" he said.

"However, I do want to talk to you about a possible transfer down to the LA office."

"The LA office? You gotta be kidding? Why on Earth would you want to move down there?"

Charles was a Bay Area native who rarely had a kind word to say about other parts of the world outside of the Bay Area, especially LA.

"Something personal has come up, and there's a chance that I may need to move down there. If so, I want to know that I can stay with the company."

"Ethan, I don't know about this."

"Listen, Charles, LA is in the same time zone, so, this wouldn't cause any major problems with coordinating schedules, and as you know, most of my client presentations are now done over the web, which means I can do them from anywhere. It's also a short plane ride, so if I need to, I could make it back here quickly for any HQ activities."

"What about Alex? You know how heavily he relies on you, especially for his onsite presentations, and a lot of his clients are up here. I don't have the budget to keep flying you back and forth from LA all the time."

"I've already talked to Alex about it and most of his growth is in his Southern Cal accounts. Starting next quarter, he expects to do about seventy-five percent of his business down there and he thinks that percentage will grow each year based on his sales pipeline. So, in the long run, you'd actually be saving on airfare if I was based down there."

Charles came up with a few more reasons why it might not work, but I easily shot them down.

"Well, Ethan, it sounds like you've thought this through." He paused for a few moments before continuing, "But from a selfish standpoint, I'd miss having you in the office." Charles and I didn't really have a close relationship, so I felt this was his way of saying that he'd miss having my neck nearby to choke when needed.

As he stood up and shook my hand, Charles said, "You have my support. Just keep me posted. If you want to go ahead with the move, I think I can get the final approval you need with the big boys upstairs."

"I will, and thanks, Charles."

After getting the thumbs up from Charles, I spent most of the day in meetings with various teams about our presence in the vendor exhibitor area of an upcoming conference. I was expected to spend most of my time at the conference in our booth to answer basic questions that our sales and marketing people were bound to screw up. But, my mind was only focused on one interaction that had to go perfectly: my call that night with Anna.

His Hands

"Anna, it's Ethan. I really need to talk to you. Please call me back as soon as you can."

After leaving several unreturned voicemails, I sent a few text messages. When it became apparent that they weren't going to be answered either, I decided to drive over to Anna's place. Although I was ready to talk, she clearly wasn't ready to listen, and, most likely, wouldn't be in a listening mood when I showed up at her doorstep late on a Thursday night. But that wasn't going to stop me from saying what I should have said a long time ago.

I rang the buzzer for her condo several times before I walked around to her balcony and noticed that the lights were off, which was strange, because she'd normally be watching TV around this time.

I heard the sound of the building's garage door opening, but when I looked over, I saw it was just one of her neighbors pulling into a spot that was right next to Anna's empty spot. I had no idea where she could be, but after placing another call that went straight to voicemail, it was clear that we wouldn't be making any progress that night. I finally drove back home.

At work the next morning, I was putting the finishing touches on a new company white paper when I was interrupted by the buzzing of my cell phone. I touched "answer" when I saw who it was.

"Hey, Mia. What's up?"

"Have you been able to contact Anna?"

"No. She hasn't returned any of my calls or texts."

"Ethan, she's decided to move down to LA this weekend!"

"This weekend? That's crazy. How do you know?"

"She just sent me a text a few minutes ago and told me that she'd contact me in a few days once she's settled down there. Ethan, what are you gonna do?"

The wheels were spinning frantically in my head as I weighed my options.

"Help her move."

"What? Ethan, what are you talking about?"

Anna had to know that Mia would contact me immediately, which meant there was a good chance that she was expecting me to try and stop her or do something before she left. If so, I wasn't going to let her down.

"I'll explain everything later, Mia, but right now, I've gotta go."

I rescheduled the two morning meetings I had on my calendar before I hopped in my car and headed to MeMove, a nearby moving supply store. When I got there, I saw seven people in line, and only one open register. My future with Anna was slipping away with every second and since I was desperate, it was time for me to make a desperate move. I ran up to the front of the line as I pulled out my wallet. The guy who was waiting to be served next looked at me as if I had lost my mind, and for the moment, he was pretty much dead on.

I didn't want the other customers in line to hear me, so I lowered my voice and said, "Hey, I know this sounds weird, but I'm really in a hurry and if you'll let me get ahead of you, I'll give you this $127 I have in my wallet." I may have sounded crazy, but I fanned the bills out so that he could see that there was nothing strange about the money that I was offering.

Without saying a word, he started reaching for the money, but stopped when he heard a voice behind the counter.

"Hey, you!" said an employee who had seemingly popped up out of nowhere.

"Me?" I asked as I pointed to myself.

"Yes, you! Get over here!." I doubted the company had a stated policy prohibiting what I was trying to do, and even if they did, I wasn't expecting anyone to enforce it. When I met the employee at the side of the store, he whispered, "I can help you out, but I can't do it in front of anyone. What do you need?"

"I need some boxes, and I wanted to also ask you about something else, but I really need to take care of this quickly."

"All right. Just come around to the side door and I'll meet you there."

"Thanks, I really appreciate it!"

The fact that I was about to get an unexpected favor from a nice guy helped to strengthen my resolve, but as soon as I turned around, I heard him whisper one last thing: "And don't forget to bring my money."

After I finished up my transaction, I scooped up the boxes and sped off in the direction of Anna's condo. If she was moving this weekend, I thought there was a good chance that she had taken the day off to prepare.

When I arrived at her building, I looked up at her condo and noticed some movement through her balcony window.

I dialed her unit on the intercom system. "Anna, it's me. I need to talk to you. Will you please let me in?"

I dialed two more times before Anna finally answered. "Ethan, I'm kind of busy right now."

"Yeah, I know. Mia told me about the move. But can you at least give me five minutes?"

Anna didn't respond, but a few seconds later, I heard the buzzer that unlocked the door to her building.

When I made it to her condo, she unlocked the door and, without looking directly at me, told me to come in. She was wearing a Cal baseball cap, a light blue T-shirt, black sweat pants, and flip flops. Judging from her clothes, she was ready to move out of her apartment, and judging from the look on her face, she was ready to move out of my life, for good.

"Ethan, why are you here?"

"Give me one second." I turned back into the hallway and grabbed the boxes that I had laid against the wall. "I'm here to help you move!"

"What?"

"And if we need them, I've got more boxes in the truck."

"Truck, what truck?"

"The truck outside."

Anna went over to her window and placed her hand over her mouth when she spotted the fourteen-foot MeMove truck that I had just rented. When she turned back toward me, there was a different expression. She had clearly been irritated at me when I stepped in the door, and now she looked ready to throw me back down the stairs I had just climbed.

"Anna, if you want to move to LA, that's fine and I'll help you in whatever way I can, but just know that I'm going to follow you down there."

I unfolded one of the boxes before I grabbed another one.

"Follow me? Ethan, don't be ridiculous."

"I'm dead serious."

"What about your job?"

"I already talked to my boss, and he's approved my transfer down to the LA office."

"What about your mom and your family?"

"LA isn't that far from the Bay Area, and I can still see them as often as I do now. Best of all, Malcolm and I finally convinced Mom to move in with him next year, so I don't have to worry about her trying to live on her own."

"Ethan... what about us? I meant what I said on Wednesday. I'm not so sure that you're the right man for me, and I don't think that following me down to LA or anywhere else is going to change how I feel."

It took her a while, but I was glad Anna finally voiced her real concern so that I could say what I had come to say.

"And I don't think that your move to LA or anywhere else is going to change the way that I feel about you. Anna, I know you have some serious doubts, but there's absolutely no doubt in my mind that we are right for each other." She didn't look convinced, and I didn't know if I was capable of convincing her, but I knew that this was my last shot and I wasn't planning to hold anything back.

"Anna, do you remember back when we shared our thoughts about kids and a family at Fine Vine?"

She nodded her head.

"I don't remember exactly how you put it, but you basically said that if I really wanted something or someone, I should act quickly before my window of opportunity closes."

I could tell from her silence that Anna remembered the words verbatim.

"Well, I've followed your advice," I said.

I pulled out a piece of paper that I had hidden in between two of the boxes and handed her a printout of an email receipt confirming the two round trip tickets I had purchased for us to fly from LAX to Hattiesburg, Mississippi, for my family reunion. She looked up at me with her mouth open in disbelief.

"Anna, I want you to be a part of my life, and I'm willing to do everything in my power in order to make it happen, not just today, not just tomorrow, but for the rest of my life. And I want you, and my family, and everyone else to know it."

I was hoping to see an expression of love in her eyes, but it wasn't there. "Ethan, you just don't get it! You're still making decisions for me and not giving me choices. First you come in here and tell me that you've decided to move to LA, and that you want me to move today with you, whether I'm ready or not and regardless of what I think, instead of using the professional movers my company has already hired and paid for. Then you decided that I should come with you to your family reunion, and you go out and buy tickets without officially inviting me or asking me if I even want to go."

"But, I thought you said you wanted to go?"

"No, Ethan! I wanted you to tell me about it and then I wanted us to make a joint decision. Don't you get it? I'm looking for someone to be an equal partner in a relationship and there's nothing equal about the way you've been treating me. I know that oftentimes you mean well, but you can't go on being the sole decision maker for both of us."

The more I listened, the more it seemed like I was fighting a losing battle. Anna was right. In my short-sighted attempts to navigate our relationship alone, I had refused to let her even touch the wheel, and had set a disastrous course for us. In the past, I would've just given in and walked away in defeat, most likely blaming the conflict on our height disparity and her hidden disinterest in dating a shorter man. But this time was different. This time, I was in the fight of my life to save my relationship with my soulmate, so, instead of just giving in, I decided to keep fighting.

"Anna, I get it. I didn't see it before, but you're right. You deserve an equal partner and up until now, I haven't been that person. At first, my issue with our height difference literally prevented me from seeing us as equals, and since it was beyond my control, I started focusing on the other aspects of our relationship that I could control. At times, I tried to control where we went, what we did, who saw us, who you were introduced to, what I shared with you, what I kept from you, when we would have sex, and as you've just pointed out, whether or not we'd be together in LA. I know I'm missing some things, but the point is that there was no equality in our relationship, only my desire to control every aspect of it."

In the midst of pouring out my heart, I felt I was in danger of even controlling our conversation, but when I paused to give her a chance to respond, Anna seemed content to let me continue. Before I could, my thoughts briefly turned to Fritz. He couldn't change what he had been through with Tracy, but instead of learning from it and turning it into a positive growth experience, Fritz had become bitter and had allowed his life to take a dark turn. I wasn't going out like that.

"Anna, I can't change any of that now, but I can change what I do and how I treat you going forward. I'm not saying that my control issues will disappear overnight, but I don't want to lose you. So, if I have to let go in order for this to work, I'll gladly do it. If you'll have me, I would like to join you in LA and build a life together. If you'll go with me, I want to bring you with me to my family reunion, and if you want me to be part of your life, I'm ready to join you in your commitment to God. And one more thing, you asked me at Yoshi's if I thought I could be the type of man you need after you described him and explained where I fell short, and I'm here to tell you that the answer is 'yes,' I can. I know that I'm not there yet, but I promise you that I'll work my ass off every day, and won't stop until that gap is closed for good."

"Ethan, it's good to hear that you finally realize that you're dealing with a control issue, but it's not just about you controlling our relationship; it's not about giving me more control or even having joint control; it's about putting God in control. That's the only way I can see a relationship can work."

I thought back to the night at Anna's place when she told me about her decision to remain abstinent until marriage. She said that she hadn't had any luck trying things her way, and that it was now time for her to try it

God's way. I wasn't having any luck either, and my annual ritual of prioritizing football over my faith made me feel like I was living my life on a meaningless, never-ending treadmill. It was time for me to make a change, starting right now.

As I nodded my head in agreement, I looked deep into Anna's eyes and tried my best to read her poker face, but I couldn't. I wanted Anna to wrap her arms around me and start showering me with kisses as a sign that she wanted what I wanted, however, I couldn't help but notice that she had just said "a" relationship, not "our" relationship. I was hoping this didn't mean she had already decided that we no longer had one, but I wouldn't have been shocked if she was about to tell me that it was too late for us. All I knew is that I had done everything that I could. I had laid all of my cards on the table and had followed it up with a silent, heartfelt prayer. Now, it was in His hands.

Takeoff (two months later)

Walking through airport terminals had always been an endless source of entertainment for me. Watching business people breaking their necks to find available power outlets, little kids struggling to pull suitcases that outweighed them, and overzealous employees blasting horns and racing carts through the crowds, all helped to temporarily take my mind off my final destination. But eventually, it drifted back to the asylum-like atmosphere that was awaiting me in Hattiesburg.

In the weeks leading up to the reunion, I had never heard my mother sound so excited. Her slow demise that I had witnessed since my father's death was long gone, and had been replaced by a boundless amount of energy that had me tempted to check her medicine cabinets to see if there was another explanation. But, there wasn't. Mom was simply in her element as she worked tirelessly with hotel managers, caterers, and travel agents to ensure that people would be saying great things about this reunion for years to come.

Mia was coming along with her new boyfriend, Stephen, who was turning out to be a decent guy with a good sense of humor. When Wall Street rumors came out about his company's interest in acquiring a small company in our space, he suggested that I start sucking up to him as soon as possible, just in case. In addition to his wit, I really liked the way that Stephen treated Mia, and assuming their relationship kept progressing, I expected to see us all screwing up the Electric Slide at their wedding one day.

Before heading to the airport, I met up with Eric, a young high school student I had been mentoring for several weeks. I wanted to make sure that he would stick to the study plan that he had committed to following while I was away. From the start, our relationship had been mutually beneficial. I had helped Eric with his math and sciences classes, while he had helped me stay up on the latest texting terminology, along with all the release dates of the hottest "kicks," which, in turn, had helped me to impress the heck out of my nephews.

Unfortunately, neither they, nor anyone else in Malcolm's family was coming, despite personal pleas from everyone my mom thought could convince him. I thought for sure he would change his mind a few weeks ago when I made my final pitch.

"What about this, Mal: what if I paid for my nephews' tickets? Would you come then?"

"It's not a money thing, Ethan, it's a safety and sanity thing. It's not safe to have my family trapped in an area with so many insane people."

I had to admit that my feelings might have been different if I had my own family to look after, and for the first time in a quite a while, just thinking about the possibility brought a smile to my face. As I continued to take in the amusing sights at the airport an hour before takeoff, I remembered that Malcolm had made it clear that he still expected a full recap of all the crazy, YouTube-worthy moments when I returned, and although I didn't make any promises, the warmth of Anna's hand in mine had me confident that there would be many wonderful moments to remember from here on out.

The End